# I Am Me

A Collection of Short Stories

By Ram Sundaram

iUniverse, Inc.
Bloomington

# I Am Me

*iUniverse books may be ordered through booksellers or by contacting:*

*iUniverse*
*1663 Liberty Drive*
*Bloomington, IN 47403*
*www.iuniverse.com*
*1-800-Authors (1-800-288-4677)*

*Because of the dynamic nature of the Internet, any web addresses or links contained in this book may have changed since publication and may no longer be valid. The views expressed in this work are solely those of the author and do not necessarily reflect the views of the publisher, and the publisher hereby disclaims any responsibility for them.*

*Any people depicted in stock imagery provided by Thinkstock are models, and such images are being used for illustrative purposes only.*

*Certain stock imagery © Thinkstock.*

*ISBN: 978-1-4620-7273-6 (sc)*
*ISBN: 978-1-4620-7275-0 (e)*
*ISBN: 978-1-4620-7274-3 (dj)*

*Library of Congress Control Number: 2011962286*

*Printed in the United States of America*

*iUniverse rev. date: 12/18/2011*

# Contents

Prologue: Dreamless xi

Earth's Child 1

Fifty Cents 10

At First Sight 22

Reality's Dream 36

Reflection 43

An Apple Branch 55

Touch of Reality 61

Soul Mate 73

Hangman 79

Immortal in Death 87

Epilogue: Absolution 101

# *Author's Note*

*I Am Me* is a two-way book: it begins from either end and meets in the middle. It holds a collection of twenty short stories, or ten pairs that are split into either half of the book. The two stories in each pair share the same title and reflect a similar theme, but are depicted in two contrasting yet congruent ways. One half of this book represents reality, while the other borrows from fantasy; similarly, one half depicts an individual nestled within a collective world, while the other half represents a collective consciousness entrapped within an individual existence. Each reader might prefer one version of a story over the other, or else will find harmony in their combined reading. The purpose of this "two-way" arrangement though, ultimately, is to challenge the segregation of "fact" and "fiction." These two labels are not as mutually exclusive as we deem; for the world of fiction borrows heavily (if not entirely) from existing fact, while the factual reality we perceive in our daily life is tainted with lies, fantasies and the artful brush strokes of an entire population's imagination.

The field of literature is so callously split into two halves, and yet if art indeed imitates life, shouldn't life be divided into the same categories as well? But it isn't. The world we perceive is not black and white, not even in the facts that we allow ourselves to trust implicitly. One single lie can tarnish the validity of several truths, and so when taken into account the countless number of lies that are created around the world each day, how can a "fact" retain any form of legitimacy? It would be easier perhaps to regard the world with a more open-minded perspective, to breathe in its every message without pausing to wonder whether it is authentic or not. The themes presented in these stories reflect the inherent nature of the "individual," and the passages that *each* individual goes through, from birth to friendship, love, desire, ambition, spirituality, death, and eventually the afterlife. *I Am Me* is both factual and fictional; yet the choice of reading a particular story as a truth or a lie rests solely with each individual reader.

# Acknowledgments

I would be remiss if I didn't take this opportunity to thank some people who contributed to the creation of these stories (so if you don't like the book, *these* are the people to hunt down). First and foremost my parents, my twin pillars of strength and stability, who gave me life (and then reminded me of it), who passed on their talents to me (and then denied it), and who have supported me relentlessly all my life—while I climb the ladder of fantasies and reach for the stars, it is they who make sure I never fall. My sister, who though would no doubt love to give that ladder a little shake (what red-blooded sibling wouldn't?) has always tempered her natural instincts with genuine affection and loyal support—it is her vision and hours of effort that led to the design of this book's cover. Mona Nikhil, the chatterbox, the clown, and the girl with the heart of a child, who appeared like a light amid the darkness, and showed me altruism in a world where there was none. Diane Wynn, my best friend, my confidante, my sounding board, and my treasure chest of infinite insight and impatience (you read that correctly), with whom I shared many profound conversations between sips of deliciously sweet iced-coffee. Chris Dueck, who played C.S. Lewis to my Tolkien, and imparted upon me the wisdom to create stories that are inspired by ideas rather than plots; it is he who showed me that life exists on different levels and that we rarely see past the first. A special thanks to Rick Bayer, my favorite tennis player and good friend, who found time between crushing forehands to lend me shrewd advice and persistent encouragement. I would further like to acknowledge every person I ever came across, whether we shared words, or merely caught a glimpse of one another through a sea of traffic, for you have *each* poured water into the sea from which I borrow my tools of creation. And one final acknowledgment, if you will bear with me, for the overweight, self-conscious fourteen-year old, who sat alone in his room and attempted to pen his first novel between mouthfuls of potato chips and chocolate cake—you made it, kid.

# Prologue:
# Dreamless

# One

My name is Ishvar.

I am alone on an apocalyptic sea, adrift upon a leaf. The leaf looks familiar—I have seen it before. It comes from a Banyan tree that had stood defiantly against a flood on a virgin patch of land somewhere... had I been there once? What happened to that tree?

Memory is an estranged friend of mine. It never visits when I am at my most lucid, and seldom stays long enough for me to remember. Perhaps it has become obsolete in the absence of time, for time itself is an estranged friend. The Banyan tree therefore stands comically in my thoughts, anchored neither to time nor to memory. It is adrift, aimless and unheeded, within the sea that is my mind. We share a similar plight, the Banyan tree and I.

# Two

He had once shared a name with God.

Every person in that world had known of God, but few (if any) had *known* God as Ishvar had. Ishvar had known God within a separate world altogether, a world that was replete with colour, love, joy and possibility. But alas it was a world that had always been destined to fall, for it had been built upon the fragile, feeble legs of imagination.

The imagination is a villain in the real world. It is perceived unfairly as a friend to those that defy the truth, and thus declared a servant to those who lie. Truths and lies are actually the same, only they hail from separate worlds. In Ishvar's world, the lie would be true; and yet in the world he was now imprisoned in, his truths were declared lies. For how could he prove a truth that was invisible in that world? And how could he defend a lie that bore neither merit of possibility nor of practicality? So when

Ishvar declared that he knew God, the non-believers doubted him. "Prove what you say is true," they demanded, but he couldn't.

Their faith evaporated, and God was duly forgotten.

Faith is a strange phenomenon. It lurks in trivial rituals and idle superstitions, yet it is ignored in matters larger than life, such as in dreams. In Ishvar's world, faith and hope were best friends; they walked arm-in-arm through the clouds, as one. But in reality they are bred for different purposes, and thus live apart from one another. Faith is considered to be belief, a trust set in stone. But hope is perceived as a flimsy quality, a naive game-of-chance. Yet Ishvar had known that in a world where possibility translated seamlessly into actuality, and where dreams blended artfully into reality, faith and hope could share the same meaning. In such a world, there were no lies and therefore no truths. Such had been Ishvar's world.

He now looked remorsefully at the sea...

What had become of that world?

## Three

There is a flower on the water.

*How did it get there?* Ishvar wonders. His world has been stripped of its powers and its defining qualities; the very basic aspect of thought becoming reality has been broken. And yet there lies now this undeniable symbol of illusion:

*A flower in the midst of a flood...*

He wants it to be real. The need is beyond desire, beyond the mere desperation he usually endures. It claws at his insides, urging him to make it a reality. The feeling is strangely familiar—it reawakens an old realisation, one he has long kept suppressed.

*He loves this flower...*

He sprawls himself onto the leaf, and paddles towards the flower. It bobs teasingly, just an arm's reach away. He reaches for it, but the current pulls it away. He paddles closer still, but again as his fingers reach out, it coyly drifts away. The current seems intent on working against him, and the flower intent on eluding him—it is ever more than an arm's reach away. He sits up and stares longingly after it. *"You're real,"* he mutters. *"Too real."*

The flower's veracity is a significant realisation, for it means that he truly is in danger of drowning in this apocalyptic flood. And it means that he cannot dream or imagine an escape.

*How has my world turned real?* he wonders…

The sea is thinning in the distance.

## Four

The sea.

It has swallowed everything graciously: man, woman, child, life, death, and even time. It has left nothing behind but the imagination. *My* imagination.

But without the sea, I can no longer imagine…

An old memory surfaces:

*In a world without imagination, God cannot be found.*

The words resonate within my thoughts. I try to remember where I'd heard them spoken, but my memory is weak and disjointed. *In a world without imagination, God cannot be found.* I realise just how true that is, for I hadn't been able to find God inside the other world. *Religion* and *Reality* limit the reach of the soul. It is only after this sea swallowed me in its forgiving embrace that I saw God standing before me, smiling.

In an existence devoid of imagination, the senses perceive only *one* dimension. They see the world in only one form, and in only *one* translation. The true meaning of God's rich and generous message is therefore distorted and eventually lost. But imagination enables the senses to search beyond the present, beyond the physical and the real; it highlights the impossible, which is where truth usually lurks. The imagination is a tool of translation; it works endlessly to bridge the two worlds, and it is a lens through which those with faith can find God.

I looked through that lens a long time ago, and I saw God,

yes; but I saw so much more too… I saw myself. I saw the entire Universe within Him. I was within that Universe, looking through the lens at Him. It is only then that I understood I had been blind thus far. I had been blind to faith; I had been blind to imagination, to perception, and to the truth.

*God is real.*

As real as dreams.

As real as lies.

As real as life.

That truth is the only fortification I bear in these fading moments of existence. I watch sadly as the sea thins around me. The water is disappearing rapidly, as if a large drain-hole has been unplugged far below. I wonder what will happen when it turns dry, when the sea no longer is? Will I still remain, or will I be jettisoned on an unforgiving beach of cruel pragmatism?

*Stay with me*, I implore of the sea.

It does not hear me. A whirlpool appears. It won't be long now…

I stare at the leaf, floating beneath me. I blink, hoping against faith that when my eyes reopen it will disappear. But it remains stubbornly by my side, defying illusion and awaiting its absolution. The sea will not drown it, I decide. No, that is *my* job.

I fold my arms and glare at the leaf.

I need an axe…

## Five

He has no axe.

So he plants his feet apart and pushes down on the leaf—it submerges momentarily under the water, but then rises up again with renewed vigour. He jumps on it with all its might, hoping to sink it. But it does not even tremble under his weight. So he claws and hacks at it with his bare hands, hoping he can tear and rip it to shreds. But its edges are strong, and his arms are weak.

Exhausted, he sits back down.

*It's just as well,* Ishvar tells himself; *I don't know how to swim anyway...*

## Six

My story isn't about idealism. There are definitely no dreamers in this tale, but it is littered with pragmatists. It's much like how the world once used to be: billions of pragmatists, convinced they were dreamers. They learned the truth near the end. So did I.

I know so much now, so much more than I ever did. But I still don't know enough... this Banyan leaf knows more than I do. It could tell me a story or two about dreams. Its very existence is a story worth telling, for it floats alone upon a sea that is now abandoning it; it came from the earth that is now reclaiming it; it breathes into the air that was never a part of it. And yet, despite all the improbabilities it has endured, it is *real.*

*We are real.* It is nothing more than wishful thinking that we are dreamers, thriving with imagination, creativity and a desire to ponder. We dream while we survive, but—and here's the rub—we are *not* dreamers. *We are real.*

We dream to escape the harshness of reality, but it is within reality that our lives begin and it is within reality that our lives must end. We cannot escape our fates, not through dreams, not through illusions, not even through hope. Dreams help us understand reality, but our lives are too short and too meaningless to enable any significant understanding. Perhaps existence is about survival then... Is life about accumulating enough resilience to survive? Answering such a question requires the aid of imagination, and that is a luxury I no longer possess.

*Do you have a dream to share with me?* I ask the Banyan leaf.

It lies still, drifting lifelessly upon the sea.

It can sense the end coming.

So can I.

# I

## Earth's Child

The events of that night precipitated from an incident that occurred two days prior, when I was separated from my company by a snowstorm. The winds destroyed any tracks they may have left behind. The storm raged relentlessly for two days and only slackened on the third. When the winds subsided, I left my shelter and made my way north, hoping to reunite with my company. It was then that I reached the canyon. Long and narrow, it was a mere cleft between two mountains, and our camp was to its north. I would have to pass through it to reach them.

I slid down the side of the hill as noiselessly as I could. Using the rifle butt for support, I edged down to the western side of the gorge, behind a large slab of rock. I dropped my rucksack and lay on my back, facing the mountain. The rifle sat on my chest and my finger tightened around the trigger, while my gaze drifted to the skies. It was snowing again and the wind began to howl. I readjusted my helmet and mopped the sweat off my face. I marvelled at the absurdity of sweating in the middle of winter—war did crazy things to men.

It was very quiet. My thoughts felt somewhat disjointed and I could discern no particular pattern to them. I pondered the snow first, but then my thoughts wandered towards my family back home, and suddenly I found myself thinking of food. I thought of steak and potatoes, of meatloaf and gravy, of the thousands of dinners I'd had, without ever pausing to relish every bite and every morsel. I promised myself that if I made it out of here alive, I would learn to celebrate every moment of my existence, no matter how small or insignificant it might seem.

"I'm starting to think like a dying man," I said aloud and chuckled wryly.

I held my breath for a few seconds, straining to listen for any sounds in the ravine. I knew there might have been dozens, maybe even hundreds of enemy soldiers scattered through these mountains at that very minute. But how many were in this canyon, and how many were near me?

I got to my feet and edged around the rock to peer out. It was then, by sheer chance, that I looked down in my stride and saw pink skin searing through the pale earth. The colour, so strange and out of place amid this miserable, decaying battlefield, filled me with a sense of hope. I assumed it was some kind of small animal, long dead and claimed by the frozen depths of the earth. But then I realised that the snow covering the carcass was fresh, so the animal had probably died recently, perhaps even a mere few hours ago. It most likely wasn't edible, but after two days of eating nothing but jerky, even the *thought* of frozen meat was appealing. I knew I wouldn't be able to eat it right away, for I would have to thaw it out first. And even after it thawed, cooking it would require lighting a fire, and that would be a dangerous thing to do in the middle of this gorge, with enemy soldiers all around. But I decided to dig it out anyway, and strap the carcass onto my rucksack, if only as a reward for when I made it out alive.

I began brushing some of the snow aside, to assess how large the animal was, and how deeply it had been buried. As I cleared a bit of the snow, I found five tiny fingers lying in the earth, attached to a small, stubby hand. It didn't look like the hand of a man… no, it was smaller, hairless, and delicate. I began digging further, tugging at the earth's stubborn grip on it, before extracting a tiny, baby boy into my arms. I knelt in the snow, holding him against my chest, shocked and confused. Coupled with remorse for the fate of this child, I was enraged at the thought that he had died here in the middle of nowhere, alone and unheeded. I wondered how he'd ended up in this gorge, and why he had been abandoned. Had he been left here after he'd died or had he been buried alive? Even as these questions encircled my head, his tiny fingers stirred slightly, his head turned towards me, and his beautiful eyes opened wide.

I stared at his lovely face, dumbfounded by this absurdity. He was dead… He *had* to be. He'd been buried naked in the snow for hours at the very least. He shouldn't have survived, and he shouldn't have been looking up at me right now, enchanting me with his presence. I am not too proud a man to admit I felt weakness then, and had tears lurking within my eyes.

I sat down behind the slab of rock and examined him. He didn't look frostbitten, pale, or even cold; he was pink, full of colour and vitality. He appeared unharmed, calm, and surprisingly happy. I estimated that he was about six or seven weeks old.

"Jesus, they're starting the draft early these days," I said, and gently tipped his head up so his eyes could meet mine. "Did they draft ya? You come out here to fight a war?" He cocked his head to one side. "I'm Sergeant Connor," I said, and gently shook his tiny hand with my own, "Pleased to meet you." I imagined how ludicrous this scene must have seemed to an observer—a soldier, saddled with a rifle, a pistol, grenades, knives, and other tools that were designed to take lives, sitting cross-legged in a snow-covered canyon, cradling a baby in his arms.

I smiled at the little tyke with as much warmth as I could muster. "What platoon you from, marine?" I asked, poking him gently in the belly and then blowing a raspberry—that made him giggle. "You know a Jacobs? Surly fellow he is—smokes a

3

lot of cigars and likes his women. He ever show you a picture of Annette? That's his girl… She's *beautiful*. Never understood what she saw in a washed-up loser like Jacobs. But they say love's blind. You hear that before?" I could have sworn he shrugged just then. "You ever been told that love's blind?" I asked again. "If not, you remember me telling you, 'cause it'll take you a long way in life. *That* and knowing that a woman will rip your heart out and eat it for dinner if you let her. Them's the two things you've gotta remember if you wanna survive this world."

He shivered. "Where's my head?" I said, giving my helmet a reproachful slap. "Here you are shivering your tiny fingers off and I'm yammering on about Jacobs and cannibalistic women." I pulled a rolled-up blanket from my rucksack. "But that's what war does to you. It makes you forget yourself, know what I mean?" He didn't seem to follow. "War makes you forget who you are, what you ought to be doing and even where you belong," I explained and spread the blanket out next to him. I gently placed his body in it. "War's a damn curse."

I looked into his face, which was radiant with youthful colour. His eyes, wide and expressive, regarded me attentively. I reckon I'd never seen anything more beautiful in my life than him. "What's your story?" I asked him. "I wish you could talk, so you could tell me just what happened to ya. Because you shouldn't be here, boy," I said, wrapping the blanket around his tiny form. "This place ain't fit for a man, let alone a baby. You should be home with your momma, listening to her sing to you, spitting up and laughing; then when she falls asleep, crying your head off like a siren. Know what I mean? You should be living and growing, not dying."

I lifted him, blanket and all and placed him on my left, to keep out the wind that was blowing from the west. Then I put the rucksack on his other side, hoping that it would keep him somewhat warm. "Ya doing good?" I asked. "You're probably hungry, but all I've got is some jerky, and there's no way you're going to be able to eat that. I don't even have water." I looked around at the snow. "Soon as we get out of this canyon, I'll melt some snow. I'd light a fire now, but it's dangerous. I'd be risking a lot of eyes seeing the smoke and finding us. Besides, I'm not leaving you here, alone and unguarded, while I traipse around looking for firewood."

The funny thing was that he seemed to agree with my reasoning. Perhaps it was just my imagination, but I genuinely felt like he understood every word I said.

"I've got a son your age back home," I said, as thoughts I'd been trying to keep supressed, leaked through my mouth. "Or rather, I *had* a son until recently. He died of pneumonia when he was just a few months old. I was real sore at God for that. I figure a child is like an angel, ya know? And the world needs as many angels as it can get.' I shook my head with bitter remorse. 'Ain't right when God lets angels die."

A gunshot sounded in the distance and the blast echoed loudly through the canyon. A moment later, a volley of gunfire erupted and the noise was deafening. I placed my hands over the baby's ears, hoping to muffle some of the sound. He remained surprisingly unaffected, except that he grimaced slightly when the gunfire began. "You're a brave boy, you know that?" I said to him, in as soothing a voice as I could manage. "Braver than I am. But I need you to be even braver now, 'cause I'm going to look out and see where the trouble is. 'Cause if they're moving down the canyon, we're gonna be caught. We don't want that. So you stay brave for me, while I go and check where they are." I left him and edged around the rock to look. I saw hundreds of small black shapes sidling down from either side of the canyon, their figures lit by blasts of muzzle flash. It was too dark for me to recognise any of the men, but I was certain the rest of my company were in that ravine. They had probably been hiding in this canyon the past two days, a stone's throw from the enemy, waiting out the storm. Had they known of the enemy's presence, I wondered? It didn't matter now. This canyon had turned into a battlefield.

I crept back behind cover and considered my options. Our

camp was about a day's march south from here, but there was no way I could cross this canyon now, with a battle raging within it. I could have just retreated the way I'd entered this canyon, but then I would have to climb back up this hill, carrying the baby. I'd be risking several minutes of exposure through open ground, with no cover. No, that *definitely* wasn't an option.

"It looks like we're stuck good," I said to him, as gunshots raged behind us. "What're we gonna do, bud? I guess we just have to sit here and wait it out." I held him in my arms again, smothering him against my chest to keep him warm. He tucked his face into my shirt, and gripped the fabric with his tiny hands. I didn't know why, but I found tears in my eyes again. It embarrassed me, and I looked away from him. I pressed my cheek up against his head.

He made a soft noise, like a murmur. I turned to him, and he was looking up at me questioningly. He began speaking gibberish, but with the utmost conviction, as if he were making a point in a debate. When he was finished, he giggled and nodded his head in agreement.

"You're a little weirdo, aren't ya?" I grinned at him.

He grinned back, and bounced happily in my arms.

"Yeah, you know you're beautiful, don't ya? That's why you're grinning," I said, teasingly. "You know you've got big, beautiful eyes, a little button nose, and the cutest little lips. And look at those pudgy cheeks… you're a darling." I kissed him on the forehead and he grinned happily, and bounced in my arms again. "My son probably looked a lot like you," I told him. "Sometimes I lie awake at night and just try as hard as I can to picture his face. Did he have my nose? Or did his ears stick out like mine did when I was a kid? Did he laugh a lot? I want so badly to know…" my voice trailed off, and he giggled after a pause. It was the sweetest sound I had ever heard, and it felt even sweeter here in the middle of a battlefield. "You really are an angel," I told him. "That's the only way I can explain you being here with me. I think God sent you to me because of what happened with my son and—" I heard gunfire close to me, *alarmingly* close. Bullets struck the rock we were behind. I crawled to the edge and peered out; a bullet struck the ground just beneath my head, and shot snow into my face.

He giggled as I crawled back into cover.

"Yeah, you think this is funny, do you?" I said, loading my rifle. "It'll be funny when they shoot me dead, won't it? Who'll take care of you then?" He paused, and the smile left his face. His eyes widened, and he seemed to regard me pensively. "No, I'm kidding, that won't happen," I said, hastily. "I'm not leaving you, bud. We're getting through this, you and me."

I heard a soft crunch behind me, and turned to see a soldier edge around the slab of rock. The moment his eyes fell on me, he pulled out a knife. I leapt to my feet and charged him. We struggled, fell over each other, and then slid down the hill. We struck each other fiercely, but the blows landed noiselessly amid the cacophony of the battle. The knife fell halfway between us; we both crawled to reach it, and then grappled over it. Gunshots whizzed past us, but we were too brutally determined in our struggle to worry about being shot. He wrestled the knife out of my hands and in one quick motion stabbed me just below my left shoulder; the pain seared through my chest, paralysing my will to fight back. But while he paused with relief to realise what he'd done, my right hand reached for the pistol I had tucked in my belt; pulling it out, I placed it right against his temple and fired. Even though the valley was overflowing with gunfire, this shot echoed with particular significance. His body fell limply beside me.

I got to my feet and trudged back up the hill, even as gunfire peppered the hillside around me. I ducked behind the slab of rock and crawled beside the baby. I pulled the knife out of my shoulder, but didn't bother to try and stop the bleeding. My life and the life of this child were at stake; what did a mere knife wound to the shoulder matter? My hands were covered with the enemy's blood though, so I picked up a handful of snow to clean them; but the blood didn't come off—it never did. I expected it would soak through the skin, into my very soul, and remain there forever. Death is disturbing enough, but the haunting memories of murder never fade. I still remembered every single person I'd ever killed, remembered every last detail about each one of them, for their blood still remained on my hands, and their sins were etched onto my spirit.

I turned to the baby. He looked worried, palpably worried, and I realised it was an expression I had never seen on a child his age before. Babies show like and dislike easily, but worry is an emotion far beyond them. Anxiety requires a level of cerebral intelligence, and an almost adult recognition of the fact that expectation does not always translate into fulfillment. But his young face was nevertheless lined with concern, as if he understood the tragedies of war and lamented its existence as much as I did.

"I don't like seeing you worry," I said to him. "You've got a lifetime of that ahead of you, so don't you dare trouble yourself with it now."

There was a sudden explosion to the south of us. Large flames erupted into the night sky, and heavy smoke rose steadily. The camp had been blown up. I could hear cheers from within the canyon, no doubt from the enemy. There was less gunfire now, but more chatter, more yells, and a great deal of bustling. My worst fear had come true: they'd won the battle. I'd be discovered and murdered perhaps within minutes.

I looked down at the child, at his troubled, grave expression. "You know something?" I said, with resignation in my voice. "It has been a pleasure knowing you. A few weeks ago, I was lying in my bunk, staring at the ceiling, when I got the telegram from my wife. She told me she'd found out she was pregnant after I shipped out. She'd then had the baby while I'd been off to war, and had raised him for six months, before he died. She hadn't even told me she was pregnant before that, not in the two years I'd been away. In one telegram, in *four* lines, she gave me a son and took him away. I've spent the last few weeks thinking about him, about what he must have looked like, what kind of a man he would have turned out to be, and how we'd have gotten along together." I smiled at him. "Then tonight I found you, my little angel. I thought when I saw you that God was giving me a chance to be a father again. But now I think he was just showing me why he took my son away."

I looked around at the gloom, the darkness, the heavy smoke, and the ever present shadow of death. "This is an ugly world," I said. "Angels can't survive in it; they shouldn't survive. I think the only reason you survived was to save my soul, and you did. You saved me…" I heard voices, *lots* of them—soldiers were moving up the slope towards us.

"You know they'll kill you," I told him. "They'll destroy you. Doesn't matter if they're my men or the enemy's, they won't spare you. Even if they do, this world will kill you." I searched his eyes for a sign of understanding, perhaps even of acceptance, but I only saw confusion. "You've only been in this world a short time, and already the smile's gone off your face. I don't want you to turn out like me. I don't want your soul tainted." I placed him back into the ground, blanket and all, into the very hole I'd pulled him out of, and began packing snow around him. "If we're lucky, you and I, we'll see each other real soon in a different world: a world without war, without death and without worry." Only his face remained exposed now, the rest of him was buried. He suddenly smiled. Hot tears streamed down my face as I looked at him. "You know the best part of that world you and I are going to? There'll be angels like you everywhere. *Everywhere.*" He nodded and giggled. "Sleep, my little angel," I told him, as I took the last handful of snow and covered his face. "We'll meet again."

A soldier crept behind the rock just then, and shot me twice in the back. I didn't fight back; I didn't even struggle. I fell limply onto the earth, atop where he'd been buried, protecting him from view. My blood stained the pure, white snow. I just hoped it wouldn't soak through the earth and taint him. Angels must remain unblemished after all.

# II

# *Fifty Cents*

My pa was real sore at me for being born stupid. He said he had bricks in his shed that was smarter and a whole lot cheaper too. He wanted to give me away but Ma wouldn't let him. It didn't matter none 'cause one day when I was four years old, we found him face down in the cereal. Ma said that he made some kind of a stroke or something, which made him fall asleep for a long time. We went to the hospital every day for two years after that, but he never opened his eyes or spoke to us, but we spoke to him all the same. And then one day the doctor told us that he wasn't going to wake up at all. I don't know much about my pa, but I know he didn't like me. I decided to ask Peter more about him today. That was the nice thing about having a brother; Peter was the only one I could ask about my ma and pa. He knew and remembered things I never knew. But then that's why Peter was so smart, 'cause he knew so much.

I hadn't seen him in twenty years though, and I missed him a lot. He sent me a letter a little while back, saying I ought to come visit him and his family. Peter had a family, but I didn't.

He had a wife and two children. He wrote me about them. He said whenever he saw them play it reminded him of me and him when we was that age. He said he missed his little brother. So I took the bus to Minnesota, and I was sure glad I did, 'cause it was going to be nice being around family again. I had been alone for so long that I missed being around people.

When I knocked on his front door, a maid asked if she could help me. I said I was looking for Peter. She told me to wait, so I sat on the porch swing, which was like the swing on our old porch. That was where Peter first called me an *idjit*.

We was sitting on it one day, watching folk go by on the street, when Peter got sore at me for stammering. "You sound like an *idjit*," he told me. I asked what an *idjit* was, and he said I ought to look in the mirror. I asked why I was an idjit, and he said it was 'cause I spoke so slow that the meaning came out before the words did. "So why bother saying anything at all?" he said, after calling me an *idjit* a couple more times. "Just think of what you want to say, and people will get what you're saying without you saying it. You get what I'm saying?"

Peter had a way with words. He could speak in a way that made sense to me, and not much made sense to me usually. So I took his advice and I didn't say anything for about six weeks. Ma reckoned I'd gone mute, and the pastor came over every weekend to pray with her for me to get my voice back. I wanted to tell them that I wasn't a mute, so I would think it around them all the time, but they still didn't seem to get what I was thinking. Even Peter didn't know; he kept asking me if all the times he'd hit me in the head had caught up with me. Then one day Peter said perhaps I wasn't mute as much as I was deaf, and so he wrote down a question for me, asking why I never said anything. When I wrote back "Because you told me to just think what I'm thinking without saying it," he laughed so hard that I reckon he swallowed three bugs. When he told Ma about it, she said I was about as sharp as a ball of cotton, whatever that meant.

Peter and me was always together; our teachers at school said we looked like we was glued at the ship, but I never found out what ship that was. The other boys teased us sometimes, and whenever they did Peter pushed me away and told me not to talk to him. Peter had lots of friends but I didn't have any, so I followed him around at recess, except on those days when he told me not to. Those days I walked around the school grounds, climbing trees or picking flowers. Sometimes I'd be so into picking flowers that I'd miss my next class. Then Mr. Marcus, the Vice-Principal, would call me into his office to yell at me. I liked Mr. Marcus, even when he was yelling, 'cause he was a real friendly person. He was always putting his arm around students, especially the girls, or else he was slapping them on the backside, and I even saw him kissing some of them. I wished Mr. Marcus was that nice to me, but I reckoned he would never like me enough to kiss me. That's good though 'cause his moustache would have tickled.

Mr. Marcus was the first person that said I had cheese for brains. Peter got mad when I told him he said that and threw stones at Mr. Marcus' car after school. He got caught though, and got suspended for two weeks. Ma had to pay a big fine she couldn't afford. Peter said he would get Mr. Marcus back, but I don't reckon he ever did, 'cause a week after Peter came back to school, someone took a bunch of photographs of Mr. Marcus giving special lessons to a girl after class, and he got fired. It was around the same time that Peter borrowed Ma's old camera, so I reckon someone stole it from him and took pictures of Mr. Marcus giving those special lessons. But I never understood why a teacher would get fired for giving special lessons, and Peter said I wouldn't understand until God mailed me the other half of my brain.

Peter looked out for me. He said that's what big brothers was supposed to do, and that if I had a little brother, I'd have done the same. Peter was a good brother; he got me a Mickey Mouse pencil sharpener for my birthday once. It was the first gift he ever got me, and I reckon it was the only gift I ever got. I thanked Peter and said he was a good brother, but that made him uncomfortable and he said it was too bad the sharpener wasn't bigger, or else I could have stuck my head into it. Peter didn't like it when I talked about my feelings, or said things that was "semimental." He said I was too "semimentally" attached to everything to turn out a real man.

Peter said friendship had a price. I asked him what that price was, but he said every friendship had a different price. "That's why you go through life bargaining back and forth with everyone you come across," he said. "Sometimes you catch a break, and sometimes you don't. But one thing's for sure," he added, leaning in closer, "It's always more than you can afford."

I like to believe Peter and me was friends, more than we was brothers. He said we wasn't friends though 'cause we didn't *need* each other. I told him I needed him, but he said that was only 'cause I was too dumb to go through life alone. But he never said he needed me.

Until I was nine years old, I never had friends. Ma told me it was 'cause everyone was jealous of me, but I don't know why they was jealous—*everyone* in town had a mickey mouse pencil sharpener. When Peter left for boarding school, I had no one to sit with at recess and that made me lonely. So one day I told myself to make friends with the first person I saw in the cafeteria. Well the first person I saw was a boy named Jimmy, who was the most popular person in our school. Jimmy was real good-looking, and he spoke well and played sports and Peter said once that all the girls had a rush for him, though I don't know what they was rushing for. Well I walked up to Jimmy and asked if I could sit with him. Then everyone at his table started laughing, but I never made a joke. I told them I never made a joke, but they laughed harder.

"You got fifty cents?" Jimmy asked, rubbing his chin.

"I think so," I said, and pulled out the drawstring pouch I kept in my underwear. The people at the table started laughing again. I gave Jimmy the money.

"Go ahead, sit down," Jimmy said, pocketing the coins. So

I sat next to Jimmy. He never said nothing to me after that, and no one else at the table said nothing neither. It was like I was... what's that word now? *Indivisible?* I was indivisible, so I sat and ate my lunch until the bell rang.

I sat next to Jimmy every day for the next few months. I gave him fifty cents every day and Jimmy always took the money without a word. I reckon he and his friends was used to me now 'cause they never even laughed at me anymore, but they didn't speak to me neither.

Ma gave me three dollars a week but I still never had money 'cause I spent most of it paying Jimmy. I didn't tell her that 'cause she would have gotten mad. So she figured I must have been wasting my allowance on something bad and stopped giving me money. I still had some coins saved up though and I paid Jimmy with that, but one day I clear ran out of money. So when I went up to Jimmy that day and he held out his palm, I told him I didn't have any money. He said I could pay him tomorrow. But I said my allowance was cancelled, so I couldn't pay him no more. Jimmy shook his head and said, "Well, then you can't sit here anymore."

Jimmy was the only friend I had besides Peter, so I was sad I couldn't sit with him no more. I tried to get a job so I could pay him again, but the pastor said I couldn't clean his windows 'cause God hadn't meant for me to work with glass. And the librarian said she would rather hire a monkey. I even wrote to Peter asking him for the money, but he said he was about as broke as me. So I lost my friendship with Jimmy and I was very lonely.

Ma died my last year of school. She died a day after she told me I had missed-a-point-at her. I asked her what point I missed, so she spelt it out for me: d-i-s-a-p-p-o-i-n-t-e-d, but I reckon she spelt it wrong. She said she thought me being dumb didn't mean I couldn't be something, but that I proved her wrong. She said I was too soft in the head and too soft in the chest to be something. The next morning she wasn't in the kitchen for breakfast. I went up to her room and saw her lying on the bed, not moving. That was the first time I ever cried, was when Ma died. I sat by her body for two days until the pastor came over to see why she missed church.

Peter came home for her funeral. That was the last time I saw him 'cause he took a job out in Minnesota after that. I was eighteen then, but I was still in school 'cause I failed three times. The good thing was I was old enough to live alone. When he left after the funeral, Peter gave me a hug and said we would always be brothers, forever and ever. I asked him to stay.

"I would, bud, but I got work to take care of."

"Ain't we friends, Peter?" I asked him. "Can't you stay for your friend?"

"We're *brothers*," he told me. "And I *would* stay for my brother, but like I said, I got me a lot of work. Tell you what, I'll come back one day and take you with me. How's that?"

I believed him, 'cause I didn't think Peter would lie to his own brother.

After the funeral life became quiet. I didn't see anyone except when I was at school and no one talked to me there anyway. I went weeks without saying a word and no one seemed to really notice. I didn't know how to cook so I didn't eat much except for bread and cheese. I wrote to Peter a lot, asking what he was doing and where he was. He wrote back sometimes, and that was nice 'cause I got to know he was okay. He always said he would come visit me soon.

The only person I saw was the pastor, and that was 'cause he brought me groceries every Sunday after church. He brought me milk, bread, cheese, and some fruit. He talked to me for a few minutes, but he was always leaving, even when he was just coming in. I reckon he only took care of me for my ma, 'cause she would have asked him to if she was alive. I don't think he liked me much, or maybe he just didn't like talking to me. I wish he did 'cause I didn't need bread or cheese as much as I needed a friend. I reckon Peter was right about friendship having a price and all, 'cause I could afford bread, but I never could afford a friend.

But then one day I met a girl named Emma in school. She

was sitting next to me in math class, and when the teacher asked a question I didn't know, Emma explained it to me. The other people was laughing 'cause I was dumb, but Emma didn't laugh. She was kind. She listened when I spoke, and so I spoke a lot and I spoke things I never spoke before. She didn't laugh except when I was funny and even then her laugh wasn't mean. She was the nicest person I knew, except for Peter and my ma, but I didn't have them in my life anymore. Emma said I was like her brother who died in the war. She said when she spoke to me she felt like she was speaking to him. I asked if he was dumb too and that made her laugh. But then she said both of us weren't dumb, and that I shouldn't let anyone call me dumb.

Emma was real pretty and when she smiled at me I forgot where I was. She was nice to me, even though her friends never was. I was never smart around her though, and I always said wrong things. One time I came up to her when she was reading in the park behind school. She looked up at me and smiled. "Here, sit down," she said, patting the bench.

I reached into my trousers for the drawstring pouch. Emma smiled when she saw it, and said her grandma had a pouch just like that. Then I gave her two coins and sat down by her.

"Fifty cents?" she said, looking at the coins. "What's this for?"

"For sitting beside you."

Emma laughed. She had a pretty laugh—it sounded like a song. "You think you have to pay to sit next to me? What do I look like to you, some girl from an escort service?"

I didn't know what she meant, but I said yes 'cause I was confused. But that made her angry, and she called me a jerk and walked away. I followed her when she went back into the school and then when she went home. I followed her so much that she stopped and told me to stop following her. "Stop following me," she said. "I don't want to talk to you."

"But I paid you."

She looked more angry now. "You're not a gentleman," she

said. I was confused 'cause she had tears in her eyes even though she was angry. "What kind of girl do you think I am?"

"I think you're pretty." Her eyes rolled, but I didn't know if that meant she was more angry or more sad, so I kept talking. "I think you're nice to me, when no one else is. I reckon you have a big heart, 'cause you smile a lot and my brother Peter says it's more hard to smile than to frown. So I reckon you got to have a big heart to smile more. And you smile good, Emma."

She looked surprised now. "Thank you," she said. "But why did you give me fifty cents?"

"My brother Peter said every friendship has a price. And I paid fifty cents to my last friend every day, so I reckon I ought to do the same for you. I didn't mean to make you mad."

"Your brother was wrong," she said, wiping her eyes. "Friendships come free. Trust me."

So I did. I trusted Emma and we became friends, and I never had to pay her nothing.

I sat next to her at recess after that. She was different from Jimmy, 'cause she actually spoke to me. She spoke to me about her life, about things she had seen and things she wanted to see. She said talking to me was like throwing stones into a well. The more stones she threw, the more "semimental" feelings I had inside came up. I reckon that was true 'cause I even cried around Emma a few times and I never cried around no one else before except Ma. Sometimes I talked so much around Emma that my throat closed and then she would tell me to calm down and get me water. She said I was always getting excited and that I should be calm. But I told her I only got excited when she was around and that made her laugh.

Emma and I was friends even after school ended. We was good friends, and I made her laugh a lot. We took long walks and we swam in the lake and saw movies. Emma was a lot like Peter, and when I was around her I didn't miss Peter much. I still wrote to him lots—I told him about Emma but he reckoned I was making her up. He said no girl who had all her marbles would be

17

friends with me. I showed Emma the letter and she reckoned Peter was mean, but I told her he was just being Peter. "That's how big brothers are," I said.

Emma said things I didn't understand sometimes. We was sitting in a meadow once watching seagulls fight over bread crumbs and I said this was romantic. Emma said it couldn't be, 'cause there was nothing romantic about our friendship. I think she thought romantic was something between lovers, but I thought anything was romantic whether I was with a friend, or my ma, or a stranger, or a hundred strangers, or even if I was just by myself.

She said that romance was anything from a nice song to a bouquet of flowers, or even just a piece of paper with the words "I love you" on it, as long as it was between lovers and not friends. That confused me 'cause I always thought romantic things was bigger than life.

That moment with Emma was special 'cause it felt like it was bigger than my life. In that moment, I forgot my ma was dead, that I hadn't seen Peter in years, and I even forgot I was stupid. I think any moment that makes you forget everything is romantic.

I reckon Emma was romantic, 'cause she made me forget everything. In fact, when I was around her I only remembered good things. I felt love for Emma and that scared me, 'cause I never felt love before. I wrote Peter asking him what love felt like, and he said if I felt something funny in my pants, then it was love. But I reckon he was wrong about that, 'cause my pants never told jokes. So I asked Emma what love was.

"It's a drug," she said, and smiled. "Be careful you don't take some of it, because you'll forget where you're going and where you came from. Know what I mean?"

I didn't know what she meant 'cause when she smiled then, I forgot if I was coming or going. I told her that and she laughed, 'cause I reckon she figured I was making a joke.

One day I told her that I felt love for her, and that made her uncomfortable. She acted the way Peter did when I talked about feelings, and then she said she didn't love me, not the same way I loved her. I asked if she was my girlfriend, and she said she couldn't be 'cause we wasn't right for each other. I didn't understand what she meant, 'cause I thought we was right for each other. But she said it was like how you go shopping for hats; you got to find a hat that's the right size, the right colour and the right look. She said I wasn't the hat for her.

"I know what you're saying, Emma," I told her. "You're saying I don't have fifty cents."

I was real sad I wasn't Emma's boyfriend, but I was happy she was happy, 'cause she found a boyfriend a little while later. When she told me about him I saw a look on Emma's face I never saw before. She spoke about him like he was the only man she ever saw, and I figured he was very rich 'cause he could afford Emma's love. I told her that and she said it was wrong for me to keep calling her a hooker. I told her I didn't call her no hooker, and I meant it; Emma sure wasn't some kind of a ninja or a fisherman.

She married a real nice man, tall, handsome and rich. They had lots of children too, and they had a happy life. Some folks said she was sad 'cause he was cheating on her, but I don't know how you can cheat on a marriage, so I reckon they were wrong.

After Emma was married we didn't see each other much. So I stayed home most of the time, where I felt like Ma and Peter was both still with me. I didn't have a job but I lived off the money Ma left me. The pastor got me work sometimes, mowing lawns and cleaning gutters and building fences, but I always seemed to lose the jobs, even when I was working hard. Peter wrote me a letter once a year, telling me what he was doing. He had a wife and children now. He said they would visit someday, and that made me happy, 'cause I wanted to see Peter again and I wanted to see his family. Then for two years he didn't write me at all, until last week, when he sent me a letter saying I should come see him. So that's why I was here. I was real excited, too.

Sitting on the swing, waiting for Peter, I thought about all the friends I had and all the friends I lost. I thought about my pa, my ma, the other boys in my class, the girls I tried to talk to, the teachers that were nice to me, and the teachers that weren't. I thought and I thought, and I thought until my head hurt. I thought that I paid everyone in my life to keep them with me, and the ones I couldn't pay left me. Pa left me 'cause I was stupid and useless. Peter left me 'cause I was too dumb to go along with him. Ma left me cause I missed-a-point-at-her. Jimmy left me 'cause I ran out of money. Emma left me 'cause I wasn't good enough to marry her. I was alone now 'cause I didn't have nothing left to pay no one else. I never talked to God before but I wanted to talk to him then; I wanted to ask him why I was so poor I couldn't buy a friend.

But then I thought that people had paid me, too. Ma paid me by taking care of me; Peter paid me by explaining things to me; Jimmy paid me by sitting with me, and Emma paid me by being nice to me. I started to understand what Peter said about friendships having a price. Only, I think people pay each other when they're friends, and not always with money.

The maid came out then with a pretty woman who was Peter's wife. I said I was Peter's brother and she took me into the house and showed me their children. They was beautiful, just like their ma and Peter. Rose and Samuel they was called, and they was four and six. They was real smart, too. They told me stories, showed me games and sang songs.

I asked where Peter was and his wife took me to see him.

Peter died the day he wrote me the letter asking me to come see him. His wife showed me his grave. She said he had been dying slowly for many months now and that he asked her just before he died to tell me he was sorry he never came to see me.

After she left, I stayed at Peter's grave. I thought about how Peter had always been in my life, even when he wasn't really there. He was the only friend I had all my life but he always reckoned we was never friends. I don't think Peter wanted to be my friend, 'cause maybe he didn't like me. Even now when I came to see him, he had died and left me behind.

"I miss you, Peter," I said to him, like he was right there, but I knew he wasn't. "I never got to talk to you before you died, but I got something for you," I reached into my pocket. "You were right, Peter, friendship *does* have a price, and I figured out what it is." I put fifty cents on his grave. "But you were wrong about something," I said, "It's a price I can afford."

# III

## *At First Sight*

Robert Duncan was about to turn to the financial section of the evening newspaper, when she first smiled at him. He wasn't usually the attention of women like her: someone tall, slender, elegantly dressed, and obviously attractive. She reminded him of someone like Audrey Hepburn, or some other actress who was old enough to have lived in times when women chose to behave like a "lady." Truth be told, Robert regretted the fact that both the times and the women had changed. In his thirty-seven years of drawing air, he had yet to come across a woman who wore one of those round hats with a rose pinned in the middle—not that he particularly liked those hats, mind you, for some of them were downright ridiculous. But the fact was that he had rarely ever met a woman who had the etiquette to use a simple expression like "pardon me."

However, there was something about this particular woman that suggested she was different. She hadn't said a word to him, nor he to her, but he *knew* that she was unlike any woman he had ever known. There was something about her posture and her cultured smile that made his hopes rise high (among other things). He wanted to make eye contact with her.

The evening train was predictably crowded and there were dozens of people crammed into the small carriage. Robert wondered how he could possibly initiate any kind of contact, without drawing everyone's attention to him. So he chose the very basic and simplest of all gestures: he smiled back at her. "Good," he thought to himself, as she looked up at the right time to catch his eye, "Give her your best smile, and then see what happens."

She turned away.

Robert frowned, feeling deflated. Well, then why had she smiled at him in the first place? Had she perhaps aimed that beautiful gesture at someone else, maybe someone behind him? He cast a look at the men standing around him, and after a quick scan, he decided that unless she was the kind of woman who fancied tattooed men that wore more jewellery than she did (which, unfortunately, a lot of women *did*) that she couldn't have been smiling at anyone else.

Or perhaps he had just imagined the whole blissful event? Maybe he had wanted her to smile at him so much that he had imagined it. Robert felt that that was the most plausible explanation. Annoyed and disgruntled, he bent down to the evening paper once more, hoping he would become invisible in the noisy crowded carriage.

"You play soccer?"

Robert looked up. The beautiful woman was now sitting across from him. She had perhaps purposely found herself a seat in his vicinity. "Er... yes, I do," Robert replied, finding his mouth suddenly very dry. "Or that is I *used* to, back in the day," he said. "Well, not *that* far back... I mean recently, but obviously not *very* recently. Not 'obviously' as in I don't look like someone why plays soccer, but obviously in that I don't look young enough to—well I *am* young I suppose, relatively speaking, depending on whom I'm compared with. I don't mean *you*, of course," he added hastily, stumbling through his words. "Because *you* look unbelievably young, like I… I can't even believe you're old enough to ride the train alone. Not that you look like a child, or even that I would talk to a child on a train. I mean, there's nothing wrong with talking to a child of course, unless he's unaccompanied... or *she*, that is, not *just* a 'he.' Not that—"

"It's okay," she said, putting a hand on his arm to calm him. "It's all right, I'm sorry if I startled you by asking that. It's just that I couldn't help but notice your gym bag."

Robert looked down at the bag he'd put between his feet: it bore the emblem of the Telford Soccer Club. "Oh," he said, understanding dawning on him at last. "Oh yes, well like I said I … I used to play, back in the uh…"

"Day?" she grinned.

"Yes," he nodded, grinning back nervously.

She smiled encouragingly. She was even more stunning up close, he thought. In addition to her beauty, there was also a very kind, comforting manner about her, as though she was someone who talked to people purely for the pleasure of the conversation.

"Do you still play now and then?" she asked him, in a brisk yet polite voice.

"Yes, occasionally," he said. "Even if it's a busy week, I try to make time for it. Once or twice, you know… keeps the blood pumping."

"Does your wife approve of your hobby?" she asked, a mischievous twinkle in her eyes.

He grinned. "I'm not married."

She raised an eyebrow. "I'm not sure she *would* approve, if you *did* have a wife," she said, a tad pointedly. "But we all need our hobbies though, don't we? And soccer's a sport worthy of commitment," she told him. "I personally prefer cricket."

Robert grinned like a cheeky schoolboy. Like most red-blooded Englishmen, his love for the game of cricket was in-born. To hear this beautiful creature compliment what was to him more of a religion than a sport, was a truly gratifying feeling. "I'm so pleased to hear you say that. Not many American women would share your views on that, though," he told her.

"American? Am I that transparent?" she laughed.

"Your accent's *almost* undetectable."

"But I couldn't fool you."

"Not everyone is such a neurotic observer of speech patterns like I am," he commented, eliciting a short laugh from her. "What part of the States are you from?"

"New York."

Robert put down his paper while marvelling at how almost every American he ran into claimed to always be from New York—considering that the U.S. was the fourth largest country in the world, one would imagine that there would be other places in the nation where an American tourist could be from. "I had a feeling you might be from New York," he said.

"And you're from Wales, I reckon?"

He was impressed. "Born and raised. How'd you know?"

"My neurotic observation of speech patterns is fairly strong as well," she said, easing into yet another effortless smile. "Does that make us even then?"

"You sound like you've been in England a long time."

"Fourteen years," she nodded. "I feel like I'm one of you 'blokes' now."

"Ah well, if you watch the Ashes instead of the Super Bowl and spell colour with a 'u' then you might be," he said, amazed at the fact that he even *knew* of the Super Bowl. About as many Englishmen followed the NFL as the number of Americans that knew of the Ashes.

In fact, there were probably more British people that cared about American football than the number of Americans that might have even *heard* of cricket. Robert had once been stunned when he'd mentioned the sport to an American colleague, who had quite promptly said (and that too in an unabashed voice), "Oh, cricket! Is that the game you play on horseback?"

Robert of course bore a small knowledge of the NFL thanks

to the three years of his youth that he had spent living in Denver, Colorado. It was there, incidentally, that one of his University professors, a historian too at that, had commented, "Ah yes, cricket. I tell you, I've looked in all the sporting goods stores here, but I just can't find a cricket paddle anywhere." Those who aren't well versed in the game might be tempted to wonder what the learned professor had said wrong; others would realise that cricket is played with bats, not paddles.

"I don't follow sports, but I *do* like cricket more than football," Emma agreed, even while Robert's thoughts momentarily meandered away from her. "But I'm afraid my spelling hasn't quite made the transition to England that the rest of me has."

"It takes some getting used to, no doubt," he remarked, politely.

Both paused and stared at one another, almost as though they were searching for even the slightest flaw in the other that would prompt them to end this conversation immediately. They found none. Robert gazed down at her hand to see if a wedding ring lurked anywhere on those long, slender fingers. When his eyes produced no sign of one, he lifted his gaze to meet hers once more, and they smiled together.

"Do you take the train every day?" he asked. No sooner had he said the words that he inwardly admonished himself for having asked such a pointless question.

She nodded. "It's a miracle I haven't lost my senses yet."

"You probably have, or else you wouldn't take the train every day," he remarked, and enjoyed hearing her laugh once more. "I'm afraid I'm in the same boat as well—almost *literally*. I'm a daily commuter, too."

She shook her head sympathetically. "You know, I haven't come across a good transit system yet, not in all the places I've travelled to."

"Germany isn't half bad," he said.

"No it isn't. You know, I think their airports might have been the first—"

26

"—to install the little train that connects the terminals?" he broke in. She stared at him, her expression unfathomable, and then nodded.

"It's a very sophisticated airport," he said.

"I haven't seen a better one," she agreed. "Although I am a bit partial towards the airport in Birmingham, but only because it has some of the best cafés and restaurants."

"I like the drinks they serve there," he nodded. "There's one café in particular that serves the best Suada over ice. You don't get that at many airports."

"You like that as well?" she asked, looking incredulous. "That's my favourite drink!"

He nodded, equally amused. "I know it's just basically an espresso with condensed milk, but you'd be surprise how many coffee shops make a mess of it."

"I know!" she said. "I usually just make it at home, but then you miss out on the café experience, know what I mean? You can't seem to get the best of both worlds."

"Isn't that true?" he agreed.

The train disappeared headlong into a dark tunnel and the carriage became brighter as the indoor lights kicked on—but they flickered poorly and often left the passengers on board stranded in a few moments of darkness. "One thing you Brits haven't conquered yet is the workings of a proper electrical system," she commented.

"'You Brits?'" he laughed. "I thought you said you were *one* of us."

"Only when it's favourable to be so," she winked. Robert noticed that her eyes were a captivating shade of brown, almost hazel but a touch darker.

"What part of the city do you live in?" he asked her.

"South side."

"Could you be more specific?" he grinned.

A playful smile came upon her face; it was different from the others she had shared with him that evening, but no less enticing. "I don't know you well enough."

His hand jerked forward in almost an instinctive reaction; "Robert Duncan," he declared proudly. "Investment banker by day, poet and playwright by night."

"Duncan? Duncan..." her eyes danced playfully as her mind worked swiftly. "I know that name... ah yes, *Midsummer* and *Henry meets Harietta*, not to mention the collection of three-line poems entitled *Apathy to Zen*, hmm?"

"I'm flattered," said Robert, amazed to find that one of his readers was actually a smart, beautiful, interesting woman. His publisher's marketing reports had suggested that his typical reader fell into the "lonely, depressed and suicidal" demographic.

She now took his hand and shook it affably. "Emma," she told him. "I'm afraid my job's not nearly as exciting as yours, but it *is* related to your line of work."

"Oh?"

"I'm the chairman—*chairwoman* rather, of New Line Publishing House."

"No wonder you knew of my works," he smiled.

The train rumbled out of the bridge and sailed through the heart of the city's core; the first downtown station pulled up and at once a visibly large portion of the passengers stood to their feet and filed to the door. "I hope your stop doesn't come up soon," she said, looking out through the tinted windows. "We were just getting to know each other."

"My thoughts exactly, Emma."

Maybe it was because she hadn't expected him to say her name, or maybe it was because of the way he had said it, but it seemed to Robert that he had caught her off guard. She looked away shyly and nervously fiddled with the straps of her purse. He broke into his warmest smile, and then kept the conversation going in a soft, soothing voice. As they talked, her every word felt electric to him, and she in turn gushed at everything he said, like one of the young girls at the college where he taught a literature class once a week.

"And what part of the city do *you* live in?" she soon asked him.

"South side."

They smiled together. "Do you live alone?" she asked.

He shook his head. "Married with three children."

Again, they both laughed.

"And you?" he asked.

"The same," she replied. She then crossed her legs, folded her arms and frowned at him in a scrutinising manner. "Do you smoke?"

He shook his head.

"Drink copiously and crash your car into lampposts?"

"Only on the weekends."

"How do I know you're not just some kind of psychotic rapist?" she asked.

"Oh, I'm not psychotic."

"And what are your views on politics?"

"Er…that guy had it coming?"

"Views on global warming?"

"I like wearing shorts."

"Endangered species?"

"They aren't going fast enough."

"Inflation?"

"Without it, I'd never have a date."

She fought back a smile. "Same-sex marriages?"

"I'm sorry, could you repeat that? The word 'sex' distracted me."

"Rise in teen pregnancy rates?"

"I'm glad *someone's* getting laid."

"The candy company *Jambles* going bankrupt?"

"*Finally*, a topic that's close to my heart."

Emma laughed.

"My turn to ask you," he said, sitting up straight.

"Yes, I *am* a psychotic rapist," she declared.

"Good, next question: thoughts on the Mid-East crisis?"

"Where *is* the Mid-East?"

"Effectiveness of the U.N?"

"They look good in their uniforms."

"Favourite basketball player?"

"Er…the tall guy?"

"Favourite movie?"

"The one with… the woman and the tall guy?"

"Romance?"

"I'll take it to go, please."

"Do you own a TV?"

"What do you think all my furniture points at?"

"Do you believe in love?"

Emma stopped for the first time, and then slowly grinned. "Trick question," she said, after a pause. "Just when things were going so well."

"It's a fair question," said Robert.

"Like I said before, I don't know you."

"You know me well enough now," he said, piercing her with his eyes alone and hoping it would be enough to overpower her defences. Robert suspected that like most women, she secretly enjoyed being challenged by a man.

"Why don't you give me *your* answer first?"

"You mean do *I* believe in love?" he asked and then promptly shrugged. "I don't know. I don't think I've ever been in love before, to be quite honest."

"No?" she looked sternly at him, almost disapprovingly.

He shook his head. "I thought I was in love once, but it was just an ear infection."

She laughed. "Well okay then, I've never been in love either."

"It's not a contest," he laughed. "There's nothing wrong with being in love."

There was a pause, and then she said, "It *is* high up on my "to-do" list."

"What, falling in love?" he asked, and she nodded. "Well, it's not like grocery shopping or picking up the laundry. I believe in fate more than I do in love, so I believe if there *is* such a thing as love, then it must be dependent on fate. So you can't fall in love, unless fate helps you."

She rolled her eyes at him, "Kismet and all that nonsense?"

"You don't really think that it's nonsense, Emma."

"How do you know?"

"Because I know *you*."

She shook her head. "But you don't."

He paused and leaned forward, "Then give me a chance to know you."

She stared at him, unwaveringly. "Robert, do you believe in love at first sight?"

"No, I'm short-sighted."

"Be serious and tell me the truth, Robert, for I expect nothing *but* the truth from you: do you really believe that love at first sight exists?"

He sighed. "I believe that attraction at first sight exists; so if two people are truly compatible, and the circumstances favour a suitable partnership, then love will duly develop over time. But no, I don't think that you can just meet someone and instantly fall in love."

"Then you and I disagree."

"You think you can fall in love with someone like *that*?" he said, snapping his fingers.

"I did once, long ago," she confessed.

"Really?"

She nodded. "A *very* long time ago."

"Let's just agree to disagree on the matter, shall we?"

She nodded and Robert quickly veered the conversation away from love.

What happened next seemed much like a dream to Robert. The train was now almost empty around them; they spoke for another half an hour and rode the empty carriage till the last stop on the line, where Robert led her to his parked car. They drove to a café two blocks away where Robert claimed they served the best Suada over ice in the country. Afterwards, they drove to a restaurant that turned out to be a mutual favourite.

Over dinner they discussed anything and everything, from their families to their work, their ambitions, their childhood dreams and aspirations, and even went as far as to reveal each other's innermost secrets. It didn't seem to Robert that they were strangers, and what transpired between them was more akin to a pair of soul mates conversing than two complete strangers getting to know each other. Before they finished dessert, Emma's foot was sliding up Robert's leg and his hand was caressing her thigh. When they left the restaurant and headed to his car, they stopped underneath a tall lamppost as soft rain pattered around them. Robert pulled her close into his arms and they leaned into a perfect kiss, one that he was certain he would never forget. It was as though he had kissed her every day for years and years—such was the comfort and familiarity with which he cherished that moment.

Within the hour they were in the nearest motel, under the sheets with the lights dimmed low. Neither spoke a word—it wasn't necessary. It was eerie how well they seemed to know each other's desires; Robert felt like he knew exactly what Emma wanted and she seemed to know what he needed. He couldn't imagine two souls and two bodies merging more completely. When at last he paused to look into her eyes, he knew they were meant for one another.

"This was a perfect night," she remarked, when he kissed her neck.

"Beyond perfect."

"I love you."

"I love you, too."

They had said what no two strangers would have ever said to one another in so short a time, but such was the connection that Robert and Emma shared. It was another hour before they were dressed and ready to leave. They held hands and shared many kisses on the way from their room to the lobby. They looked so comfortable with one another that an unsuspecting observer might have assumed they were a honeymooning couple.

Robert went to the front desk and paid the bill. Emma stood by his car, her coat wrapped tightly around her as the wind picked up suddenly. He made his way back to her, smiling as he saw her playfully unwrap the coat and flash him (though she was fully clothed inside anyway). He kissed her and she put her arms around him. They felt comfortable, warm and close.

"Let's go," he said at last, opening the passenger door and watching her step into the car.

In an hour they were out of the city and heading towards the suburbs. The roads were empty, and apart from the odd little car, they didn't come across any traffic until they reached the south side of the city. They didn't say much to each other in car; they appeared to be lost in their own thoughts, and Robert for his part was reflecting back upon the evening and smiling whenever he remembered a special moment. He felt truly, blissfully content.

Robert drove through a neighbourhood now, moving confidently through the maze of little streets and blocks of houses before stopping before a house well-guarded by a row of trees. He pulled into the drive and turned off the engine. He opened Emma's door and helped her out; again, they said nothing to each other. She waited as he moved the car into the shed, locked it and came back out to her. Together they went into the house and turned on the light.

Robert went to a sleeping figure on the sofa of the living room and gently roused it; a young woman stirred and stared at the couple. "Back so soon?" she murmured.

"It's been hours, Natalie," he smiled.

The woman rose to her feet and stretched. "The children went to bed around eight—poor darlings were so tired after re-enacting the battle of Waterloo all evening."

Robert and Emma smiled. "Go on and get some sleep; sorry to be so late."

"No problem at all, sir," said Natalie, before picking up her pillow and blanket and moving out of the room. "Good night, sir, mum."

"Good night," said Robert and Emma together. They went upstairs and made their way to one of the bedrooms. They peered in and saw two sleeping figures huddled in separate beds. Emma was about to step in, but Robert stopped her.

"You'll wake them," he said. "We'll see them in the morning." She nodded.

They closed the door behind them and went into the adjacent room, where another small figure lay huddled in an aptly proportionate bed. They closed the door behind them once more and went into the room at the far end of the landing. A much larger bed rested in the middle of this room, but no figure lay huddled upon it. They closed the door behind them and turned on a soft light. Robert disappeared into the changing room while Emma moved into the bathroom.

In a few minutes, both were dressed in pyjamas and under the covers of the bed. Robert and Emma sighed with contentment as the comfy mattress soothed their weary limbs. "A perfect end to a perfect night," said Robert, as he took two wedding rings off the bedside table, put one on his finger and then took Emma's hand so that he could slip the other one onto hers.

"Feel good to be Mrs. Duncan again?" he asked her.

She smiled and nodded. "I missed Mrs. Emma Duncan terribly."

He slipped his arm around her, "So what's the verdict on tonight?"

"Perfection," she laughed. "Except for when you said you hadn't been in love before—don't think I've forgotten about that. And what was that bit about an ear-infection?"

He laughed. "Were you worried?"

She nodded. "About leaving the kids for so long, yes. I missed them."

"You're right. We'll just make this a monthly thing."

"Yes, I think that would be good." Robert kissed her good night and turned off the bedside light. Emma rolled over and slipped her arm around his. "Robert?"

"Yes, dear?"

"Do you believe in love at first sight?" she asked, with a hopeful smile.

He sighed. "When I met you, I didn't even believe in love at all." And then he paused to reflect on his own words. "It's not like it's there to see in black and white. It's not *there*, you know? It seemed too bloody far-fetched so I didn't believe in it until I fell in love with you."

Her face fell slightly and she looked down. "So what *did* you feel when you met me?"

"I can't say for sure, Emma. The day I first met you was years ago, and I don't remember whether I fell in love with you at once or not. I knew I was completely enamoured by you, by your beauty, your grace, and your intelligence, which shone through your presence without you even uttering a single word to prove it. That was as close as I'd ever come to love."

"But it wasn't love at first sight?" she said, disappointed.

He shook his head. "Maybe, but I just... I don't know, Emma. I just know that I love you *now* more than I've ever loved anyone or anything. But I don't know what I thought when I met you." He lifted her chin to meet her eyes, "I doubt this will be much of a consolation to you, but for your information, I *did* fall in love with you all over again today."

She smiled bashfully. "At first sight?"

"At first sight." They leaned forward and kissed. "Good night, Emma."

"Good night, Robert." She snuggled up close in his arms. "Robert?" she said.

"Yes dear?"

"Next time, you be the American."

# IV

## *Reality's Dream*

He stood on the beach, lost in every sense of the word. Across the sand, a mere twenty or thirty yards from him, sat a bottle of cold, frothy beer. Perspiring underneath the afternoon sun, his limbs screamed for rest—what had he been doing, he wondered? He had no memory of anything before this moment, or *besides* this moment. He remembered nothing of himself or his past, save for this beach and that bottle of beer. Thirst invited him forward.

A towering wall rose from the earth, parting him from the beer. He began scaling it with the nimble grace of an athlete. He reached the top with relative ease and then dropped down to the sand on the other side. He took a step towards the beer again, but once more a wall rose from the ground and fenced him behind it. This time the wall was lined with thick, metal spikes that would make climbing it impossible. He looked helplessly at its formidable height.

It was then that he noticed a blueprint by the foot of the wall. He laid it open on the sand—it showed two walls, him in between, and the bottle of beer just a mere ten feet away. The instructions at the foot of the diagrams were clear: he would have to build a structure that would first enable him to reach a height greater than that of the wall; then he would have to build a second structure that could cross the breadth of the wall; and lastly, he would have to build a third structure that would enable him to climb down to the beer and retrieve it.

"Well that's just stupid," he said aloud, scratching his head. He had no tools on him, or any kind of materials to work with. He was stuck on a beach, between two walls that he couldn't climb over. How on earth was he to build even *one* structure, let alone three?

He picked up the blueprint again: there were some instructions written on the bottom left hand corner: *Only creative and distinctive designs can be used. Imagination is key.*

He read and re-read the instructions to himself, until it made sense. So he was to design a structure that was distinctive, and he had to use imagination to achieve it? It sounded deceptively simple, he realised. He imagined a stack of a hundred two by fours, two buckets of nails and a sturdy hammer. The materials appeared by his side the moment he thought of them.

He didn't know how, but he felt quite familiar with the idea of construction, as though he had devoted a lifetime to it. Even though he was in the middle of a bizarre and unsettling situation, he found comfort in hard work. He even felt confident about the task ahead of him. He began building a vertical structure using the tools and materials that he'd imagined. Before long he had built a wooden structure just taller than the wall parting him from the beer.

But even as he put the last few nails into the tower, the entire structure fell out from underneath him. He landed on the beach and found that all the two by fours, the nails and even the hammer had disappeared. In their stead he found a pink slip: it was a citation explaining why the structure had been torn down: *Structure lacked original, creative thought.*

He crumpled up the piece of paper angrily, wondering why he couldn't have been told that before he had built the entire thing. He paced back and forth below the wall now, wondering what other structure he could devise that would be creative and original. He couldn't imagine a simpler or more effective structure than a tower of two-by-fours, but since that apparently showed a lack of creativity, he would need something similar in shape and size, yet distinctive enough to show originality. Perhaps it was because he was fantasizing about sitting in a pub with a mug of beer in his hand and a bowl of pretzels before him, but it suddenly occurred to him that he could build an entire tower out of pretzel sticks.

He imagined himself a stack of pretzel sticks as large as the two-by-fours, along with vats of steaming hot cheese, and a moment later they appeared by his side. Eager and thirsty, he set about building his tower. He placed the pretzel sticks in a crisscross pattern, such that each pretzel was perpendicular to the next, but with a slight overlap in relation to the pretzel beneath it. He then used cheese to mesh the pretzel sticks together and hold them in place. Soon he had a towering structure built. With a bit of apprehension, he sealed the last pretzel in place. Then he waited… Fortunately though, this time the structure didn't collapse. He stood atop it proudly. He could now see the beer sitting beneath him, just beyond the wall, unharmed by either the sun or the warm, beach air—it still looked icy cold. He grew thirstier just gazing at it.

Now atop the stack of pretzel sticks, he wondered how he could create a second distinctive, imaginative structure that would lead him across this wall. He thought of crackers, for that would certainly match his theme of food, and compliment the pretzel sticks nicely. Soon he had built a bridge of sorts out of enormous crackers and cheese. But when he put the last cracker in place, the entire structure vanished beneath him, and he was pulled behind the wall and dropped onto the warm sand in between the two walls. Not only had the crackers been torn down, but the pretzels were gone too! Another pink slip of paper floated down by his side:

*Food items already used in first structure. Each structure must be distinctive.*

"Well why did you have to tear the pretzels down too, then?" he demanded aloud, crumpling up this second piece of paper and tossing it aside. "Now I'm back to square one…" He was tempted to try the pretzel sticks one more time, but he didn't think he could bear to see another citation, so he tried something completely different: monkeys.

The idea was highly impractical and a poor choice of construction, but he figured it was in keeping with the theme of "original thought," for who else would have thought to build a tower of monkeys? But once he'd begun, he regretted having used live monkeys. After what felt like an eternity, he had finally organised them into a suitable formation and began climbing them. The monkeys were quite animated, however, and kept bickering with each other. He urged them to be quiet but they were hardly obedient, and made faces at him or ignored his presence entirely. He had just about reached the top, when their fighting worsened, and before he could think of a way to pacify them, they broke out of their positions and the entire structure collapsed. He fell amid a sea of raining monkeys, but when he hit the ground, he was alone. The structure had disappeared. He waited for the citation. Sure enough, the pink slip floated over his head.

*Using monkeys was a pretty idiotic idea…*

"Great, lip service," he muttered, throwing the paper aside. "That's all I need."

He tried to focus yet again and think of a better, more original structure than before. He stared at the wall in frustration—just beyond it was the beer, cold and refreshing… The task before him shouldn't have been that difficult, really. How hard was it to build some kind of a tower using original, creative materials? But the more he thought about it, the more he was inclined to believe he had been given a hopeless task. He felt that his ideas would almost always be shot down, purely because he was expected to fail. If so, then what was the point of trying?

Much to his surprise, a yellow slip of paper floated down to him. He read it:

*Don't be yellow, you dirty fellow.*

He ripped the paper to shreds and buried it in the sand. Sand… Sand, of course! Why hadn't he thought of that before? Within minutes, he imagined a tower made of sand. He even designed a sturdy sand-ladder to take him to the top of the tower. But when he reached the top, almost predictably, the tower collapsed and disappeared. He was left lying face down on the beach. "What was wrong with using sand?" he cried aloud into the silence.

The pink slip found him a moment later:

*Must not use existing materials: you're on a beach, remember?*

He stared at the note in outrage. "But where does it say so on the blueprint?" he demanded, as he pulled out the sheet from his back pocket.

Yet another pink slip drifted down; he caught it briskly and read it:

*Read the fine print. Dunce.*

Many attempts later, he was ready to give up. He wasn't sure how long he had spent on that beach, or how many structures he eventually tried, but he felt defeated. He had used tires, coconut shells, Legos, books (which, the pink slip informed him had been a disrespectful use of knowledge) and eventually even tried large onion rings with a three foot diameter, at which point the pink slip suggested he was a little food-obsessed. So he now resigned himself to what seemed an inevitable defeat and surrendered aloud.

A green slip floated down to his side. Hands trembling, he read it:

*You know, you could have just* imagined *drinking the beer…*

Even as he read the words, the walls before and behind him disappeared, and he found himself staring at the bottle of ice cold beer. He walked forward slowly, as if in a trance. He touched the bottle tentatively, for he was afraid it would disappear. But it was real, and it was still cold. Grinning in spite of himself, he picked up the beer and raised it to his lips.

He awoke with a start.

It was late in the afternoon. The warm sun was beating down on his face; he had fallen asleep on his lawn chair, with a cold beer (now warm) in his hand. He sat up and brushed his eyes. He'd been laying the patio in his backyard and had paused for a break, which he realised as he glanced down at his watch, had lasted almost two hours now. Admonishing himself for his tardiness he got up and stretched lazily. He thought back over his dream as he resumed work. It had been the residue of an argument he'd had with his son, earlier in the day. His son had insisted that they had different personalities, that while he was someone who enjoyed the practical, logical side of life, such as building, planning and working within a rigid, structured environment, that his son was eccentric, and thrived on creating a space that defied all logic, purely for the sake of being different. His son was imaginative, while he was not.

The argument had ended with that very accusation, with his son insisting that the reason they had never met eye to eye, was because he lacked the imagination to *truly* see the world.

He paused in his work and mopped the sweat off his forehead. He wondered if his son had been right. In the dream he'd been mentally restrained, left unable to visualise the reality he desired. He couldn't help but wonder if that was also true of his real life. Was he lacking in imagination? And more importantly, was this shortcoming affecting him negatively?

He glanced down at the patio floor he had just laid out: a large square, built with hundreds of tiny tiles. Four sides—four equal, perpendicular sides: a perfect, boring square.

"I can do better," he told himself, and frowned in concentration as he tried to envision a more imaginative and distinctive shape. It was a simple task, he told himself: all he had to do was imagine a fun and creative design for his patio. Simple really, nothing to it...

He grew thirsty and went to reach for the beer, but then held himself back. "I won't even take a sip until I come up with an idea," he told himself, feeling that the addition of a clear incentive would prompt the wheels in his mind to start spinning rapidly.

He sat on the ground and stared at the bottle of beer, while his mind worked tirelessly to conjure up an original, imaginative idea for a patio structure. In a small corner of his mind, he thought it funny that his reality had taken on the nature of his dreams.

To his immense astonishment, a pink slip floated down by his side. He picked it up slowly, in utter disbelief. On the paper was written: *Pete's Patio Designs: When you feel you've run out of ideas, call Pete's Patio Designers!* He crumpled up the flyer with disgust.

Imprisoned within reality's dream, he stared longingly at the beer...

# V

# *Reflection*

I was six years old when I announced to my father that I wanted to be a magician. He responded by offering to show me a magic trick that would turn me black and blue. Then, turning his angry glare back to the newspaper, he said, "No son of mine is going to play Houdini for a living." Thirty years later, I was about to go on stage for my 1000<sup>th</sup> performance. The bruises on my body had healed long before my first performance, but the scars on my memories still remained. I didn't blame my father for what I had become, though I certainly didn't credit him for it either. I was what I was because of my *own* choices.

A psychiatrist I had been assigned to a few years back attempted to attribute every one of my "flaws" to my turbulent relationship with my father: my anger, my excessive drinking, and even my womanizing tendencies. She said that though he'd passed away several years ago, his shadow still loomed over me and said it always would. I chuckled wryly as I remembered her asinine conclusions and wondered how such an absurd field like psychology could be considered a science. I hated my father, perhaps more than he hated me, but his shadow, along with the rest of him, was six feet under. The scars I wore from our time together were nothing more than reminders of a nasty childhood; but the scars weren't wounds—they didn't bleed.

I checked the clock above the dresser—I had a few more minutes before my cue. I scrutinised my reflection in the antique cheval mirror. "A thousand performances," I said to myself, with a sly grin. "No one ever gave you a chance of even going past a dozen." But then the grin slowly left my face, "Least of all your father," I added.

*The silence was deafening.*

*An intimidating air of expectation hovered over the entire theatre, as the spotlight fell upon him, standing in the middle of the stage, alone but for a single, ordinary prop.*

*"Behold," he said, gesturing to the orange bucket. Picking it up, he turned it over in his hands so that the audience could see there were no false bottoms, tubes, pipes or any machinery attached to it. It was quite simply a plain, unremarkable orange bucket that he would perform magic with. He spat once into the bucket, covered it under a white sheet, and then muttered an incantation while twirling his wand over the sheet in clockwise circles. When he was finished, he glanced at the audience for a moment, to further intensify the anticipation, before removing the cloth with a grand flourish. The bucket was filled to the brim with water.*

*The resounding applause filled the theatre with an overwhelming sense of achievement, as he bowed and received due praise from his spectators. But even as he raised his palms to modestly quell their appreciation, a gurgling noise rose from the bucket. At first he ignored it, but then he noticed several people shifting in their seats to look past him, their eyes wide with awe and alarm. Slowly he too turned to look behind.*

*A dim silhouette rose from the bucket, its shape transforming steadily as it emerged into the air. It took on the form of a man, a man he knew and recognised very well: his father. He moved forward, entranced by this inexplicable occurrence. His father stood with his feet submerged in the water, still blurry and see-through, but his identity was unmistakable. His eyes screamed with disapproval as he pulled a gun from within his jacket and aimed it at his son.*

*A shot fired and the audience screamed in horror.*

A magician's life, like the trunk he carries with him from show to show, is full of secrets. And these secrets, if exposed, would not only reveal the workings of his tricks, but would also reveal the workings of the magician himself, whose very existence is a trick. But I knew, as I checked my appearance in the mirror, that my own secrets were safe. I had paid my dues in life, and this was the time to enjoy what I had earned.

These few minutes before each show were my favourite moments of the entire night. The anticipation was at its highest point, as was my confidence. After working hard to practice my tricks again and again, these final few moments before the performance were about relishing the prospect of undeniable success. It was a moment when I could reflect upon my existing accomplishments and be proud of what I was now about to achieve.

Standing before the floor-length mirror, I deemed my appearance decent enough—still, it never hurt to look perfect, so I took a brush to my jacket in an effort to make it spotless. It was then that I noticed something odd: the man inside the mirror, identical to me in every detail, did not brush his jacket as I did. I frowned at him, but he did not frown back.

"No," I sighed heavily. "Why're you doing this to me now?" I tried to ignore the aberration and straightened my tie. The tie in the reflection remained crooked.

I closed my eyes and took a deep breath. I hadn't had a drink in years, I was certain of that. My mind couldn't have been playing tricks with me, not now, not so close to the show. I told myself that there had to be a reasonable explanation. In fact, I *forced* myself to believe that when I opened my eyes, everything would be normal and my reflection would behave normally.

My eyes opened, but the man in the mirror still had his eyes shut.

"*Damn* you!" I cried, kicking my dresser in anger.

I felt like this had happened before, but it hadn't. I had seen strange things when I'd been drunk, but nothing like this and definitely nothing when I was sober. So if it wasn't alcohol that was producing these visions, what else could it be?

My gaze fell upon the divorce papers I'd received that very morning, a parting gift from the cheating wife that had left my side over a year ago. Next to the papers was a bottle of gin. I had carried this bottle with me from show to show for many years now. It was still full and the seal hadn't even been broken, though there had been many times when I had contemplated succumbing to its temptations. But the fact that I hadn't lapsed in my self-control was precisely why I carried it with me wherever I went. It was a reminder of the sacrifices I had made and the demons I had vowed to evade. I turned back to the mirror.

In the reflection, the bottle of gin was half-empty.

"No, don't do this," I begged, falling to my knees, but I wasn't sure who I was pleading to—maybe it didn't matter. I could hear the applause of the audience from the stage, just above my dressing room—the show was starting. My manager was introducing the programme now. I only had a few moments before my cue. I had to get myself together... I *had* to...

*He was the best magician in the world. He believed that... he had to. Underneath all his doubts, his weaknesses and his lack of any confidence, there lurked a stash of self-belief that was paramount to his success. He needed to borrow from that stash now, to regain lost ground; and perhaps most importantly, he needed to become the magician he knew he could be.*

*A cabinet stood on the stage. It had been raised about three feet from the floor, so that the audience could see there were no trapdoors leading beneath it. Similarly, apart from the strings that held it suspended in mid-air, there was nothing else touching the roof of the cabinet. It was now rotated in a full circle for the audience to get a good look all around it, and learn that it was quite simply an unremarkable wooden cabinet. He now opened the door and showed the audience the inside of the cabinet. He stepped in and ran his hands along the back and side panels, to show them that these panels were smooth and devoid of any mechanical rigs or features. Then he finally leapt out and asked if they were satisfied. Without waiting for an answer, he closed the door and pulled out his wand. He aimed it at the cabinet and muttered an incantation. He then tapped the door with his wand and pulled it open with a flourish.*

*His lovely assistant stood inside, clad in conservative clothing (conservative in length, not in style), which elicited a lot of howling and whistling from the men in the audience. He helped her down from the cabinet, closed the door, and allowed her to take her bows, while he stood smiling behind her. But then the cabinet door flew open again, and this time there was a couple inside, kissing passionately. The audience, thinking this was part of the trick, began applauding and whistling even louder. But he knew it wasn't a trick, at least not his own. The woman in the cabinet was his wife, and the man kissing her was his brother.*

*Slamming the cabinet door shut, he set it on fire, disregarding the commotion this caused among the audience, and ignoring the screams that came from within.*

*The funny thing was he didn't even have a brother...*

I paced in front of the mirror, but my reflection stood still, with his hands behind his back, grinning at me with a kind of perverse amusement. I tried to ignore him, to focus instead on getting myself together, but my mind kept throwing obstacles in my path.

It had been a little over a year since my wife left me, but the pain still lingered. Why was I thinking of her now, I wondered? I had more pressing concerns than her adulterous nature, a label she would have been quite offended by, for it had never been proven that she'd had an affair. Instead, it was *my* apparent unfaithfulness and numerous scandals that she'd pointed her finger at when filing for a divorce. But I'd always noticed the way she'd looked at other men, not just strangers, but even my friends and colleagues. They were looks of admiration, of desire, and of approval… none of which I had earned from her in all our years of marriage.

The psychiatrist had met with me again a few months ago, by court order. She had told me that in addition to the scars left on my character by my father's abuse, I was also suffering from abandonment issues. According to her, these issues were a direct result of my mother running out on our family when I was a child. Apparently my impending divorce had now further exacerbated the condition. She said that I felt emasculated by my wife's rejection and that it'd hurt my already weakened self-esteem even further. I'd told her that she was daft and that it hardly took a medical degree to realise a cheating wife would hurt the husband's self-esteem. I had stubbornly maintained that I'd made my peace with my wife's rejection, and that I wasn't suffering from any sort of psychological issues. The sessions had ended and I had returned to my life, untreated. Watching my reflection stare coldly back at me, with the kind of hostility only a stranger could express, I began to wonder if there had been any truth to her conclusions.

I stared at myself in the mirror, at the tired, gaunt face, wan complexion, and dishevelled hair. My eyes were hollow, practically lifeless, and there was a defeated expression on my unshaven face. *Unshaven…* I felt the smooth contours of my *own* freshly shaven chin… this wasn't me. This man in the mirror definitely wasn't me—he *couldn't* be me. Was I hallucinating? Or worse, was he a *real* person? What if there had been a schism in my existence, splitting me into two different halves. What if my reflection was a different person altogether? I took a deck of cards from my breast pocket; good, he was doing the same thing. We both shuffled the cards deftly and then split the deck; we held up the top card on each deck for the other to see: I had the three of hearts, while he had the ace of spades.

I threw the deck at the mirror and cursed him. He was still holding onto his deck, eyeing me smugly. "Don't do this to me..." I implored of him.

He shrugged, as if my plea meant nothing to him.

I turned away from the mirror.

I thought practising another trick would calm my nerves, so I chose a short but effective routine. I pulled a white silk handkerchief from my right sleeve; then I pulled a blue silk handkerchief from my left and tied the two together. I displayed them to an imaginary audience with my left hand, and as I did so, I pulled a third handkerchief out of my breast pocket with the right. This third handkerchief was made out of red silk and so was the most striking of the three. Keeping both hands separate, I tossed the joined handkerchiefs and the single red one into the air, and caught them both in a flourish with just my left hand. Grabbing either end with either hand, I revealed all three handkerchiefs joined together, with the red one tied in between the blue and white. I imagined the theatre erupting into tumultuous applause, and this eased my anxiety.

I turned back to the mirror.

He seemed to be waiting for me. When he had my attention, he repeated my trick, but with *five* handkerchiefs, all shown to be distinct pieces, and *all* tossed into the air at once. The effect was astounding, for five separate pieces of cloth rose clearly and yet fell as one single strand of five fabrics, knotted together. I gazed, dumbstruck by his impossible feat. He smiled at me smugly and I noticed that the defeated expression on his face had vanished, replaced instead by a look of arrogance I had often glimpsed in myself

"We should be working together as *one*," I told him. He said the words with me, adopting the same gestures and facial expressions that I did, and yet when we finished, he stepped back and shook his head. I collapsed onto the floor and tore at my hair in frustration. Why had my own reflection suddenly turned against me?

There was a knock at the door and my assistant Amelia's beautiful face peered into the room. She scanned the room cautiously, before finding me huddled on the floor; her lovely eyes couldn't mask either the shock or the sudden revulsion she felt.

"Are you all right?" she asked, dropping down to my side rather hesitantly.

"What're you doing here?" I said, sitting up and leaning against the dresser.

"You missed your cue," she informed me. "Charles had to promote the singing group ahead of you. So you have another ten minutes before you're supposed to go on again. In the meanwhile, he asked me to check on you."

I felt a prick of disappointment, because I'd hoped that she had come in here out of her own concern for me. Amelia was quite beautiful, in many ways the *most* beautiful woman I had ever beheld. She had an innocent, virginal quality that I found irresistible. I wondered if it was this very innocence that kept her from realising my feelings for her. Many of the assistants before her had succumbed to subtler advances, but Amelia had obliviously (or else skilfully) evaded my every determined effort to win her affection.

She peered at me closely now, her expression hard to fathom. "You look ill," she said, sounding more critical than worried. "Are you sure you're up to this tonight?"

I glanced at the mirror. My reflection was kissing Amelia passionately. He had one hand on the small of her back, while the other caressed her long, black hair. I felt a new surge of bitterness towards him, coupled with poisonous envy.

"Are you okay?" she asked, a look of clear disgust on her face.

I managed a watery smile and a weak nod. "I'm fine. I'll be out soon."

She wasn't convinced, but she didn't linger either. "You have a few minutes before your cue. Call if you need anything. We're just down the hall."

I nodded. As she closed the door behind her, I felt the emptiness within the room grow stronger, until it slowly began to suffocate me. I realised that beneath the façade of carefully practised routines, my life was in shambles. I had lost my wife, had been shunned to this small theatre in a corner of the city, and I no longer had the charm to win the affection of beautiful women. The frustration reduced me to tears.

*He tossed a notebook, with a small pencil attached, into the audience. An old woman in a large hat caught it. He asked her to write down a single word and then return it to him. A few seconds later, the notebook made its way back onto the stage and into his hands. He read the word to himself and then called out his assistant. Amelia strode out onto the stage, looking stunning as usual. A few whistles and howls came from the audience, followed by embarrassed laughter. Amelia indulged them with a quick smile and a wink, before a solemn look of concentration came upon her features and she closed her eyes.*

*He raised his wand silently; the audience held their breath as he circled it over her head and then tapped her on the shoulder. "What's the word?" he asked her.*

*She frowned in concentration and a heavy silence fell over the theatre. Then her eyes opened and she smiled. "Arraigned," she answered.*

*"Amazing!" the old woman in the audience yelled and the audience erupted into applause. There were those that no doubt suspected the old woman had been planted there and been given a previously decided word, so he prepared to repeat the trick by tossing the notebook into the theatre at random again. It was then that Amelia suddenly uttered yet another word.*

*"Impotent," she said.*

*He froze. The theatre fell into a heavy silence.*

*Amelia was looking right at him, with a look of disgust. "Impotent... Ugly... Small... Weak... Pathetic... shall I go on? Or are those words sufficient?" she said and then laughed cruelly. "What woman in her right mind could possibly love you?"*

I stared at the bottle of gin... it had been so many years since my last drink, but the memory was fresh in my mind. The taste, the feel, the potent effect... Alcohol was forgiving in a way nothing else had ever been, or ever could be... it erased everything negative from within the mind and replenished everything that was good and heartening. I could feel my disheartened spirit calling out for help... dare I break so many years of self-control to answer its plea?

I took the bottle of gin and broke the seal. My hands trembled as I lifted it to my lips and then a moment later the heady liquor rushed past my throat, immediately lending vigour to my limbs. I placed the now half-empty bottle back on the dresser. The effects of the liquor were oddly short-lived, for no sooner had I felt a sense of renewed strength invigorating my limbs, that the sensation evaporated and I felt weaker than even before.

I glanced at the half-empty bottle and realised I was a failure... It occurred to me that this was the reality I'd glimpsed within the mirror, for hadn't the bottle in the reflection been half-empty to begin with? The one consolation, if I could call it that, was that I had now probably matched the reality of my reflection. I was right, for turning around I saw that the bottle within the mirror was still half-full. My reflection, meanwhile, stood with his hands in his pockets, regarding me with a kind of pity. He looked better now, healthier, and even happier.

But I felt sick, both physically and mentally. I felt guilty about having had that drink, and I didn't think my body had agreed with it. I felt intensely weak, as if my legs weren't my own anymore, and they wobbled unsteadily as I tried to find my balance.

I glared at my reflection, at his perfect, unaffected appearance. "This is what you wanted, isn't it?" I hissed at him. "You wanted what I had for yourself."

Feeling oddly disoriented all of a sudden, I took my hat off the rack it hung on and placed it on my head; he did the same. Then I took my wand out and clumsily tapped my own head with it, while muttering an incantation. His hand was steadier as he echoed my movements and as we both took our hats off in a flourish, a rabbit sat atop his mane of lustrous hair, whereas the top of my flat, lifeless hair lay empty. I glared at him and hatred burned strongly within me. He had stolen *everything* from me: my health, my looks, my fantasies, and now he'd even robbed me of my magical talent—not just robbed it, but as he showed with the handkerchief trick, he'd even gone far enough to surpass anything I had ever achieved before.

I paced unsteadily around the small room, my anxiety deepening. He took the time to smarten his appearance by running a razor through his stubble, combing his hair and tidying his clothes. I watched him with fascination. He looked quite sharp when he was finished, and even I had to admit that it was a pretty impressive transformation. Colour had returned to his cheeks, his features were fuller, and his eyes sparkled with promise and talent.

He came up to the mirror and I followed to see what he was doing. Standing inches from my face, he straightened his tie and brushed the loose strands from his hairstyle back into place. I mimicked his movements, hoping to annoy him. But he wasn't annoyed. His eyes, though fixed on me, seemed not to regard me at all. I don't think he even noticed me. When he was satisfied with what he saw in the mirror, he turned and walked towards the dresser. The bottle of gin in the reflection was full again, and had even been resealed. But as I turned to the bottle atop my own dresser, I found that it was still half-empty. I couldn't make sense of this madness…

He was living the life I had always wanted for myself, the life that *we* had always wanted. And yet now that he had attained it, he refused to share with me. It seemed that I would have to make peace with the fact that we were different people. We were inherently the same, yes, but we were living different lives, in different realities.

The door behind him opened and I saw Amelia enter the room again. I turned around expectantly, but there was no Amelia in *my* room. I listened to her asking him to be ready for his cue in two minutes. He nodded, and she wished him good luck with a kiss that told me their relationship was different than the one I shared with her. When she left the room again, he turned back to the mirror and looked at me… yes, directly *at* me.

"You're it," he told me, but did not explain what he meant. When he left, closing the door behind him, my eyes fell on his dresser. This time there was no bottle of gin on it, empty or full. A part of me wanted to turn around to see what I would find on my own dresser. But I no longer had the luxury of observing two realities. For somehow in the past half hour, I had stopped being the magician and the performer; instead I had become the man in the mirror, a reflection.

# VI

## *An Apple Branch*

Faisal Anwar waited for the garage door to open. The machine made a loud grating noise as the enormous metal door lifted laboriously into the slim space overhead. Anwar waited for the noise to end before he started his car. The '98 Prelude whirred to life and white smoke lifted into the hazy skies overhead. Anwar buttoned his coat, slipped on his gloves and picked up his shovel. City by-laws had been revised recently to dictate that the portion of sidewalk belonging to each home owner ought to be cleared within twelve hours of the most recent snowfall. Back home in Pakistan, Anwar never had to worry about snow, let alone clearing it. But he didn't complain. There were many things that were different between his life in Rawalpindi and his life out west. It was, he realised, as if he had lived two distinct lives.

He ploughed his way down the length of the long driveway and stepped onto the sidewalk. He began the arduous task of clearing the white burden off the concrete, cursing every time the wind howled around his ears, and smiling every time his metal shovel struck the hard ground beneath the thick layers of ice.

Within a few minutes he had cleared his driveway and the pathway directly before it. He now moved to the stretch of sidewalk that circled around his front lawn. To his great surprise, Anwar found that the sidewalk was bare, bathed in a soothing dark shade of concrete gray. He smiled and glanced at his neighbour's house. Henry Maurice had beaten him to it. Anwar put the shovel back in its place, got into his '98 Prelude and slid out of his garage. Just before he drove off, he shot a quick glance at the enormous apple tree that stood proudly on his front lawn. Its branches were frigid and bare, but it still appeared proud and somewhat regal. It seemed as magnificent to him then as it had when he'd bought this house seven years ago. Anwar drove off into the cold, wintry dawn.

That evening, after a long day at WADE corporation, a procurement and consultation company where Anwar was a junior-level engineer, he returned home in his '98 Prelude and kissed his wife as he came in through the door. He had his dinner while they talked over his day at the office, and he detailed how difficult his co-workers had made his job for him, but how he had risen above them and won the praise of the lead engineer. Farah, Anwar's wife of eleven years, listened to him with a smile on her face and a frequent nod of her head to show she was following him. It was a reflection of her loyalty, Anwar knew, that though she had heard this story before (it was the same story he told her almost every night at the dinner table) she had never once succumbed to the temptation of asking, "If the lead engineer is always so pleased with you, Faisal, how come you haven't had a promotion in six years?"

After dinner, Anwar spent an hour flipping through every channel on the television that was running a reality show of some sort. Soon after, Anwar and Farah retired to bed. Before slipping under the covers, Anwar reset his alarm clock from the daily call of 5:30AM to 5AM. When Farah asked why, he simply said, "I have an early chore to get done."

Henry Maurice slipped under his rising garage door and and started his '94 Civic. The engine roared to life and white smoke lifted into the hazy skies above. He stared at the fresh layer of snow that had accumulated on his driveway and cursed to himself. Little Peter Maurice, all of seven years old, came up and reminded him gently that "Mom wouldn't like to hear you swearing like that." After buckling up little Peter and four-year old Jessica into the car, Maurice picked up his shovel and began attacking the driveway. He worked painfully to clear a path for his Civic and soon approached the sidewalk. In a few minutes he had cleared the sidewalk beneath his driveway and as he approached the stretch that curved around his front lawn, he was met with a surprise. Dark concrete beamed up at him. Maurice looked over at the Anwar house and smiled. He replaced the shovel and backed his Civic out the driveway.

As he prepared to drive off, Maurice's gaze fell on the enormous apple tree that his neighbour proudly owned. Every fall, Anwar and his wife brough basketfulls of ripe apples over to his house and apologized for the leaves that had inevitably fallen over the fence and onto Maurice's yard. But Maurice had never minded the leaves or the apples themselves that fell into his yard. The apple tree was the oldest resident in this neighourhood—rumour was that it was almost two hundred years old. If anything, Maurice considered it a part of his own yard.

Spring came late that year, and then summer reared itself over the city and memories of the bitter winter faded away in above-seasonal temperatures. The driveways and sidewalks around the Anwar and Maurice household were bone dry and their lawns were bathed in golden light. The apple tree, always a late bloomer, looked full and beautiful with the promise of a healthy yield of apples. Anwar and Maurice invited each other's families over for barbecues almost every weekend. They talked, ate and laughed like they were best friends.

Summer waned slowly and by the last week of August, the tree was full of apples. That Saturday morning, Maurice collected the apples that had fallen off his neighbour's tree and all over his front lawn. He put them in a basket and ushered them to the Anwar household. Anwar was wheeling his lawnmower out of the garage when the two met.

"Another basket for you," Maurice smiled, panting a little with the weight of the basket. He placed it in Anwar's garage for him. "Fresh off the lawn."

"No, no, my friend, that is yours," Anwar said, raising two palms politely. He then slipped into the garage and returned with a larger basket of golden-red apples. "These I had picked for you early in the morning. Now you must take both."

"I can't eat so many apples, Faisal," laughed Maurice.

"Give it to the children, or to Marie."

"How many apples do you think my wife can eat?"

"As many as mine, if she's hungry enough."

They shared a laugh and then settled on a compromise; Maurice took his smaller basket of apples back with him and Faisal took the larger basket into the house. This kind of exchange was a yearly ritual, and had been going on for all the many years that Maurice and Anwar had been neighbours. And perhaps naively, they expected it to continue forever.

Fall came much too soon that year. Barely two weeks after Maurice and Faisal had exchanged the baskets of apples, the golden green stretches of endless lawns and fields had turned to a rusty bronze. The enormous apple tree though was still full of fruit, even though it had begun shedding leaves on either side of the wooden fence. Anwar had just come home from work to a lawn that needed more raking than mowing. Farah wasn't home, and Anwar didn't feel like watching television—he knew what news would be on every channel. Deep in thought, he decided he would tackle his lawn and get some chores done. He was standing in front of his garage, rake in hand, when he noticed Maurice striding up his driveway, almost red with rage.

Anwar regarded his neighbour with surprise. "What's wrong, Henry?"

"I'll tell you what's wrong," Henry yelled. "Your damn tree, that's what's wrong."

Faisal gazed over at the two-hundred year old apple tree, at the leaves steadily falling off its expansive arms. "Yes, I don't know why the leaves are falling so early this year."

"It's a bloody nuisance, Faisal, and I've had enough."

"Enough of what?"

"That pesky tree. It's always dropping things on my side of the lawn and I'm through picking up after it. Either you start making sure that no more leaves fall on my side of the lawn or else I'll have to call the city and lodge a complaint."

"A complaint?" sputtered Anwar, in utter disbelief. "You're joking."

"This is no joke. Like I said, I've had enough of that damn tree of yours."

"But Henry, that tree has been here for two hundred years!"

"So what? Now it's on *your* lawn and it's affecting mine."

"But you know that I can't control where the leaves fall, Henry. I've lived here for years and until today I've never heard you complain about it."

"Look Faisal, enough is enough. Clear my lawn right *now*."

Anwar bristled with indignation. "I will not."

"Then I'm lodging a complaint."

"Be my guest," said Anwar, calling his neighbour's bluff. "There is no judge in this world who would give credence to such a complaint."

The two neighbours stood there and argued for several minutes, before retreating into their houses under fits of intense rage. Maurice never did lodge a complaint but the damage to their friendship had nevertheless been done. From that day onwards, Anwar and Maurice never spoke to each other. There were no more baskets making rounds between the two neighbours, nor any invites to barbecues or dinners. Every winter after a snowfall, each neighbour cleared the sidewalks up till their respective property lines, but never an inch more.

Maurice and Anwar parted ways that afternoon, forever. And the 200-year old apple tree was cut down in anger that very evening. The evening of September 11, 2001.

# VII

## Touch of Reality

There is something undeniably cathartic about being in the midst of a large and boisterous crowd. It might be the sense of community that produces the catharsis, the overwhelming gratification one obtains from being an accepted member of a large group: an evolutionary throwback perhaps to the age of hunting in herds. Or it might be the endless assault on the senses: the hundreds of faces, expressions, gestures, and clothes to study; the barrage of noises, music, screams, laughter and conversations to observe. At the very least, the mood of a large crowd is infectious—it imprisons every member of its group, participant or not, within its communal energy. Standing within that crowd of several hundred, perhaps even over a thousand, I felt intensely alive, as though every inch of my body had been set alight by an invisible current. When they laughed, I laughed giddily; when they cheered, I screamed myself hoarse joining in; and when they clapped, I pounded my hands together till they turned raw.

At the moment though, the crowds were subdued. We were

gathered outside a large stadium, where the performances of some of the top celebrities from around the world were scheduled. A glamorous red carpet (glamorous only in terms of the societal connotation a red carpet holds, for in actuality the carpet looked worn and unimpressive) stretched from the steps of the stadium to the ends of the street, where limousines and expensive cars would soon pull up, carrying the few individuals who alone dictated the sheer importance of this night.

I will admit that the entire occasion echoed with frivolous vanity, of over indulgence and empty gestures. I found the idea of celebrating individuals—people who were no different to the thousands gathered here, nor to the millions glued to their televisions around the world, except through mere circumstance—mildly absurd at the very least. From the ridiculously large stadium, furnished lavishly, decorated with expensive, glittering objects, and outfitted with high-tech media equipment, to the outrageously monstrous limousines, most of which resembled buses and yet carried no more than two passengers, the whole event reeked of excessive waste.

But standing amidst that crowd, I was in a position to witness firsthand the sheer power of blind, unyielding devotion. Many of the fans around me had flown thousands of miles, spent anywhere from a tidy chunk of their vacation budgets, to even a few *months'* worth of wages, and had suffered through unimaginable inconveniences quite simply to share in this event. They didn't lament the excessive waste or the frivolous vanity of the occasion—they were here to simply share in a tiny portion of the celebration. What saddened me though was the knowledge that when the night was over, when the celebrities would return in their limousines to their five-star accommodations and luxurious lives, that these loyal fans would have to return to their realities, to their unglamorous lives, and work even harder to regain the ground they had yielded to this occasion. They would spend days, weeks or maybe even months recovering from the financial, physical and emotional impacts of the night. A few would perhaps never recover. But none of that mattered to them at present; reality would always find them tomorrow. Tonight was about fantasy, about stars and divine circumstances; tonight, they would dream.

I too was there to dream.

My story isn't about vacation budgets or financial discomforts; nor is it about celebrity worship. I was there that night to solidify a dream I had long ago relinquished to the all-consuming chasms of pragmatic thought. On that night and perhaps on that night *alone*, I would be no different than a child: idealistic, ambitious, and filled with innocent expectation.

"You're such a dork," a woman's voice said, from just behind me.

Ah yes, I forgot to mention that I wasn't there alone that night. Through a considerable lack of prudence, I had brought my wife Meena along with me. When we'd first been married, Meena had been everything I'd ever wanted in a bride. Slim, tan and beautiful, she had charmed me with her elegance, sophistication and gentle personality. Of course, marriage had changed all that. The beautiful bride I had eagerly carried up to the bedroom on our wedding night had transformed into the Meena now standing beside me: she was still tan, though no longer *as* slim, and she would perhaps have still been beautiful if her features weren't always arranged in some kind of a menacing expression. The elegance and sophistication had decayed into borderline crudeness, and the gentle personality that had promised me a lifetime of civility, had been ravaged into the kind of frightening disposition commonly found amid mobsters.

She was glaring at me just then, her strong hands folded across her broad chest. It was funny how marriage had transformed our physiques: on our wedding night, I had effortlessly supported her slender body with my strong, muscular frame. But things were different now; Meena could have held me upside down by the ankles and shaken every remaining ounce of pride out of me if she so wished. It was why I kept a suitable distance between us now.

"I don't think you should call me names in public," I told her.

"I'm not calling you names. I'm calling you a dork, because you *are* one."

I thought Meena was being rather harsh, and that too in front of so many people. Two teenage girls in front of me were giggling, apparently tickled pink by the fact that they'd just witnessed a wife calling her husband a "dork" in public.

"Would you keep your voice down, Meena?" I said, in a low voice.

"Why? Afraid I'll embarrass you?" she retorted.

"I'm afraid that horse left the barn years ago, my dear."

"Oh? So I've been embarrassing you for years then?"

"Your words, not mine."

"And you think I'm not embarrassed standing next to *you*?" Meena shot back, rather scathingly. "You're single-handedly downgrading the reputation of immigrant East-Indians living in the U.S. and *that* in itself is saying a lot."

I glowered at her, but wisely thought better of replying.

It's not as if her point lacked validity. Even those who did not know me would have guessed from my appearance alone that I was a man well-acquainted with embarrassment. I was not gifted with a body that would look good in clothes. I was also not gifted with flair. Hair parted comically, wearing old sneakers beneath corduroy pants, while sporting a flannel shirt, a baseball cap, and the largest pair of horn-rimmed glasses in existence, I no doubt appeared the true portrait of a man who was estranged with the art of style. I will admit that my idea of "good fashion-sense" was simply to tie one of my bulky sweaters around my waist on long hikes. But my unfashionable appearance never bothered me, for it's not a sense of style that I want to be defined by, but other qualities. Unfortunately, one of those qualities wasn't foresight.

For instance, the purpose of inviting Meena on this outing was rather straightforward: she always complained that I never took her anywhere, and in theory a trip to the celebrity capital of the world should have appeased her. But considering the fact that *my* personal motive for this trip was to gawk at a pretty girl, bringing the wife along had been a foolish idea.

Now, I wasn't a *total* idiot. I knew I was old, unattractive, and most undeniably married, so it wasn't as though I had a chance of forging some kind of an acquaintance with any one of the beautiful starlets that would be gracing this red carpet soon. No, my *actual* goal was merely to see them in the flesh, up close, to solidify fantasies I had long ago surrendered to pragmatic thought. Incidentally, just to make things clear, the fantasies I refer to don't involve whips and chains or role-playing, but the sort of romantic scenarios that logic and cynicism ensure reality will never possess. During my youth, I had naively assumed that such romance was not only possible in a marriage, but would probably be a frequent occurrence. Of course, wisdom and Meena had together cured me of that misconception.

She was turned away from me just now, and was fanning herself with a magazine. I was momentarily distracted by the picture of a beautiful woman on the cover of the magazine: a dark-haired beauty, with coffee-coloured skin, long, slender legs, and a pretty face. She was smiling, with an expression that was at once seductive and innocent, a feat that I considered rather impressive. In fact, I considered the woman herself to be impressive: she was the celebrity I was most looking forward to seeing today. Actually, she was really the *only* person—

"Pervert," Meena said, and I realised that she'd caught me gazing at the magazine cover. She promptly flipped it over so that I was left gazing at an advertisement for toilet paper. What an odd choice for the back cover of a magazine, I thought. Although, I suppose considering most of these magazines *are* read in the bathroom, it's—

"You're *so* perverted," Meena said, with a disbelieving shake of her head.

I pretended to ignore her.

"You heard me," she said, annoyed further by my refusal to

take the bait. "I saw the way your eyes widened when you saw the magazine. The woman is *half* your age."

I heard a few snickers around me and felt rather sorry for myself. "I *told* you to keep your voice down," I urged her, through gritted teeth.

"She is 23 years old, and you are 46!" Meena said, with no change in her volume.

"Yes, I understood what you meant by 'half your age,' *thank* you," I said, as a fresh batch of giggling ensued. "And there's nothing perverted about admiring someone's talent."

"Well you wouldn't have to admire her 'talent' if she didn't always wear such short dresses," Meena said, eyeing the magazine cover with clear disapproval.

"I meant her acting prowess," I said, as an old man with a monocle peered over Meena's shoulder to catch a glimpse of the talent my wife had referred to.

"Oh please," said Meena, with a derisive chuckle. "You don't give a damn about her acting. You watch her movies with the volume turned down, and you only ever watch the scenes when she's at the beach wearing a bikini, or in some filthy club, doing—"

"I *get* your point, thank you," I cut across her, pointedly. Thankfully, Meena didn't press the matter further, and seemed content to merely burn a hole through me with her glare. This luxurious moment of silence gave me a chance to ponder where this evening had gone wrong.

Inviting Meena had definitely been a mistake. But perhaps this *whole* evening was a mistake. I was standing amidst a hormonally charged mob, with vocal capacities far beyond even the shrillest banshees, suffering personal humiliation at the hands of my wife—a woman who should have been looking out for my well-being—and I was left with the realisation that all this misery was self-inflicted. But, as Meena was unfortunately aware, my reasons for being here centered around *one* particular person: the woman on the magazine cover. If at the end of tonight, I could leave with the knowledge that I had gazed upon her in the flesh, from as near as a few feet away, then all of this suffering and humiliation would have been worth it.

I knew she was half my age and that my "crush" was somewhat inappropriate, if not downright revolting, but in my defense she reminded me of a best friend I'd had when I was in college. Mona was the first girl I'd ever had feelings for, and I'd been quite enamoured by her through all our years of our friendship. Regretfully though, I'd never mustered enough courage to confess my feelings to her. We'd gone our separate ways in our early twenties, and now it had been many years since we'd even so much as heard from each other. This young actress not only physically reminded me of Mona, but her personality was frighteningly similar. Whenever I saw her in a movie or even quite simply on a magazine cover, I felt like I was an impressionable, easily excited twenty-year old again. She renewed my decaying sense of idealistic love and filled my head with naïve dreams that the adult inside me frowned upon.

"You'll swallow a pigeon if you keep your mouth open like that," said Meena, her voice slicing through my little reverie like a saw through a comfortable pillow.

Fortunately no one seemed to have heard her, for the first of the night's celebrities had just arrived at the end of the red carpet, and a volley of screams and excited cries were ringing through the air. I placed a finger on my lips to inform Meena that she shouldn't speak.

"Don't silence me! I am a free-thinking, independent woman with a voice," she insisted.

"That can cut through a metal bar, yes," I said. "But *please*, let's not argue in public."

"Why not? Let the world know we are fighting," she said, raising her voice even further. "I sit at home and slave all day, preparing your food, ironing your shirts, cleaning your house, and cleaning our children, but you spend all day ogling other women without a care—"

"I do not *ogle* other women," I hissed at her, as the old man with the monocle brought out an ear trumpet now. "Listen, *every* person in this crowd is here to see their favourite movie stars. I am no different from them, except that I suffer the misfortune of having my wife—"

"Oh my God, look!" Meena suddenly cried, with a most unnatural squeal of delight.

I looked to see what she was pointing at and comprehension dawned on me as I saw a tall, tan, muscly-looking thing stroll down the carpet in what can only be described as an "ape's walk." In his defense, he was definitely quite handsome, with strong features, thick, black hair that was sleeked back elegantly, and a smile that was at once confident and charming. Yet, despite his bronzed good-looks, there was something theatrical about his every gesture, as though he was in the middle of a performance even when greeting his loyal fans. Mind you, no one else seemed to have noticed this synthetic behaviour, for a cascade of excited squeals and screams flooded the air as he made his way down the carpet. People cried his name, sang songs from his movies, whistled, screamed, laughed, wept, and some even tried pointlessly to scale the barricade parting us lowly normal citizens from the stars on the red carpet, only to be tossed back by the ever-alert policemen. I had never glimpsed such madness before, and all for what? For a man that was no different than any other in this crowd, except through mere circumstance.

I had never seen Meena so excited either. She seemed to have forgotten all about our argument, and for that matter all about me entirely, for she was busy trying to peer over the heads of the considerably taller people before her. But what she lacked in height, she made up for in a sturdy frame, and so jostled her way through the crowd determinedly to reach the barricade and scream louder than any of the shrill-voiced teenage girls gathered around us.

I had to pause to consider the odd feeling in the pit of my stomach... was it jealousy? Could it be? I had always known of Meena's crush on that Fabio-wannabe, but I'd never been bothered by it. But there was something distressing about seeing her express her infatuation towards him in the middle of a crowd. I *was* her husband after all—didn't she owe me the simple courtesy of discretion? I saw her giggling and screaming till her Casanova sashayed down the length of the carpet and disappeared into the stadium. Only then did Meena return to my side, her face flushed with excitement and (I guess?) embarrassment. She avoided my eyes as she fanned herself with the magazine, not even bothering to keep the front cover away from me.

"So…" I said, in a teasing voice.

She still avoided my gaze. "What?"

"You did a marvellous impression of a fourteen-year old girl that sees a poster of her favourite vampire or werewolf," I said, and was glad to hear a few chuckles around me.

"I admire his acting," Meena replied.

"How could you not? He never *stops* acting," I replied, and looked around for more congratulatory smiles, but instead received a bunch of disapproving glares. Apparently Meena wasn't the only loyal fan that heathen-in-a-suit possessed.

Meena ignored my little jab. "Shall we?" she asked, turning to me.

"Shall we what?"

"Leave."

"You've got to be kidding me," I said. "I'm not leaving yet."

"Waiting for your girl, are you?" she asked, waspishly.

"I'm not here for any girl, Meena," I lied, with what I considered a pretty impressive poker-face. "I simply want to soak up the experience of this night. Now just because you've had your hormonal fill for the night, doesn't mean that *I* have."

"Look—"

"No, *you* look," I said, indignation giving way to rage. "I have had to put up with your torture for years now and I have had enough! Do you realise that—"

"Will you look…"

"Stop interrupting me!"

Meena grabbed my face with her right hand and turned it towards the red carpet. "Look," she said, nodding to a limousine that had just pulled up. I felt my jaw hit the floor.

At once I seemed to forget everything, including myself, as I pushed the old man with the monocle aside, and fought my way towards the barricade. People complained, some groaned, others yelled, a few even tried to push me back, but I was relentless in my pursuit and my eyes were fixed solely on the woman that was now gliding gracefully down the length of the carpet. Dressed in a gleaming, pearl-white saree, atop a stylish, velvety blue blouse, she practically sparkled in the dull, twilight atmosphere. The saree, draped over her right shoulder, circled back around her to eventually rest stylishly over her left arm; not many women would have looked as sophisticated and as effortlessly beautiful as she did in an outfit that was the perfect blend of a traditional design reworked with modern flair. Her dress aside, the rest of her appearance was equally flawless: her long, black hair fell in elegant, wavy curls just below her shoulders, and I was greatly impressed that she wasn't one of those women who used every special occasion as an opportunity to lacquer her hair up in some kind of a ridiculous shape. Her make-up, if there was indeed any upon her, was barely discernible, and served only to accentuate her already beautiful features. She wore simple jewellery in the form of silver earrings, which matched the colour of her saree, and a matching bracelet upon her exposed left wrist. Her look in its entirety was unassuming yet mesmerizing, for it allowed her natural splendour to shine through. Her radiant smile flashed brighter than the cameras that clicked furiously in a futile attempt to capture the full effect of her limitless beauty. Her eyes, large and reflective, conveyed more emotions and expressions than the faces of anyone else that had walked this carpet before her.

In what can only be described in hindsight as a trance, I gripped the top of the barricade and pulled myself over in an almost unconscious effort to reach her. I didn't even feel the sting of the police baton that rapped my knuckles, or the shove of the forceful arms that pushed me back repeatedly from the barricade. She paused at an enthusiastic group of children a few feet from me and signed their autographs for them. There were squeals and screams and whistles all around me, so I couldn't hear what she was saying to them, but her smile and her expression suggested that she was being kind, humble and effortlessly charming.

As she turned away from them and edged along the barricade to briefly touch the outstretched hands of her many fans, I felt as though time had been slowed to a bare minimum. I held out my own hand, reaching as far out as I could, with as much desperation as I would have shown had I been reaching for my utility belt, with my arch-rival closing his hands around my neck. She walked closer, waving to people around me, smiling at them, touching their hands, and even speaking words of gratitude to some. As she came up to me, our eyes met for the briefest moment, a moment that nevertheless lasted a lifetime. I gazed hungrily into the face of a woman who reminded me of all the youthful qualities I had surrendered to the past. Within that one short instant of eternity, I saw myself married to Mona, leading a life of unequivocal bliss, where neither one of us were left wanting for affection. We were partners in every sense of the word. There were no fights or arguments, not even disagreements. Every moment was spent in romantic indulgence. We were just as life had meant for us to be: two people that were linked by love, and turned not so much into a couple, as into *one*, living, feeling being.

Her hand, which had brushed the fingertips of many of her fans, now drifted near mine. I held her gaze as our hands touched and the illusion strengthened. She smiled at me, directly *at* me, and my fantasy turned real. But then her gaze drifted away, her hand passed beyond mine, and was lost forever. The illusion shattered, and my life with Mona became what it had always been: a wistful dream, built upon the feeble legs of an unfulfilled desire: the road not taken.

I came out of my reverie, and saw her glide down the carpet, waving to fans, touching their extended hands much as she had mine, before she filed into the auditorium along with the rest of the celebrities. The fans remained outside, packed into thick crowds, deflated by the departure of their favourite stars, yet elated by the memories they would cherish forever.

I turned to find Meena standing with her arms crossed, looking jealous and angry.

I hadn't realised lately just how much I loved her. Yes, I loved her. Despite all the tension that seemed to incessantly plague us, and all the insults we threw at one another, I sincerely loved her. I remembered now that there was a reason I had married Meena, and a reason why I had pursued her with the kind of fervent desire I had never wasted upon Mona: it was because I'd always known that Meena was my other half, my partner, my (for lack of a better term) soulmate. Meena was the bird in the hand; Mona was the pair in the bush—no pun intended.

I took my wife's hand in mine and smiled. She turned her exquisite eyes upon me, surprised and touched by my simple gesture. "Sometimes," I told her, "I forget how beautiful you are. Movie stars are glamorous and exciting, but they're not exactly *real*, are they? They don't love us the way we love them. Besides, they've got nothing compared to *your* beauty."

I leaned in and kissed her; she wore an expression akin to having been clubbed on the head. "Now, I think maybe we should go home."

Uncharacteristically mellow and tongue-tied, Meena nodded, and we made our way through the crowd back into reality. As we reached the car, I turned and cast one last, wistful glance at the distant auditorium. Her performance would begin shortly. Perhaps in another life, another existence, or merely just within a different reality, I would be in there with her. I might spend the evening with her, become her friend, and maybe even share the stage with her. But for now, within this reality, I knew I would never forget that one moment we had shared together; a moment where she'd smiled at me, held my hand, and shown me a life that could have been. It was her touch I would always cherish and remember: it had been the touch of reality.

# VIII

## *Soul Mate*

My consciousness awoke suddenly, though I had no memories of having been asleep. I was in the middle of a school gymnasium during P.E. class. Dressed in those god awful red shorts, beneath that dull grey t-shirt, I felt like an awkward, out-of-shape teenager. I didn't recognize any of my classmates, but I did recognize Coach Simmons, our teacher. Short, squat and unusually pink, he looked rather like a cartoon character. I tried to remember why I was here, back in school, back in a gym class. But I seemed to have no tangible memory of myself prior to this moment, only awareness of odd details like gym class and Coach Simmons.

There were both boys and girls in today's class, which was unusual, because I somehow remembered that Coach Simmons usually kept the sexes separate. The only times when he ever brought the entire class together was for dancing lessons. A shudder ran up my spine at the thought, because I hated dances. I couldn't remembered what I hated most about them, the prospect of walking up to a person and asking them to spend a few minutes moving with me rhythmically, or the embarrassment of standing against the wall of the gymnasium, *waiting* to be asked. Either way, dances were nerve-wracking. Coach Simmons never made the process any easier either for he usually kept up a barrage of incessant taunts and jokes throughout the duration of each class. Today's class would unfortunately be no different.

"All right, princesses, gather around," he called, aiming his first insult at the boys.

We filed in around him, boys and girls alike, all nervous yet oddly excited. Though it was nice that the sexes had been brought together in *one* class, this union led to such moments of awkwardness and discomfort. The girls gathered together in tight packs, giggling and whispering amongst each other, while the boys grinned stupidly, each one wearing an expression similar to having walked headlong into a brick wall (which considering they were boys was a possibility).

"Today's dance class is going to be different," Coach Simmons declared in that loud, robust voice of his, which despite its commanding authority still sounded squeaky. "We're not just going to have you paired up to dance. No, today you're going to find your soul mates."

An excited murmur ran through the class, but I was startled. Soul mates? How were we to find our soul mates within a class this small? And anyway, this was hardly the sort of atmosphere that would breed romance and soulful union. We were in a large, intimidating gymnasium, surrounded by basketballs and oddly-colored jerseys, with Coach Simmons barking orders at us in that squeaky voice of his. How could we possibly find our soul mates like this?

"Now I don't want any funny business," Coach Simmons continued, wagging his fat finger at us. "We will pair you up according to our list. Each person will dance with three different people, and we will be watching how well you dance. The couples that dance *best* with each other will most likely be soul mates. But *we* will ultimately make that decision."

"Sorry sir," a little mouse-haired boy said, raising his hand tentatively.

"What is it, boy?" Coach Simmons barked.

"Sir, does that mean we don't get to *choose* our soul mates?" the boy asked, timidly.

"That's exactly what it means," Coach Simmons said at once. "I'll be choosing your partners, along with Miss Wilkins here." A woman who looked rather comically like Coach Simmons in a blonde wig, nodded curtly at the mention of her name. "You will dance for five minutes with each partner, before we make the decision at the end of it. Ready?" He didn't wait for an acknowledgement, nor did we provide him with one. He merely looked down at his list and then walked around us putting people together. I waited nervously for my turn.

It was then that I caught sight of her in the corner, standing with a group of girls, yet looking detached from them. She was easily the prettiest girl in the class, and by far the prettiest girl I'd ever seen. Tall and slender, with a coffee complexion, black, wavy hair, and the most expressive face I had ever seen, she was causing many heads to turn in her direction.

I didn't remember anything of who I was, or what my life had been before I'd woken up inside this gym class, but I was certain that I did not have the kind of luck needed to ensure that this beautiful girl would end up being my soul mate. It was too much to hope for.

True to my expectations, my first partner proved to be anything but suitable. He was a tall, gangly looking thing with a bad case of acne. He didn't appear to be even remotely coordinated, and promptly tripped over himself three times before he took my hands. When the music began, he tried hopelessly to lead me around the dance floor, only to end up stepping on my feet three times before the first minute was up. It didn't help that he was so tall that I was forced to stare into his chest as we tried to make conversation. By the time the music ended, I felt a mad desire to run from his side and hide behind Coach Simmons.

"All right, change up!" Coach Simmons cried, and he and Miss Wilkins moved about the floor arranging everyone into new partners. I wasn't sad to see my partner paired up with someone else, and I tried to catch her eye to warn her about what was to come.

My next partner was a pretty, red-haired girl with green eyes and cute freckles. She seemed pleasant and confident, and when the music started we moved around rather fluently at first, until the tempo of the song picked up. Suddenly, in the middle of our interesting conversation, she began tripping over herself, causing me to stumble. Annoyed, I tried to focus on our feet so that I could keep out of her way and avoid further mistakes. It was then that I noticed her feet, strapped tightly into a pair of red heels: two feet… to be precise, two *left* feet. We'd stopped dancing by now; the music still played idly in the background, and I was dimly aware of the other couples swaying around the dance floor together.

"You have two left feet," I told her. "*Literally*! How is that possible?"

She shrugged. "I don't know."

"Well… we can't really dance if you've got two left feet."

"Why not? This isn't about dancing."

"Yes it is!" I said, hotly. "It's how well you dance together that determines whether you're soul mates or not. So if you can't dance, then clearly we're not soul mates."

"Oh no, how tragic…" she said, contemptuously.

"Bite me."

"Back at ya."

It was a good thing the music ended when it did, for we looked about ready to lunge at each other's throats. I was a little pleased to see that she was paired with the tall, gangly guy for the final dance: a match made in hell. I was so engrossed with observing how they would get along together, that I didn't notice who Coach Simmons had led me to. When I turned to face my partner, I found myself gazing at the stunning, dark-haired girl I had ogled at before.

"Hi," I said, almost breathlessly, just when she herself mouthed "Hi" to me.

I never dreamt I would be so lucky as to be paired with the prettiest girl in the class. I smiled at her and she smiled back. We stepped closer and held onto each other's sides; her face remained impassive, and she merely regarded me with simple courtesy. The music started, and we began to move around. It was easy to hold onto her, for her sides weren't soft and fragile like the others. However, slender and beautiful though she was, she felt heavier than the others, and unwieldy. She did not move lightly, but thankfully she didn't fight my efforts either, and came willingly. She matched my smile with one of hers, and laughed when I did. We didn't talk, for somehow it didn't feel necessary. The few minutes I spent with her felt like a happy marriage, like a flawless union of two souls. I was rather disappointed when I heard Coach Simmons' whistle announce the end of the dance. I let go of her reluctantly, and we stole glances at each other while Coach Simmons and Miss Wilkins conferred to choose our soul mates.

Much to the satisfaction of my childish thirst for revenge, I saw that the tall, gangly guy I had first danced with, and the annoying red head I had subsequently been paired with, had been declared soul mates. They seemed happy together though and beamed at one another. I thought it was a miracle that they had managed to dance well enough together to be deemed soul mates. Perhaps their mutual deficiencies as dancers had enabled them to dance fluently? It didn't make sense, but then who was I to question the larger, cosmic powers at work here?

I was more concerned about my own soul mate. I watched impatiently as others in the class were put in pairs. There were squeals of delight and laugher from the decided pairs, and the "soul mates" broke into kisses and hugs, much to Coach Simmons disapproval, although I did notice Miss Wilkins give him a look that plainly suggested she felt left out. As I tried not to think about what any offspring of Coach Simmons and Miss Wilkins would look like, I was led to my partner, my soul mate and eternal companion. It was the pretty, dark-haired girl.

I couldn't believe my good fortune! We smiled happily at each other. I knew that she *was* my soul mate, and not just because of how well we'd danced together, or because Coach Simmons had said so, but because it *felt* right; it truly felt like she was my other half. I didn't know my past, my identity or my purpose. I didn't know what the future had in store for me… I only knew that having my soul mate by my side would ease my path towards salvation. I did wish she came in a more pocket-sized version though… antique mirrors are pretty, but they sure are difficult to dance with, let alone carry around through all of eternity.

# IX

## *Hangman*

It is dawn. The field is empty, but won't be for long. The people here are always starved for entertainment, and nothing entertains better than a hanging. They'll be marching out of their homes soon, chatting merrily on their way to the gallows. I sometimes find a bit of mirth in the knowledge that I can so easily upset their plans, for there can be no hanging without me. The task of hanging a man isn't difficult, nor does it have to be done properly—a man can be strung up repeatedly if need be, till life drains out of him. It will be anti-climactic, not to mention painful for the poor bastard hanging by a rope, but eventually he'll die like he's supposed to. So why then does the town have a designated hangman? Maybe it's because no one else wants to do what I do; for who would want the stains of so many killings on their hands?

I have killed *many* men. I do not know the glory of shooting the enemy in the middle of a battlefield; I do not know the sport of hunting a trophy through a dense jungle, and I do not know the gallantry of challenging a rival that competes for my love. The men I have killed were defenceless, had their hands bound, and begged for mercy. It was not my choice that they die, nor was it my choice that I be the one to kill them. But as a hangman, it is my duty.

I have learnt the faces of many dying men in my daily work. The face of a man that has looked death in the eye is different than any other; for it is when confronted with his mortality that a man's features fully echo the nature of his soul. In those final moments before he meets death, he discards everything that had once separated him from God: pride, vanity, and even hope. Unburdened, he appears almost sage-like when I tie the noose around his neck. When I ask if I should cover the face, some refuse, but others are glad for the mask. There are some who like to die with their eyes open, so that they can see every last moment of life before it passes them by; but then there are others that choose to be blind when their lives end, for they fear they might otherwise glimpse some feature of life that stirs eternal regret within them.

The ones that die with their faces uncovered are somehow easier to forget than the ones that die faceless. It is the latter that haunt me in my dreams, for they float around me like veiled servants, loyal in their intentions to remain beside me, yet not friends, for I do not recognise them. I try persistently to unveil them, to determine who they are beneath the hoods, but I am never allowed that luxury. It is the curse I suffer for having taken so many lives.

I have been a hangman for nearly fifty years. It was not a duty I volunteered for or had been *selected* to perform; no, it was a mantle that had been passed down to me by my father, and his father before him. My father was eighteen when he performed his first hanging. He told me eighteen was too young an age to begin killing. I started when I was twelve.

My first kill was the man who shot my father. His brother had been sentenced to the gallows, and my father had been the hangman—he was shot midway through the execution. I watched him die from amongst the crowd. The very next day I was ushered in to take over my father's role. I stared his killer in the eyes and searched for a sign of contrition, for anything that would give me cause to hesitate. But he stared back coldly, taunting me with his eyes alone. He *wanted* to die. I did not disappoint him. But a part of me died along with him that morning.

In the fifty years since, I have taken more lives than I care to count. There have been weeks where I've gone without killing, and yet there have been weeks where I've killed dozens each day. This job has cost me my life. The incessant killing weighs heavily on my soul, and it inhibits me from establishing any meaningful rapport with the living. I don't have any friends, and my father was the last of the family I had. I live as a recluse, hiding out in my cabin on the outskirts of town. The noise of hoof beats in the distance always makes me anxious, for I know my visitor will summon me to duty. Why else would anyone visit me? My partner in life is the noose that earns me my living; without it, I would have no identity.

I often consider leaving town. If I stay, I will likely remain a hangman for life. Sheriffs have come and gone, as have mayors, but my post seems to outlast entire governments. My life lies in pathetic shambles, and solitude seems to be my only comfort. I never married, though I partake in female companionship every so often. I normally sleep at the saloon after an execution and sometimes I get so drunk that I pass out in the street; but most of the time I sleep in a hooker's bed, after having worked my frustrations out on her. I never feel better afterwards though, and that has nothing to do with my hangovers. The endless killings haunt me, and nothing seems to cure me of it, not women, not alcohol, and not even the people in town that congratulate me after every hanging for doing my job well. If anything, that makes it worse...

There are times when I find solace talking to the reverend. I'm not normally a church-goer, and I've never enjoyed attending a sermon. But I like the reverend. Maybe it's because he is the only one in town that doesn't treat me like a hero for killing defenceless men. Or maybe it's because he is the only one that realises how helpless I actually am. He never speaks much during our meetings, not unless I ask him to; mostly he listens while I talk. There are times though when neither of us says a word, when we merely sit together and stare at the floor until the hour passes. Sometimes he reads to me from the bible, and that always lifts the fog over my thoughts. But as soon as I return to the gallows, I feel helpless again.

I have three executions scheduled this morning. I don't know how I'll make it through them. I can see people filing out of their houses now. The sheriff will be bringing the three men over from the jail. It is a beautiful, cloudless day, though somewhat cold, for the winter air is bitter. But I do not complain. Air, *any* form of air, is a wonderful luxury.

Just ask the three men who will soon find themselves deprived of it.

Within a quarter of an hour, the gallows are surrounded by the townspeople. I climb the steps to the platform and the sheriff follows. I avoid looking at the prisoners, as is usually my custom. I don't make eye contact with them until I tie the noose around their necks. The reverend nods to me and takes his place on the other side of the platform, holding the bible with both hands. I stare at my boots and inwardly ask forgiveness for what I am about to do.

"Merry Christmas," the sheriff says in a quiet voice, as he passes me.

I frown at him, surprised. Is it really Christmas? I usually don't follow the calendar but I do remain aware of important dates. I didn't even know it was *close* to being Christmas though. It's probably because I haven't been into town in so long. I knew the weather was getting colder, and that the days were quite short, but I had expected it to be the first week of December at most.

A question remains though: why is there an execution scheduled on Christmas morning? More importantly, why has the entire town assembled to witness it? Why stand around and watch a killing on Christmas morning? Have none of us earned ourselves a sinless day? Are the jails so full that I am forced to take lives on this, the day when we celebrate life and birth?

My eyes then fall upon the first man that the sheriff leads towards me. He isn't even a man—he is a young boy, no more than six years old perhaps. Yet his solemn face shows that he has endured more in those six years than most, for there is genuine sadness in his eyes, not unlike that of a man who has lived a lifetime and learnt that the world is cruel.

What crime could this child have committed to have his life taken on Christmas morning? He ought to be in his home, with his parents, opening gifts and shrieking with the kind of joy only a child would know. He shouldn't be here...

He does not ask me to spare his life; he does not cry or even show fear. Instead he meets my gaze with a steely resolve, as though he has already accepted his fate. I feel genuine sympathy for him, for he has barely lived. If not for me, he would perhaps live to be an old, withered man. But what would age bestow upon him but regret and bitterness? He has already amassed enough sadness in his six years to match a lifetime's worth of grief; why should he endure more? Life is hollow. It would benefit him to put this existence behind him and embrace the next. Let him enter the beyond, where his dreams will turn real, where his hopes will find fulfilment, and where his love will push past this ordinary realm of individuals.

I slip the noose around his neck and cover his face with the mask.

The second prisoner is a young man, handsome, strong, and full of ambition. I see in his eyes a sense of promise I'd never known in myself. He is in the prime of his life; a stallion, capable of challenging the world and defeating it. He should be thundering through life, conquering everything he deems a challenge. He shouldn't be here, facing defeat.

I hide his beautiful face and slip the noose around his neck.

The third prisoner is an old man, grey and wrinkled. He meets my eyes proudly, without any regret. It is he who saddens me the most, even though he has lived longer than the others, for I realise it is this old man that I will never become. I was once a young boy, innocent and full of dreams; I had briefly been like that young man, full of daring ambition; but I haven't lived enough to accumulate the experience this old man holds within him. It is the life he has led that I envy, when I slip the noose around his neck and cover his face with a hood.

I step back as the reverend whispers words of counsel and comfort to the three hooded figures. They do not respond. When he is finished, the reverend steps away from them and says aloud, for all to hear: "May God have mercy on your souls."

That is my cue.

Their bodies drop with sudden, loud jolts. The crowd turns away as one, unable to watch the end of a show they sacrificed their Christmas mornings for. Almost immediately, they begin to disperse, chatting animatedly amongst themselves. A few of them cast covert looks at the three hanging bodies, but then hastily turn away. The sheriff nods to me before shuffling away. The reverend puts a sympathetic hand on my shoulder before leaving. Soon I am left alone, with three more killings on my soul, and three bodies to dispose of before breakfast.

I remove the hoods off of their heads and stare into their faces, so different from one another in life, yet so alike now in death. We are all the same in the end; in fact, we're all the same in the beginning. It is somewhere in between that we delude ourselves into finding non-existent differences, and then naively form unnecessary segregations. When strung up by a rope, we all die the exact same way, regardless of age, race or gender.

I have been contemplating my own death of late. I have no responsibility to this world but for this noose and my partnership with it. However, I have learnt to realise that the noose is fickle and unworthy of my loyalty. I have taken far too many lives to worry now about duty and loyalty. What then do I have to live for? I wish to embrace death as soon as I can.

Death sits on our shoulders from the moment we enter this world. We carry death with us wherever we travel, whatever we do, and however robustly we live. Death is not an estranged acquaintance that returns to us when our bodies can no longer endure this existence. No, death is our dearest friend and our most loyal companion— perched on our shoulders, it waits for the day when we can become one with each other. I wish to be one with death.

But then I remember something from my past.

Years ago I tried to kill myself. I strode onto the gallows one night, when the town was silent and the stars were veiled. I slipped the noose around my neck and prepared for the long drop. I had tried to think of a suitable last thought... I debated whether to fill my head with pious thoughts, or choose instead to reflect over a happy moment? I decided eventually that it would be best to recount sadness, so that my spirit would be more willing to leave this mortal existence.

But I couldn't bring myself to do it. It wasn't cowardice that held me back that night, for I was more afraid to live than to die. No, it was the realisation that I was already dead, in every way a man could die. My innocence died when I saw my father shot; my ambitions died the day I was shackled to this duty; and my soul died the day I first killed a man.

I do not need to reunite myself with death now or ever, for death and I have been one for many years. In fact, it can be said that in many ways, I *am* death. Will I die one day? I hope so, but I don't know for sure. All I know is that my duty as hangman is larger than this town. It's larger perhaps than even this world. It is more than just a duty—it is my life.

I lower the bodies with the help of an undertaker, who then transports them to the town cemetery. I stay behind, watching the sun climb higher in the sky. I can hear laughter and celebration in the town. People are busy enjoying life. I stay at the gallows all day, until the sun disappears behind the long arm of the mountains and darkness falls. I do not know what tomorrow will bring. All I know is that I'll be here at the gallows, first thing in the morning.

# X

## *Immortal in Death*

A bell tinkled as I stepped anxiously into the shop. A large, tawny owl, magnificent and regal, peered down at me with lamp-like eyes; his gaze seemed at once inquisitive and accusatory. I fumbled through my mind for an explanation, for an answer that would appease his curiosity, before I noticed he was perched atop a wooden coat rack. He wasn't real.

Perhaps I should rephrase, for he was indeed real, as real as I or this shop were. But he was a mere shadow of his former self: skinned, dismembered, and then resurrected onto a hollow, lifeless shell. Yet he looked frighteningly life-like, and a part of me expected him to hoot disapprovingly at my searching stare. I hung my coat on the rack, while admiring the creature's faultless assembly, its seamless restructuring, and the smooth, intricate finish.

"He was one of my first specimens," called a voice from the end of the store.

I looked up to see my former student and old friend, Menon. He was wiping his hands on a blue apron as he emerged from

87

the darkness, with a generous smile spreading through his plain features. "I keep him by the door so that he'll be the first thing my customers see upon entering my store. If he passes their approval, and perhaps as importantly, if *they* pass *his* approval, then the odds favour a mutually beneficial partnership."

"Ah," I said, smiling as we shook hands. "And did I pass his approval?"

Menon grinned. "I think he's undecided."

As we laughed and exchanged pleasantries, I was struck by how young and resplendent my former prodigy looked, despite the dim, unflattering light. It was as if all the skins he had tanned and all the bodies he had preserved had somehow rejuvenated his own. But as my initial impression of him faded and I studied him more intently, I realised that though he looked much younger than when I had last seen him, his eyes had aged far beyond what they should have; and despite his glowing, unblemished skin, and lustrous hair, he looked disconcertingly lifeless.

"You look well," I lied.

An empty smile spread across his waxen face, but the gesture missed his eyes. "I'm glad you chose to come today," he said, and I noticed his voice had changed considerably. There was no longer a boyish softness to it, but a deep, gravelly tone that was oddly unnerving.

"I was surprised to receive your invitation," I confessed.

He raised a perfectly shaped eyebrow. "But why? I owe all my success to my mentor."

I smiled. "The store's larger than I expected," I confessed, looking around.

"Come, I'll give you a tour," he said, leading me into the shop.

I followed hesitantly, wishing the store was better lit. It was dusk, and there were only two windows in the store, both by the front door and both veiled by drapes. The only light came from the lanterns above each diorama, and that was hardly sufficient.

The place had an eerie quality about it. Taxidermy shops

were usually peculiar anyway, but the atmosphere in this store was particularly unnerving. The darkness concealed most of the animals from view, but their figures still bathed the store in heavy, ominous shadows, while their eyes danced unnaturally in the glow of the lanterns.

As Menon led me into the shop, I came to appreciate just how extensively he had branched out in his trade, for he had a diverse collection. Most of the specimens were lined up for sale on shelves, but quite a few were placed in very elaborate dioramas to attract potential buyers. These displays depicted the animals in natural poses, as part of natural situations, within their natural environments. Of course, an African lion and a Siberian tiger facing off on a riverbank wasn't exactly a *natural* situation, but it did make for fascinating viewing. I smiled inwardly at the commercial mindedness that had no doubt determined which animals would be selected for the dioramas. The lions, the tigers, the leopards and the rhinos had made the cut, whereas the less glamorous buffalo, elk and antelope, were left on their shelves to gather dust.

"After I left your class, I went to Africa," Menon said, as we passed a pair of arctic foxes, standing alertly on a blanket of artificial snow. "I wanted to see as many animals as I could, living in their natural habitats. I wanted to remember them in their active, mortal forms, before I immortalised them in plaster and fiberglass. It was a journey of discovery."

"I see," I replied, as a black panther glowered at me from beneath a bush. His eyes burned yellow in the shadows, and the malice within them felt frighteningly real.

"Then upon my return, I branched out into other areas of taxidermy," he said, leading me towards a large display case, filled with hundreds of insects, from as small as fleas, to as flamboyant as butterflies. "I learned the skills of restoring birds and insects."

I stared at the collection with genuine revulsion, for I hated insects. I was also overcome by jealousy, for I realised Menon had surpassed my own knowledge in the trade. I possessed a general understanding of the process of restoring insects, but I had never *actually* learned or practiced the skill. But Menon had a display filled with hundreds of these specimens, each real and life-like enough to provoke my natural repulsion towards them.

As I hastily turned away, my attention was caught by a rather large diorama containing a life-sized African elephant. It was a bull, a male in its physical and symbolic prime. He was a grand and humbling sight to behold, for he towered several feet over me, and since his dark body merged with the heavy shadows, he appeared even more massive. He had his head tilted back slightly, and his trunk was raised in the air as if he were just about to bellow majestically into the forest. His most distinctive feature though was a large pair of tusks, which gleamed impressively in the modest lighting, like a royal symbol of his might and ability.

"I've never had the pleasure of restoring one of these," I said, bitterness leaking into my tone, as I approached the dwarfing stature of the enormous creature. "Did it take long?"

"Indeed," Menon admitted, "Of course I was less-experienced then, so it took longer than perhaps it should have. But this is definitely my masterpiece."

I shot him a searching look. He was different to the humble student I had tutored all those years ago. His demeanour had somewhat hardened, a change I attributed not only to the fact that he was older now and had acquired more wisdom, but also to his freshly inflated pride. But thereupon I chastised myself, for it occurred to me that that which I perceived to be his ill-serving pride, might merely have been a projection of my own ill-fitting envy.

"Has the trade changed much recently?" I enquired, suppressing acrimony.

"The world makes scientific advancements steadily, and the benefits of these advancements filter down through the chains of necessity, shedding most of its worth before trickling into obscure and irrelevant art forms such as our trade," he replied, mechanically.

"Irrelevant?" I repeated, studying a leopard yawning lazily. "Personally, nothing in the world seems more relevant to me than the skill of preservation."

"Do you remember what we always said restored pieces were?" he asked.

I nodded, a smile forming on my lips. "Frozen moments of time," I said, as old memories reattached themselves to my mind. "Each specimen tells a story: what the creature looked like, what its behaviour was, what it ate, and perhaps even how it died. Of course, some pieces reveal more than others. Some are frighteningly real, to the point where you feel you know them."

"They're all the same though," Menon said.

"How do you mean?"

He was staring into the shadows, his expression one of yearning, as he said in a hollow, detached voice, "The killer and his prey are the same." He turned to me. "The fox and the hare; the cougar and the elk; the cheetah and the antelope—they're all one and the same." There was darkness in his voice and it made me considerably anxious. I noticed how strong Menon was, how his thick forearms jutted from beneath his rolled-up shirt sleeves. His hands, rough and calloused, looked more like the hands of a killer than a restorer.

Even as I considered Menon's physicality, I had a sudden vision of a cheetah, powerful and agile, thundering across the earth in pursuit of its prey. Its muscles moved with mechanical efficiency, but were driven by a pulsating desire that was human in its planning, yet animal in its desperation. It reached the antelope rapidly and leapt forward with murderous relish. Little did it know that it had just been frozen in time, for it was then that the gun fired, and the cheetah's quest ended humbly; so mighty, so magnificent, yet so undeniably mortal.

The restored cheetah in the diorama was lunging forward with its teeth bared. The antelope before it was frozen in an evasive posture. The scene looked vividly real, more compelling than video footage, and far more exhilarating than a photograph.

I realised the tragedy behind this display: the antelope would forever be pursued by its predator, and the cheetah would forever remain frozen, a mere two feet from its prey.

"You miss it," Menon said, and I saw him eyeing me with an odd gleam in his cold eyes. He knew me well and was adept at guessing my thoughts. "The instincts are still there."

I nodded. "It'll always be a part of me." I touched the skin of the cheetah, feeling its genuine texture—I will not lie and say I did not look for unconcealed seams or stitches, but there were none to be found. The finish was flawless. I wasn't sure what I envied more, the progress Menon had made as a taxidermist, or the fact that he was *still* a taxidermist while I wasn't.

I hadn't touched my cutting blade in the six years since I had given up the art. I say "art," though many would cringe at my using that word. Taxidermy is considered a dirty, crude trade. But as someone who was once immersed mind, body and soul into the practice of preservation, I cannot imagine a more rewarding experience. When a specimen is successfully mounted, the taxidermist feels a sense of godliness, of having defied death and attained immortality. Finished specimens are more than models; they are fractions of life, preserved in three-dimensional forms.

"You've improved dramatically," I told him, ushering forward the best compliment I could manage, considering the torrent of bitterness raging within me.

"I had a good teacher," he said, humbly.

But I shook my head. "You surpassed anything I ever achieved… I always thought I had the unique gift of capturing an animal's character in its recreation, but you took it further." The elephant's eyes met mine. "You've captured its very *soul*."

The word struck me with deeper significance as I said it—*soul*. That's precisely what I was seeing before me. Menon had captured every creature's soul and projected it through its recreated form. It is said that when a creature dies, the soul escapes blameless, while the body is left behind to hold all of its sins. These specimens in

Menon's store were brimming with evil, with horrific misdeeds and sinful pasts, but their souls were intact, too. Trapped within their murderous forms, these souls were in turmoil, demanding to be freed.

"Have you worked on any pieces since retirement?" he asked, as we left the cheetah and came up to two lionesses, nuzzling each other affectionately.

"No," I said, though I wondered if perhaps he had guessed it already.

"The field is changing daily," he said, conversationally. "The methods have advanced, but the attitude had regressed to a more romantic, old-fashioned time."

"How so?"

"We aren't merely content with capturing an animal's form. We want to take a living being, with all its imperfections, its malice, its greed, its cruelty... and *immortalise* it."

A lonely orang-utan caught my eye, like evidence to his statement.

I remembered an orang-utan I had restored several years ago. It had been laborious work, because like all primates, the orang-utan has a unique face that is more difficult to capture in a mould than other animals. I had struggled with the plaster for weeks, and it had been Menon who had finally solved the problem. He had had the foresight of making a "death mask" of the orang-utan when its body had first arrived in our class, and using that as a reference, he designed the clay mould and practically finished the piece all by himself. I had been proud of him then. I wondered why that pride had evaporated with time, to be replaced by jealousy.

"In the years after I left your class," he continued, "I travelled whenever I could afford it, collecting artefacts along the way. I learned to hunt, to *earn* the trophy and not merely build it. Perhaps that was what my earlier pieces were lacking. It's one thing to have an animal sent to you to be mounted, but to actually kill it yourself... nothing comes close to that experience."

I listened enviously, imagining what a kill would feel like.

I had been raised with the belief that murder was a sin, a crime so heinous that it damaged your soul. But there was something tempting about the idea of taking a life, before "immortalising" it.

I stood near a beautiful zebra that had wise, thoughtful eyes and a near-smile on its peaceful face. Though the notion of "stuffed" animals following an observer with its eyes was somewhat of a cliché, it had always humbled me to realise just how much feeling lurked within those glass eyes. The zebra seemed to regard me with empathy—no, with something more than that... with *recognition*. He looked at me as though I were a friend—a long lost friend, perhaps, but a friend nonetheless. I gazed into those empty eyes and found a Universe within.

"You see yourself in it, don't you?" Menon said, shrewdly.

I smiled and nodded. "It *is* glass, after all," I joked, though I sensed he knew I was merely trying to avoid discussing what I'd seen within the zebra's eyes.

"My latest kill," Menon said, leading me to a table. It was old and worn, its wooden grain stained with blood. I passed my hand along the surface, wishing I could soak up all that blood, and harvest the power it held within. Menon watched me closely.

On the table lay an eagle, its belly split open. I approached it with academic interest, never having preserved a bird before. "Is restoring a bird much different?"

He shrugged. "Cut the skin; clean it; tan it; and then reattach it to a mould, just like with anything else. Although for birds we use the *original* skull with the beak."

"Instead of a mould," I said, nodding. Most animals' heads were moulded out of clay or plaster, and then the skin was sewn onto the mould. But in birds, the original skulls with the attached beaks were used, because a mould was a poor substitute for the actual beak. I was surprised that I knew so much of the process. Strangely, I even had vague memories of having restored birds myself, though I was almost certain that I had never done so.

Menon offered the blade he had been using. "Go ahead," he said.

"I wouldn't know how to proceed," I told him, honestly.

"Some things you never forget," he said.

Perhaps it was the look in his eyes that convinced me, or maybe it was simply having a blade in my hand again that did it, but I pressed the sharp edge onto the bird's skin. The knife pierced the flesh easily—it was a sensation I had missed. He studied my expressions more than my work, and I wondered if perhaps he too sensed my symbolic homecoming.

"You've missed it," he said.

I nodded. "You have no idea how much…"

"You could return to it."

"It's a little too late to start from scratch."

"My store could use you," he said, taking the knife out of my hands. "Consider what it would mean to return to this… it's where you belong." As he said these words, I had a sudden, terrible vision of every animal in this store coming to life, their murderous eyes bent upon me as they obeyed his orders and lunged with the intent to kill. But then I blinked and the vision faded; Menon stood alone, knife in hand, requesting my partnership.

I took a moment to consider what I'd seen, and then decided that there was something unnatural about this store, something that I couldn't quite fathom… The lighting, the animals, the smells… everything about this place was overwhelming. It was as if the store had character, as if it were a thinking, feeling being. I sensed its spirit, its very *soul*… and I sensed the level of control it had over me. What surprised me though was that I didn't fear it. Instead I was excited, for I recognised that unnatural though it seemed, it was still my *world*.

I considered the animals again, but with a different sentiment this time. They seemed now not terrible and frightening; in fact, they felt familiar. I studied the beaver, standing on a log; I watched the hyena, bent over the carcass of a deer; a black bear stood on its hind legs, and I almost expected it to roar at me in recognition.

Yes, in recognition, for I could remember him, and I knew he remembered me. I knew how each of these animals had lived, and knew how they had died. Menon had killed them, and he had then restored him, but I felt as though I had shared in the process. He *was* my prodigy after all, so perhaps we had formed a connection deeper than I had anticipated. In the six years that I had abstained from this world, he had thrived in it, and now I was reliving his experiences through this store.

A low growl caught my attention. I looked around in surprise and caught sight of a freshly restored lion at the end of the store. I approached it cautiously, wondering if I was now imagining sounds as well as sights. It was then that I noticed a giant cage beside the restored model of the lion. Within the cage stood a similar sized lion; only, this one was *alive.*

It paced restlessly within the cage, its head bent in thought, while its muscles flexed in idle frustration, demanding to be unleashed. I was struck by its might, which though concealed, radiated through its very presence. I could distinctly notice the difference between its obvious strength and the impotent might of its twin, frozen upon the shelf. Had the living specimen not been in a cage right beside it, I would have considered the resurrected lion to be a masterpiece. But it paled in comparison to its living, breathing counterpart.

"It's beautiful," I remarked, dropping to my knees to study it closely. It paused in its pacing to return my gaze, though with less curiosity and great hostility.

"Do you want to do the honours?" Menon suddenly asked, holding out a rifle.

I leapt to my feet. "You intend to kill it?"

"But of course," he said, surprised. "This is a taxidermy shop, not a zoo. He is like a bag of ingredients, which must be cooked and prepared before becoming edible. Killing him is the first step in immortalising him. I intended to do it later, but since you're the guest—"

"But I've never killed before," I told Menon, hastily. "The

bodies were always sent to me. I don't think I *could* have killed either. I always imagined the animals living fulfilling lives, roaming freely, proudly, like knights in a medieval castle, or gods in an ancient Greece." I turned to look at the lion—I regarded his frustrated, troubled demeanour with more pity now than reverence. "I never imagined them like *this*."

"But this *is* their reality."

I shook my head. "Not in my world."

"Most of the animals sent to taxidermists aren't trophies hunted bravely in dense jungles," Menon reasoned. "Those times have long since passed. These days the animals that reach us are pets, performers, or properties. They belong to people who want them remade into a more convenient form. They aren't mighty, romantic heroes of the savannah that we glorify through art. They're ordinary creatures, weak, flawed, and *mortal*."

The lion dropped its head as if it understood.

"I can't kill it, Menon," I said, throwing my hands up. "I just can't."

"I *know*."

There was so much venom in his tone that I turned around. I found him glaring at me with his teeth clenched. "You're gutless," he hissed. "You always have been. That's what made you a lousy teacher. You could only teach me *half* of what I needed to know."

"I taught you *everything* you needed to know," I replied. "It wasn't cowardice that limited me, but lack of resources. I admit that. I didn't know how to restore insects and—"

"You're not a coward because you didn't read a book on insects," he said, derisively. "You were and *are* gutless, because you never understood what a restoration entailed."

"Meaning what?"

"Meaning," he said, stepping forward. "You never knew how to *kill*."

I edged away from him. "The kill isn't important."

"It is the *most* important thing," he said, in a low voice. "It was the kill you never taught me." I noticed that the lantern glowed in his lifeless eyes the same way it did in the eyes of the animals. "Preservation is one half of the skill; the other I taught myself."

"Is that what ruined you? Killing?"

"Ruined?" he said, and the beautiful skin on his face stretched into a cruel grin. "If I'm ruined, then why do you envy me? Why do you resent what I've achieved?"

I didn't have an answer.

"You and I are the same," he told me, "Two halves of the same person. But we complete each other; without you, I'm nothing."

"You've done all *this*," I argued. "You don't need me."

"*You* did this," he said, with sudden ferocity. "*This* is what I did."

As he said the words, the store changed.

I looked at the animals; their beautiful, impeccable forms disintegrated before my eyes. The restored lion had a gunshot wound, but was alive, while the lion pacing in the cage now lay dead. The leopard was bleeding; the bison was beheaded; the beaver had been strangled; the beetle had been crushed, and every other specimen in the store carried the injuries that had killed it. They were dead, yet alive; their wounds exposed, their blood splattered and their guts spilled, they made a hideous, gruesome sight. They moved behind him restlessly, carrying the wounds that had killed them. Their bodies were in agony and their souls were trapped.

"When you entered this store, you healed everything," Menon said, holding the knife before him. "You restored what I killed. Without you, the skill is incomplete."

I noticed now that Menon himself wasn't beautiful and unblemished; he had an old wound in the chest, where a knife had stabbed him, and his shirt and apron were stained with dried blood. He looked older now, older than he actually was: lines had appeared on his face and his skin looked stretched somehow, as it hung lifelessly from his bones.

He approached me like a hunter stalking his prey. His every

move seemed measured, calculated, and I was too inept to guess it. I stumbled against a large display case, covered beneath a black cloth. "The *last* exhibit," he said, nodding towards it.

I eyed it cautiously, and then edged away.

"We mustn't forget the original purpose behind taxidermy," Menon said, smiling that hollow smile again. "The purpose isn't merely to capture life, but to capture *trophies.*"

Saying so, he unveiled the last exhibit.

Inside was a portion of a taxidermy store: a few restored animals stood on shelves, and between them was a table with a carcass lying upon it. Bent over the carcass, with a cutting knife in hand, was a life-sized model of me. I turned to Menon in outrage, but he wasn't there.

Instead, I found that I was wearing his blue apron and had his knife in my hand. I looked around the store and found that all the animals had returned to their respective dioramas, and had frozen in their respective poses. All was as it should have been.

Menon's words echoed in my memory:

*"The killer and his prey... they're one and the same."*

I thought I heard the owl hoot by the front door. His name was Alan... I had restored him six years ago. But how did I know that? I looked at the zebra, at the shrewd, all-knowing look in its eyes—it was still smiling at me. Trapped inside this giant riddle, I wondered if Menon had ever *really* been there, or if we had both been immortalised within this store.

The bell on the front door tinkled, but no one entered the shop. I was alone.

# Epilogue:
# Absolution

## One

It is time.

Is it? I check the skies. There is no sun to mark the progression of the day. Has the sea swallowed everything, I wonder? For though it is a cloudless sky that I gaze into, there is no sun, no moon, and not even a star. In that case, even time must have been consumed.

The Banyan tree and I are alone on this world. This beach has withstood the cancerous tide thus far, but how long will it be before I too am engulfed by the ocean? If these are my last few moments of life, then I must accumulate as much knowledge as I can and preserve it.

But I have nothing to learn from.

## Two

He learns from the world.

There is much about this existence of his that he has yet to understand. It is vast and diverse, yet it is small and monotonous. What he sees is endless sea and an endless sky to mirror it; yet within this tedium there exists the diversity of currents, of infinite ripples of water, each different from the other. The sky for all its abundance is cloudless, yet it serves as a celestial mirror to the sea, echoing the elegant motion of every wave and every current.

The world is poetic. But it does not rhyme.

## Three

There are bottles upon the island, hundreds and thousands of them. They lie amassed in a little inlet on the other side of the beach, waiting to be searched. Every bottle carries a piece of paper with a message on it. Excited by the prospect of learning, I hastily uncork the bottles and read the messages within. Since time no longer exists, I cannot measure how long it takes me to read *all* of them, but when I finish the last message, I find that the world is different.

The tree hasn't moved.

The beach hasn't flooded.

The sea and the sky are the same.

Yet the world is undoubtedly different.

Perhaps it is because I myself have changed; or rather the knowledge within the bottles has changed me. There is nothing profound within the messages, nothing written with divine inspiration or matchless talent; but even the idle thoughts, the aimless theories and the random notions, crafted in a crude hand by an ordinary mind, serve to enhance my understanding of life. For the author, whoever he or she was, must have been just like me, and might have even been a part of me. For that is the gist I have gathered from these messages, is that we are all *one*.

*One plus one equals two…*

Oh shut up…

## Four

He does not understand every message. Some bottles contain papers that are essentially blank, but for a small drawing or even just a number written in the corner. Some papers are *covered* in writing, back and front, such that not even an inch of the paper lies bare.

The messages are written in a strange, factual language that he cannot comprehend. Since they were preserved in a dry bottle, and kept apart from the sea, the words lack the sensitivity required to affect him. He therefore soaks every message in the sea before reading it.

*Funny*, he thinks, *what was the point of putting the messages in a bottle, then?*

# Five

Vanity is a funny notion.

A man that spends two hours training at the gym to build an aesthetic physique is considered vain. A woman who spends two hours at a salon having her hair and her nails done is considered vain. But when the same man and woman read books in a library, in an effort to expand and enhance their knowledge, they are considered studious and enlightened.

Is reading not an indulgence in vanity as well? If improving one's physical appearance is considered vain, then isn't developing one's mental prowess also vain? For what motivates us to read and learn? We hope to gain a better understanding of the subject we learn, so that we can earn a living in that field, or so that we can instruct other students in that subject, or merely because it bestows upon us the satisfaction of knowing that our knowledge has been enhanced.

Every gesture, every action, and every breath that we take in life is driven by vanity. We are individuals, equipped through circumstance with a unique set of talents, skills, and ambitions. But one common feature we each share is an ego, an awareness of our apparent individuality, which motivates us to enhance ourselves through every moment of every day. When eating, sleeping, thinking, moving, acting or speaking, we are driven by a necessity to serve ourselves. The impulse is so deeply ingrained within our psyche that it affects our behaviour unconsciously. None of us are immune to the ego, for as long as there is an individual upon this world, there will be ego.

I am reminded of a dream where I'd entered a classroom and found that every student within that class, as well as the teacher, was me. We interacted with one another as though we were different people, yet we were all the same. I was everyone and yet, because it was a mere dream, I was no one. It is that rule that parts reality from fantasy, and the individual from the collective.

Reality features an individual within a collective world; Fantasy features a collective consciousness within an individual. Yet ultimately, there is only *one* individual in both realms.

All these fantasies… all these dreams and illusions that I have tortured myself with… what do I have to show for them except frustration? As a society we tend to believe that dreaming increases understanding, but what if fantasy actually impedes empathy? What if it inhibits our ability to accept? Why else does life grow increasingly difficult as we grow older? As children we're naive, and that innocence allows us to find fantasies within reality. But excessive dreaming eventually corrupts our reality and dilutes it. Fantasy dispels all fact, all certainty and therefore all reality. It leaves us intolerably vulnerable to that cruel nemesis, disappointment. And so whenever we stumble upon an answer, we dust it off, measure it, and then finally hold it up to fantasy's expected standards. And more often than not, the answers appear ordinary. So we discard them and move on. Until eventually, there are no more answers left.

I find all this information within the bottles washed up on this beach.

Perhaps the ultimate answer then is to stop trying to imagine, and to stop searching for dreams, illusions and fantasies. Choose instead to think, assess and survive.

Perhaps reality *is* the ultimate dream?

*Real, true, factual, honest…*

I was told once that dreamers find reality only in death. If that is true, then I must be nearing the end, for I have found my reality. I have found it within my world of dreams, where nothing has ever been real before, until now… when this beach is consumed, my world will become real.

## Six

He notices the irony of the situation. Lamenting the drastic transformation of life from reality to fantasy, he collects all the thoughts and concepts from the messages he found in the bottles, and converts them into artistic ideas. For in a world slowly becoming devoid of reality, it would serve him better to translate his ideas into art, so that his thoughts may wander time without any *real* limitations. For art is the *one* language, the *one* translation of the truth, which transcends *all* human boundaries. So he paints, sculpts, composes music, writes stories, and translates all the ideas bestowed upon him by reality, into a suitable, distinctive form of art.

And then finally, on a piece of paper, he writes not an ordinary message, but a poem.

## *Seven*

The Poem:
> To Him *We Return*

> Pale and Black.
> Unbroken and Unblemished
> But for you, and your Touch.
> Endless Sea
> No Wind to summon it
> No Land to breach it
> A timeless Quest, measured by Thought
> A blank canvass, a clear Sky, an empty Sea
> Think. Feel. Live. Accept
> This Sky and this Sea
> And Him.
> He is there
> He was always there
> Perched on that Tree
> That Tree without Earth
> That Boy without Shadow
> In His eyes you will find it: Meaning
> And in His mouth you will find

Life, The World, Yourself
Let Him swallow you
For in His chest dwells Time.
The Past never was
The Future will never be
The Tree was never there
The Sky was broken
The Sea was dry
You never were, Are not, Never will be
For He made You, This, Them
And to Him we return

## *Eight*

I see a leaf.

I stare at it from atop the Banyan tree, which has survived the flood as I have. Adrift upon the sea, the leaf contains a young boy. I wave him over to the tree. The boy leaves the leaf behind and climbs the tree. He now sits next to me on one of the branches.

He is beautiful. His skin is dark, so dark that he looks blue. Or it is fair, so fair that he looks blue. He has wide, expressive eyes, and delicate, red lips. His thick mane of curly hair is adorned with three peacock feathers, and he wears golden anklets and bracelets. He smiles at me.

I stare at him, lost for words. And then he inhales. I am swept into his lungs along with the sea, the leaf, the tree and the skies. Within his stomach I find another Universe, another ocean, another leaf, another tree and myself perched on it, staring at this beautiful boy. But there are more Universes, millions upon millions of them. He has swallowed them *all*. I find myself sitting before him again, gazing into his resplendent face, etched with an ethereal, translucent beauty. I say translucent, for though he sits before me in a solid presence and I can see his features, his hair and his body, I also see everything *within* him, as though he is transparent.

I ask him to show me *Maya*, a kind of cosmic illusion.

So he opens his mouth in response and I am once again inhaled into his stomach.

I awake in a meditative pose, alone upon a beach, beneath a Banyan tree. The leaf sits idly before me, like a mere spectator to this grand show. I examine its texture—it is the same leaf as it has always been, except there is no boy sitting on it this time. I wish he would return...

I sit back down on the beach and meditate over this world...

The sea is rising. The skies are clear. I am Me.

CPSIA information can be obtained at www.ICGtesting.com
Printed in the USA
LVOW121504120112

263426LV00001B/6/P

# I Am Me

A Collection of Short Stories

Ram Sundaram

# Contents

Prologue: Dreamer                                            xiii

Earth's Child                                                   1

Fifty Cents                                                    13

At First Sight                                                 34

Reality's Dream                                               46

Reflection                                                    55

An Apple Branch                                               66

Touch of Reality                                             74

Soul Mate                                                     89

Hangman                                                      102

Immortal in Death                                           109

Epilogue: Absolution                                        119

# Author's Note

*I Am Me* is a two-way book: it begins from either end and meets in the middle. It holds a collection of twenty short stories, or ten pairs that are split into either half of the book. The two stories in each pair share the same title and reflect a similar theme, but are depicted in two contrasting yet congruent ways. One half of this book represents reality, while the other borrows from fantasy; similarly, one half depicts an individual nestled within a collective world, while the other half represents a collective consciousness entrapped within an individual existence. Each reader might prefer one version of a story over the other, or else will find harmony in their combined reading. The purpose of this "two-way" arrangement though, ultimately, is to challenge the segregation of "fact" and "fiction." These two labels are not as mutually exclusive as we deem; for the world of fiction borrows heavily (if not entirely) from existing fact, while the factual reality we perceive in our daily life is tainted with lies, fantasies and the artful brush strokes of an entire population's imagination.

An incident that occurs is fact. But the moment it is perceived by the spectators of this world, the integrity of its truth is diluted; for no two spectators are ever the same, and perception is fraught with prejudice. When an incident is recounted, this translation of the fact is already tainted with embellishment, misinterpretation

and considerable opinion. By the time the incident makes it through its many retellings, it will have lost all trace of its original factuality. And yet the basic message of the incident, despite all the transformations it has gone through, will be the same when it reaches its final spectator as it was when the first spectator witnessed it.

Fiction is no different. Art is a translation of fact. In its entirety, it is an analogy for life. An incident that is translated into art retains its essential message as much as a factual retelling does. Both are enhanced with creative license, with colorful embellishment and emotional prejudice. Fact and Fiction are therefore no different from one another, not in their conception or their perception. The only difference is us, the spectators that study both mediums.

*I Am Me* presents ten stories in each of these two mediums. It is up to the reader, the impartial spectator, to decide which medium retains more of life's essential truths.

# *Acknowledgments*

A married couple entered the café, pushing a stroller before them. By their side was a seven-year old girl, who seemed curious about everything around her, yet never wandered more than an arm's length from her mother's side. When the couple found an open table and took their seats, the young girl lifted a toddler from within the stroller and set him on the ground. The toddler's legs promptly buckled underneath him and he fell. Together, the mother, father and sister propped him up again and gave him a gentle push; he could wander as far as he liked—they would always be near to pick him up when he fell.

He did not wander far though, and did not wander willingly. As if tethered to them by an invisible string, he returned frequently to look up at his mother's lovely face and giggle, or else to have his father pick him up and hoist him over his head, from where he felt taller than everyone else in the café. At this tender age, his family was his entire world.

But life in the café moved at a brisk pace, and its customers aged rapidly; some even aged years in mere minutes. When the boy was older, and had outgrown his current boundaries, he tried to wander further away from his family. He was therefore placed inside a glass box with wheels; this way he could move around the café, observing the world from within the security of the glass

box, while remaining unaffected by whatever he witnessed. He did not hear the words of those around him, not the profanities, the curses or the vindictiveness; but the sword had another edge to it, for he also missed the wisdom in their words and the emotions in their voices.

When he grew older still, the glass box shattered and he was hurt. Where once the world had been full of sweet music and kind words, it was now harsh and painful. So he threw out the shards of glass and crafted a bubble instead. It was built much like the box, serving much the same purpose, and yet it was more pliant and therefore more resistant to harm. It curved itself cleverly over the sharp edges of reality and deftly bounced back the sharp arrows of negativity. It also expanded as both he and the world grew in tandem, and did not shatter or burst, despite how extensively he stretched its limits.

From within the bubble, he met the other customers in the café. He drifted over to their tables and spoke with them. Some invited him to stay, but others were skeptical about his appearance—they distrusted the bubble. Otherwise unremarkable in every manner, the boy garnered no particular interest or favor at any of the tables, be it from the athletes, the artists or the academics. His normality gave him the opportunity to observe the reality of the café rather than shape it, and this passive form of participation would eventually define his role as a person. He was a reflector rather than an inducer; he merely shadowed the moods, gestures and intentions of others, rather than inducing these reactions within them. This passivity enabled him to observe discreetly, without ever intruding overtly.

He made friends along the way, who each changed him in minor or significant ways. Some merely steered the bubble in a different direction, while others kept it temporarily. There were also some that tried to destroy it, for they did not trust a boy in a bubble. But regardless of how they perceived him, or even how they treated him, he considered them all to be the same, like grains of sand on an extensive beach. He was a grain of sand himself,

no different than the rest of them but for this bubble. For he noticed that unlike him, almost everyone he came across lived in glass boxes. Some even lived in cardboard or wooden boxes, and a few unfortunate individuals actually lived in *cement* boxes—as you can imagine, they didn't get very far. There were some who lived without boxes, and they were quick to suffering but equally quick to joy. They experienced the world on a heightened level, without any censorship. He longed at times to share in their experiences and to be rid of his bubble; yet he was glad for the shelter it provided him. The bubble was more than a home—it was a part of him.

Along the way he met a boy that did not wear a box or a bubble, but instead sported a brown paper bag full of holes and slits. Chris Dueck was the most interesting person he had ever met, for he did not wander around the café interacting with the others, but instead sat at his table and allowed the café to come to him. It was Chris who showed him that while planting flowers was aesthetically pleasing, planting trees would serve his purpose better. Trees could be climbed, could be built upon or built with; trees bore not only flowers but also fruit, which nourished as well as soothed taste buds. Everyone else in the café had gardens of beautiful, exotic flowers, but they themselves seemed malnourished and disoriented. Chris was healthy.

It was a little later that the boy met Diane Wynn, a young girl with a big heart that lay concealed within an enormous fortress, equipped with six moats and thirty crocodiles; walls that were a hundred feet high, with skilled archers that manned their parameters; a dozen beastly trolls, and one *very* mean dragon. When they met, the boy handed her fifty cents; she did not smile, did not hug him, or take him by the hand and promise to be his friend. She merely considered the two coins, took one and gave the other back to him. Then she returned to her table. But she hadn't taken more than a few steps before she turned around to look at him enquiringly, as if to say, "Well? Aren't you coming?" He smiled and followed her happily. Diane was the first best

friend the boy had ever had, and he was proud of their friendship, because he thought he had earned it. The truth though, was that they had earned each other's loyalty. She was the only one who let him sit at her table, though she wouldn't eat with him. It didn't seem like Diane would mind even if he sat at her table forever. But he couldn't stay, for so much of the café remained unexplored. He however found solace in the knowledge that he could return whenever he liked, and could sit with her and talk like only two best friends could.

A little while later he met Rick Bayer, one of the kindest men he'd ever come across. Rick was a fellow juggler, and he imparted upon the boy the many facets of juggling artfully, while still being an active, normal customer of the café. Rick and the boy shared many conversations while they juggled, and it seemed to the boy that he grew wiser in Rick's company, yet did not age. It was as though their partnership lent the boy the maturity he had been lacking, which he used to harvest the reckless ambition that burned within him.

The last significant person he met was Mona Nikhil, a woman who was more like him than any other he had come across. It was starting how alike they were, and this similarity enabled them to become best friends almost immediately. Mona was the first person who ate with the boy, cooked for him, and also ate his cooking. Their friendship was built on equality, and they roamed the café together, not so much as a couple but as *one* person, built with two individuals. They ordered the same drinks and the same snacks; they bought each other's meals, told each other's stories, and fulfilled each other's ambitions. Until he'd met her, the boy had thought that the café was full of attractive, normal people, while he alone was disfigured. Mona was the first and only person who held a mirror before the boy's eyes and told him he was beautiful too, as beautiful as she and every other customer in this café were.

By the time he'd met everyone in the café, the boy was a man. The bubble had been stretched as far as it would go. Every

person in his life, from his parents to his friends to even complete strangers, attacked the bubble with a needle. They stabbed at its stubborn hide, forcing it to surrender and liberate the individual within. When the bubble burst, he inhaled fresh air for the first time in many, many years. The air was sweet, invigorating, but full of dust and smog—it was the price of freedom. Once free of the bubble, he understood himself better.

To thank them for their efforts, and to preserve them in his memory, he decided to immortalize them on a canvass. Standing before an easel, paintbrush in hand, he captured every one of them onto a large, life-sized portrait. When he finished it, he looked up to find that the café had disappeared. The people, his family, his friends... they had all vanished. They lurked now only on the canvass, imprinted like scars on his aging memory. They would remain there forever. They were a part of him after all, and he a part of them. They were all *one*.

# Prologue: Dreamer

# One

His name is Ishvar.

He is sitting under a Banyan tree, gazing out into a far-reaching horizon.

The sun is sliding down the last few lengths of time. It won't be much longer now before the darkness falls, for the heartbeat of the world has already slackened, and before the Great Shadow lengthens over him, time will have drawn its last breath.

The sea is rising…

It wipes away the beach, which has forever been its friend. Now it seethes onto the land, the loam that has never known its touch. The trees fall, yielding to the strength of the conquering tide.

The virgin earth surrenders…

*"How has it come to this?"* he ruefully wonders.

# Two

I was named after God.

Millions chant my name in their prayers. They groan out my name when they stub their toes; they sing out my name when they win their lotteries; they call out my name when they can't find answers, and they hold onto my name when they take their last breaths inside our mortal world.

"Ishvar" means God.

One might therefore forgive me for having indulged in as much vanity as I once did. Their chants and prayers still ring in my memories, as they did in my ears long ago. And I still swell with pride and importance each time I hear my name being celebrated, even though the love in their voices faded long ago, as did I. Pride is a funny thing. It lingers on beyond the stretch of memory, beyond relevance, and even beyond time. Pride is

essentially existence. So as long as there is an individual squatting under the Heavens, pride will live on. But *we* will not.

By mere definition, my existence should now invoke little or no pride. I am naked, stripped of everything physical and emotional. I sit under a Banyan tree, alone in a world I neither recognise nor understand. A flood approaches, slithering closer with every beat of time. And yet, despite all of this, I am still proud. For existence—*any* existence, is undeniably special. Just ask the ant that scurries away from your thundering footsteps. We look upon that ant as an insignificant creature, unworthy of importance. If my big toe happens to hammer the life out of it, so what? Life goes on, we would say. Or rather, *our* lives go on. *My* life goes on. But what happens to the ant? Where does it go? What happens to the pride it must have taken in its own existence?

The big toe of fate hammered the life out of me many years ago. I expected to stop existing, to lose the pride and the joy I had taken out of breathing, out of living. But I endured. I endured beyond death. I have endured through a stretch of time I cannot measure, and have been deposited here on the last remaining beach of existence. Everything that sits around me here is all that is left: the land, the animals, I, and this Banyan tree. We make up one large, insignificant ant.

And the gigantic big toe of this conquering sea bears down upon us.

## Three

There is a flower on the tree.

*How did it get there?* he wonders.

The world is in its apocalyptic climax; the very essence of life has been strangled and destroyed; and yet, amid this decaying landscape, there lurks this symbol of hope and beginning.

*A flower...*

He wants it. The desire is real, and is more visceral than any feeling he has endured in a long time. It claws at his insides, urging

him to commence the chase. The feeling is strangely familiar—it reawakens desires long suppressed within his barren depths.

He straddles the enormous girth of the tree, and then his limbs work efficiently to move him up to the branch. His hand extends to reach the flower, and his fingers flex to pluck it—but then suddenly, it vanishes! It then reappears on the branch just above him.

He climbs up further, but again as he reaches for it the flower disappears—it gazes down at him from one branch higher. He frowns and drops down to the earth.

*Ah, who needs you?* he mutters angrily.

He has more pressing concerns.

The sea is drawing closer.

## Four

The *sea*.

It has swallowed everything greedily: man; woman; child; life; death, and even time. It has left nothing behind but solitude. *My* solitude. I am alone.

An old memory suddenly surfaces:

*In a world without mirrors, everyone is beautiful.*

The words resonate within my mind. I cannot remember when I'd heard them spoken, or in what context, but they suddenly seem very meaningful to me. *In a world without mirrors, everyone is beautiful.* It means that the eyes do not assign value to beauty— they don't even *measure* it. The eyes, the senses and even the mind itself, cannot *actually* measure an object's worth. It is the *ego*, which judges. It is the *ego*, which determines our perception of beauty.

So in a world without mirrors, in a world where we cannot examine and scrutinize ourselves, beauty would be worthless; or to put it more aptly, beauty would be *measureless*. How can I judge a man to be beautiful or ugly, when I cannot compare him to myself? Appreciation is inherently envy, and without proper

reflection, how can envy exist? I cannot envy another man's features, his hair, his eyes or his build, when I have no measure of myself. And if I cannot envy him, how can I judge him?

*This* world, this "existence" of mine is not only without mirrors, but also without people, without life, and without any opportunity for reflection. I am alone. And so, despite my mortal, inhibited state, my sluggishness, my arrogance, my vanity, and all the rest of my imperfections, I am still the strongest, smartest, most beautiful creature alive.

I am *perfect*.

I laugh aloud at the absurdity of the remark, and the noise echoes across the sheer vacuum that is this world. The sea hears me, but it is far too preoccupied to comment. Otherwise, the laughter goes unchecked, unheeded, and fades into silence.

*Silence…*

Another tree falls in the distance, and then another, and another…

I stare up at the Banyan rising over my head. Its gnarled branches shiver and tighten around one another, as though bracing themselves for what is to come. The sea will not harm this tree, I decide. No, that is *my* job. I place my hands on my hips and frown.

I need an axe…

## Five

He has no axe.

So he plants his feet apart and pushes the tree—it stands stubbornly.

He scratches his head and then climbs up the massive girth of the trunk. The first branch is a long one, slender yet sturdy: ideal. He grips it near its joint and heaves; then he pulls and pushes alternatively—it does not budge. With a grunt of frustration he kicks it; then he stands on it and jumps, but it does not even tremble under his weight. Exhausted, he climbs back down.

*It's just as well,* Ishvar tells himself; *I don't know how to build a raft anyway...*

## Six

My story isn't about heroism. There are definitely no heroes in this tale, but it is littered with villains. It's much like how the world once used to be: billions of villains convinced that they were heroes. They learned the truth near the end. And so did I.

I know so much now, so much more than I ever did. But I still don't know enough... this Banyan tree knows more than I do. It could tell me a story or two about life. Its very existence is a story worth telling, for it stands defiantly against this all-consuming flood, entirely alone in a world that is falling into ruin. It is joined to the earth that weakens it; it drinks from the sea that erodes it; it breathes into the air that has now abandoned it; and yet, it is alone.

*We are alone.* It is nothing more than a fanciful illusion that we are a part of families, of certain circles, communities, countries, cultures, and coincidences. We each exist individually, but—and here's the rub—we are *not* individuals. We are alone.

Our existence is about finding answers, about accumulating knowledge and understanding. For what purpose, one might wonder? But that question in itself requires the aid of an answer.

"Do *you* have any answers for me?" I ask the Banyan tree.

It shivers and ruffles its branches into the wind.

It can sense the tide growing closer.

So can I.

# I

## Earth's Child

It was by sheer chance that I looked down in my stride and saw his pink skin searing through the pale earth. He was half-buried in the snow, and we were many miles from civilisation, adrift in the vast wilderness. I thought at first that he was some kind of an animal, or the remains of one. But then I saw his tiny hands with its red fingers, reaching out as though for help. How long had he been left here, I wondered? The first layer of snow upon him was fresh from this morning's, but there was harder, thicker snow closer to his skin. I assumed he'd been left here more than a day ago. But how could someone have committed such a monstrous act?

Cursing the inexplicable cruelty of life, I fell to my knees—I wanted to see him, to learn his face so that he would be remembered. When my fingers dug into the bitter snow, fighting against its stubborn grip on him, I did not expect to retrieve anything other than a corpse. But as I pulled him free from the earth and lifted his tiny body into my arms, I saw his eyes open, and heard a small cry escape his pink lips. He was alive.

Startled, I stared into his beautiful face, so fresh with colour despite the bitter cold. His skin was warm to the touch and he looked healthy. But how could this be? Even if he had only been left here a mere hour ago, he shouldn't have survived, and he had clearly been here more than just an hour. He was quite animated considering his tender age and the ordeal he had just endured, and seemed intent on trying to grab my hair with his little fingers.

A long, menacing howl rang through the air, cleaving the stiff silence. A sudden chill of fear seized me—it was not my own well-being I feared for, but this child's. It was a miracle the wolves hadn't found him already. Setting my contemplation aside, I pulled a blanket out of my pack and wrapped his naked form in it. He did not seem to like the touch of the fabric, for he kicked the folds away; but with persistence, I coaxed him into relenting, and smothered him in my embrace. Cradling him gingerly, I moved quickly across the snow, seeking shelter. We were currently at the mouth of a canyon, exposed to the elements, so I headed for the mountains.

Thankfully, we reached a cave shortly before sunset. The winds were particularly cruel here at night, so I crawled as far into the cave as I could. Even before I could set him down, he began kicking at the blanket again; surprised, I loosened the folds slightly and he grew calmer at once. He smiled up at me with an enchanting face. I knew at once that just as suddenly as he had appeared in my life, he had also just as suddenly become my life's main purpose. I would now die for him if I had to, for our fates had become inexplicably linked, like an object and its shadow—no, something even stronger: like life and its eventual death.

Judging by his size, I would guess that he was barely a week old. And yet he demonstrated movement, dexterity and expression far beyond that age. I wondered what his story was, who his parents were, and how (or why) he had been abandoned. But what perplexed me more than his unusual circumstance was the fact that he had *survived*. This world was inherently a predator, and the elements were its sadistic hunters, ever alert for innocent

prey. How then had such a fragile, helpless creature survived the clasp of certain death? If, as I suspected, he had been abandoned several hours ago, then he should have long ago been claimed by the cold. And even if he had only been abandoned a mere few minutes before my arrival (which was an unlikely scenario, for he was nearly entirely buried in the snow when I found him), then he still should have shown some effects of the ordeal. At the very least, he should have been shivering. But rather he had been warm and healthy when I'd found him, apparently unaffected.

"You're a blessed child, dear one," I told him, and he smiled, as if he'd understood my words. I heard more howls in the distance just then, and shuddered to think what would have happened if the wolves had found him. "I won't let you fall to harm," I promised. But the immediate concern, I knew, was neither the cold nor the wolves—it was starvation. His eyes, expressive and quite alert, followed my movements with interest as I then rummaged through my pack for food. I had very few provisions to begin with, and not much that was suitable for a child so young. But by some unexpected good fortune, I found a bit of milk in an old bottle, though I couldn't remember how it had wound up in my pack. Tearing a piece of cloth from my shirt, I covered the edges of the frigid bottle before I fed him. He drank the milk without fuss, and I was glad, for I knew I could now keep him alive for at least a few more hours.

"Sleep now, little angel," I told him, when he had had his fill; he promptly yawned and closed his eyes. "You're safe," I whispered, seized by a pang of sudden affection. I held him against me until I was certain he was sound asleep. He gripped the folds of my shirt as he slept, perhaps afraid I would otherwise drift away and abandon him. I promised him that I would never leave him, but he had already drifted off to sleep. Of course, he probably wouldn't have understood me even if he *had* been awake.

I had a troubled night's sleep, mostly because I was worried for his safety. Wrapped in blankets, he seemed like such a small, delicate figure that I was afraid I would accidentally roll over in

my sleep and suffocate him. I was overawed by the task ahead. How could I, a defenceless creature with humble means, hope to protect this even more fragile being? Would the evils of this world not overpower us both before long?

When I couldn't endure the torture any longer, I sat up and stretched lazily. Despite not having had much sleep, I felt fresh and energetic, ready for another day's march. But it was still dark outside, so we wouldn't be able to leave yet.

It was then that I looked over to find a young boy sleeping beside me. He must have been about four years old, and he was sleeping in the blanket I had wrapped the infant in last night. I nudged him awake. He sat up and yawned, before slowly looking up at me. His expression was one of mild confusion. His eyes were startling, for they looked remarkably like the eyes of the infant. Was he perhaps the baby's older brother?

"Who are you?" I asked, more brusquely than I had intended to, for he recoiled. "I won't hurt you," I assured him, in a softer tone. "Just answer me."

He nodded, clearly frightened by my manner, but still said nothing.

"What happened to the baby?" I asked.

"What baby?" he replied, in a small voice.

"The one that was asleep by my side last night—he was sleeping in *this* blanket that you have around you now," I told him, gripping a corner of it as if to support my claim.

"I don't know," he said, with a small shrug. "*You* put this blanket around me."

"Don't lie," I warned him, sternly. "I've never seen you before in my life."

"You saved me last night," he said, softly. "You brought me here, gave me milk and put me to sleep. *You* put this blanket around me; don't you remember?"

I gaped at him, dumbfounded. "But... you were a baby last night," I said, trying to understand the absurdity of his claim. "How could you have aged years overnight? You were a tiny

4

baby, practically a new-born." I shook my head, "How long was I asleep?"

"I'm hungry," he said, feeling his bare stomach. "Do you have any food?"

I was prepared to ignore his discomfort and press him further for answers, but his desperate hunger showed in his expressive face, and I didn't have the heart to let him starve. Since he was older than the new-born child, I deemed my rations suitable for his consumption. I fed him the last of my provisions, and questioned him softly while he ate.

He did not seem to understand my perplexity, and insisted that he hadn't changed at all since the night before. But how could a new-born child age four years overnight and not even remember it? Or, if I am to believe his claim, then how could I have mistaken a small boy for a new-born child last night? It was a maddening conundrum…

I concluded that he was tricking me. But then I wondered what he would gain by such a lie? Perhaps he was lost, had found me asleep in this cave and rather than steal my food, had pretended to be in my care so that I would feed and protect him. But then where was the new-born child? Had he destroyed the infant to complete his plan? And then of course, there was the resemblance between them that was hard to explain. How could he look so convincingly like an older version of the infant? So then I considered if perhaps his claims *were* true. Was he indeed the same child I had dug out of the snow? But no, that idea seemed far too absurd…

He slept some more after he ate and this gave me an opportunity to ponder my thoughts. I watched the day break in the distance, beyond the long arm of the mountains. Dawn came silently. I was aware of how still the world seemed, as though all life had been vanquished from it. Yet I knew I wasn't alone, for the wolves still lurked within these hills. There was an ugly look to the skies this morning. I stood at the mouth of the cave, hugging myself for warmth. I found no comfort in the scenery around me, not

even in the sheer cloth of snow draped over the land, for its white hue seemed now not so much pure, as it did pale with disease. The reddish tinge of the mountain seemed to me like streaks of blood on a violent hand; its silver peak like the threatening tip of a murderous blade, and the murky sky like an ugly veil cast over a doomed land. This landscape was cheerless, its very spirit drowned in some kind of evil.

I went back into the warmth of the cave. He was sleeping innocently, like an angel. I felt the same pang of affection towards him that I had felt for the new-born child last night. I was compelled with a desire to save him from the perils of this land. But I knew that to accomplish such a feat, I would need fortune to fast become my most loyal servant.

I roused him an hour later, and we left the cave.

He was naked but for the blanket, yet seemed unaffected by the cold, and filled my ears with ceaseless questions as I carried him on my back. He asked me to explain everything he saw, from the snow to the sky it fell from. He was certainly curious, and rather well-spoken for his age. The depth of his intellect and his eagerness to learn more impressed me greatly, though the incessant questioning didn't. I was growing increasingly weary of answering him. Besides, I had enough questions of my own that I wanted to ask *him*.

As we marched further, his questions grew more complex; he began asking me about the world, about life, death, and the Universe as a whole. He saw and noticed things that I hadn't; his perspective, so childlike in its naiveté, was also rich with imagination. I never once felt that I was talking to a boy of four or five. It felt instead like I was in conversation with an old man, wiser and more thoughtful than I had ever been. For many hours I marched, until exhaustion crept upon me rather suddenly. I had been fine just a moment ago, but I could no longer tolerate his weight with any degree of comfort. I was forced to stop in the middle of an open dale.

"We shouldn't rest here—we're exposed," he remarked, his

voice hoarse with the cold. "It would be better if we tried to reach those hills before nightfall."

I shook my head. "I'm too tired, and besides, it's already twilight."

When I lowered him from my back, I was startled to find that he was no longer a boy of four, but a young man, old enough to shave. I realised now why the last few steps had felt suddenly difficult. "How did you age so quickly?" I demanded, astounded.

Again, this adolescent standing before me looked just like the boy I had seen in the cave this morning, and the infant I had saved last night. All three of them had the same features, the same complexion, expressions, and apparently the same story.

"I don't know what you mean," he shrugged, disinterestedly. "But you had better light a fire before the winds pick up. The temperature falls suddenly at night."

"I *never* set you down," I said, refusing to believe him this time, "Not even *once*. You were clinging to my neck for hours, so you couldn't have suddenly thrown the boy off my back and climbed on yourself. No, this isn't mere trickery—it's sorcery."

"I am no sorcerer, I assure you," he said, smiling.

"Then what are you?"

He shrugged again, adopting a helpless expression. "I am a child."

"You *were* a child, yes. But you're a young man now."

"I am still younger than *you*, so that makes me a child."

I opened my mouth to argue further, but then I wondered if perhaps he truly was a sorcerer as I feared. This land was brimming with evil, with horrific creatures capable of terrifying feats. What if he were some kind of a demon, bred by this world to perform wicked deeds? If so, then he was obviously more powerful than I was. My best chance of survival would be to wait for an opportunity to escape, rather than to try and confront him.

I did not talk to him that evening while I gathered wood and built us a fire, although I did check up on him discreetly every so

often, to make sure he hadn't aged further while I had my back turned. Once the fire was alight, I did not sit with him, though he seemed eager to continue questioning me. Ignoring him almost rudely, I closed my eyes and forced myself to fall sleep.

My dreams were haunted by visions of strange children, leading me through a cosmic labyrinth that I couldn't fathom. They all looked identical, though they were of many ages, sizes, and ethnicities. Each child tugged at my hand, offering to show me something special and magical. They allowed me to glimpse the future, which was disappointingly murky. Then they revealed answers to my questions, and explained much about the world. And then suddenly I saw myself standing in the middle of a forest. I was alone, and oddly, I too looked like the rest of the children, with the same eyes and the same features. But I could recognise myself and was able to realise that I wasn't one of them. I was glad when the dreams ended.

At first light I left to find us food. I hunted game for much of that day, until late in the afternoon when I struck a lonely doe. I noticed as she fell that she too had eyes like that of the new-born child. I convinced myself that hunger was causing me to hallucinate. Dragging her carcass back to the cave, I roasted her flesh on the open fire. I offered the boy some of the meat, but he refused. I shrugged and did not ask him again. I was hungry and this meat was already lending strength to my tired body, and clarity to my perplexed mind. I would need both body and mind to escape his sorcery alive.

"I refuse to kill a living being," he suddenly said. "I would rather starve."

"Good. Starve."

He looked across at me questioningly. "Why do you hate me?"

"I don't hate you," I replied. "I don't even *know* you." I considered him at length then, as I took another piece of the meat. "What are you? A demon of some kind?" Internally, I chastised myself for provoking him. This meat, I realised, had renewed

more than just my physical and mental strength—it had also rekindled the embers of my subdued temper. But I would have to be careful not to let my words wander beyond their intended purpose.

"A demon?" he said, sounding incredulous. Then he shook his head. "Hate me if you must, but I will not dignify your insults with a response. I believe there is still goodness left in this world, and I am quite simply a child of that goodness."

"You're not a child anymore though, are you?" I remarked, pointedly. "Ignore my insults if you want, but tell me the truth. How is it that you age so quickly?"

"How do *you*?"

I frowned. "What do you mean?"

"Since I first met you, you've aged backwards rather alarmingly," he said. "We are now of the same age—how do you account for that? Are *you* a demon of some kind?"

I concluded that he was mad. I hadn't aged backwards at all.

But then I looked down at my hands and was surprised by the sudden colour in them. They looked so young and strong! What had happened to the veins jutting out of the pale, lifeless skin? I ran my fingers through my hair and was startled to find a thick, robust mane atop my head. I rummaged through my pack and pulled out a dirty spoon; wiping it clean on my shirt, I examined my reflection in it. My face, my neck, and my body… everything looked and felt younger than they'd ever been before.

I turned back to him. "What devilry is this?" I demanded.

"It is the progression of life," he explained. "Everything ages."

"Yes, but not backwards."

"No? Is your conscience as old and wise as it is supposed to be, considering your age? Or is it misguided and infantile, deformed by years of sin and guilt?"

"Are *you* my conscience?" I remarked, annoyed.

"Are you mine?" he replied, flatly.

I leapt to my feet. "You did this," I hissed at him, clenching my fists. "You *are* a sorcerer, aren't you? You lured me to you, tricked me into saving you, and now you've stolen my age. Reveal yourself, demon!"

"I am *not* a demon," he insisted, still calm. "And I will not fight you."

"Then leave me alone, and do not follow," I said. I turned away from him, gathered my pack and left. His eyes followed me intently, but he himself did not follow. I ran for as long as I could, until my lungs burned and my limbs ached. Soon he was lost in the distance, and night concealed the gap between us. I was alone once more. The starlight showed I was nearing the mountains again, which meant that I must have crossed a few miles already. But I did not slacken my pace. I ran dangerously, without pause, for I was determined to put distance between the boy and myself. When I could go no further, my knees buckled under me and I collapsed. I lay there in the snow, contemplating my fate, wondering if I had found death.

It was snowing. I rolled onto my back and gazed at the sky. I had never felt lonelier in my life than at that moment. I was truly alone, lost and tormented by incomprehensible riddles. I longed both for companionship and an absolution.

I heard howls in the distance.

I forced myself to look up—I was near a canyon. It looked oddly familiar. Even as I gazed at it, I suddenly remembered my home. Built in a lush green dell, under a gentle mountain's shoulders, it was a place full of laughter and joy. I remembered friends and companions I had shared that home with, and I longed to be in their presence again. My home lay through the canyon, on the other side of these mountains. I was nearly there...

Mustering my remaining strength and will, I marched once more through the snow. I heard more howls and this time they were nearer. I ignored them and ran faster, losing my balance often but regaining my footing each time. When at last I reached

the mouth of the canyon, I fell to my knees in gratitude. I could *see* my home in the distance.

But then my joy evaporated.

The wolves swarmed through the canyon in terrifying numbers. Their black shapes sidled through the white canvass, assuming positions in an almost orderly fashion. If I ventured through this pass, then I would never reach my home. And yet I had no choice but to attempt it, for if I stayed out here in the wilderness another day, I would surely either starve or else freeze to death.

A large hand gripped my shoulder, turning me around.

He was standing behind me, larger than ever, his broad face kind and smiling. "I'll take you across," he offered, in a deep, assuring voice.

I shook my head. "You can't—you're just a child."

"Actually," he said, with a smile, "*You're* the child."

He stood to his full, considerable height, and I felt a mere dwarf next to him. My hands and feet were tiny in comparison, almost... *childlike.* The truth struck me just then: I *was* a child. Somehow, in the time that had passed since I'd first come across his half-buried body in the wilderness, he had grown older while I had aged backwards. I was fast becoming an infant and would soon be rendered helpless. I would be at his mercy.

"Am I dying?" I asked.

"Only if I was dying too, but I am still very much alive."

He helped me to my feet and led me through the canyon. I walked slowly, holding onto his hand. The wind howled around us, its echoes amplified with the voices of the wolves. But we were not harmed. I lost all my remaining strength about halfway through the pass, but he cradled me in his arms and carried me the rest of the way.

When we reached the other side of the mountains, I could see daylight breaking over the distant horizon. I sighed contently. There was so much of this world that I did not yet understand; however, I wondered now if I perhaps wasn't supposed to

understand it. Within this incomprehensible existence, adrift in the wilderness, hunted by wolves, I would always remain a child: innocent, unassuming and sufficiently ignorant.

"We're home," he said, as he tucked my new-born body gently into the snow, and half-covered me with snow. The heavens parted again, and the silver rain began once more. But I wasn't cold and I wasn't afraid, for I knew that I wasn't alone.

In fact, I knew now that I had never been alone.

"We'll meet again," he whispered, as we parted ways once more.

# II

## Fifty Cents

*Friendship comes at a price, and more often than not, it's a price we can afford. The problem is that we go through life bargaining with each other, trying to whittle the price below what's expected, and as a result we lose friends that ought to have stayed. Kishan and Shreya knew the price of friendship; they knew it so well that they never had to discuss it aloud. The price stayed the same through the several different lifetimes that they shared with one another.*

Under the sombre shadow of the evening sky, a soft flame grew within the hanging lantern outside Number 3 Gautami Nagar. Almost as if on cue, the lanterns outside every other house burst alight down the narrow street. Swarms of moths and fireflies rose out of the shadows and fluttered around the sturdy glass panels that shielded the flames. Children in these houses stood outside their front gates and stared at these harmless creatures with relentless fascination.

Kishan stood alone.

His once white shirt was now soiled and ragged, and he

scratched his skin through it absent-mindedly. His hair, which was neither combed nor tamed, had simply been greased back with some old lamp oil he had found discarded in a garbage pit. His eyes were sunken and rather strained, yet he stared dolefully through them at the doorstep of Number 3, Gautami Nagar.

Arun Nayar slapped him on the head as he pedalled by with a large aluminium milk-can strapped onto the back of his bicycle. "You'll go blind if you keep gawking like that," he called out. "Go home and take a bath. I could smell you from three streets away."

Kishan didn't even turn to him. He had his arms wrapped around a streetlight, which had long ago fallen out of use. His arms, like his legs, were puny and covered in dirt. He wore no shoes on his blistered feet—they had been scorched today in the afternoon sun, from the many hours he had spent underneath this streetlight, staring dutifully at Number 3, Gautami Nagar.

Arun Nayar now dismounted outside the Number 3 gate and looked back at Kishan with a triumphant grin. "You wish you had my job, don't you?" he teased, ringing the bell on his bicycle loudly. He kicked off his sandals, opened the gate and wheeled his bicycle into the yard.

The front door opened. A tall figure appeared in the outline of the doorframe and spoke to him. He was given a large copper basin. A small conversation ensued, and then Arun Nayar went back to his bicycle to fill the basin.

Kishan watched him enviously.

Within a few moments, a small figure ran down from the house to the open gate and peered out into the dimly lit street. Kishan saw her in the warm glow of the lantern: a small, pretty girl with an expressive face. He let go of the streetlight and sprinted down to the house, ignoring the aching pain in his feet. Shreya saw his scrawny figure pattering up to her and folded her arms across her chest, looking exactly as her mother did when she was similarly annoyed.

"Arun uncle told Daddy that you were standing outside,"

she said, disapprovingly. "*Why* are you here, Kishan? Go home, please! It's late."

Kishan stared at her, his tiny face impassive.

Shreya clicked her tongue impatiently. "I know you're not stupid, Kishan, so please go home! Go, *shoo*! How long are you going to stand there like that?"

Kishan slowly shrugged.

Shreya pushed her neatly braided hair off her shoulders, and then frowned as she caught the stench of Kishan's unwashed body. She took a few steps back.

"Come back next week when your mother starts work, and we can study together, okay?" she offered, in an effort to be kind. "But I'll only let you into the house if you take a bath first. And change your shirt; you've been wearing *that* for weeks now!"

Kishan nodded.

She waited, and when he still didn't move she stamped her feet in frustration. "Oh, you are *so* annoying!" she cried. "I'm going inside now—I have to eat, so *please* go home! Otherwise I'll tell Arun uncle to complain to your mother. Bye!"

Shreya turned on her heels and walked back up to her house, with her pretty pink frock dancing around her fair legs and her posh, new sandals. She quickly checked her appearance in the living room window as she passed it, skipped up the stone steps and disappeared into the house. Kishan stayed there, staring after her blankly.

Arun Nayar wheeled his bicycle out a few minutes later. He paused when he saw Kishan and smirked. "You like that Brahmin girl, don't you?" Nayar asked.

Kishan didn't answer, but merely stared back.

"Personally, I couldn't care less," Nayar said, with a shrug, "I think it's a lost cause, but it might help me. See, I have to go to Madurai for two days and I need someone to do my rounds for me. If you want the job, it's yours." When Kishan didn't respond, Nayar realised he would have to spell it out for him. "You'll get

to see your girl *twice* a day, once when you do the morning round and then once in the evening, like today."

Kishan stared at the house, contemplating the offer. Then he nodded.

Nayar grinned and pulled out two coins from his pocket. "Here's fifty paise," he said, lifting Kishan's dirty hand and putting the coins in it. "If you get a chance to talk to her, ask her if she wants to go into town with you. You can use this to buy her ice cream."

Kishan stared at the coins with wide eyes. He then shook his head wildly and tried to give Nayar his money back, but the milkman playfully threatened to tie Kishan up to a tree so that the homeless dogs could take a bite out of him, and then chased him away.

❈   ❈

It was early morning on the hillside where the Grand Tote Circus had set up camp, and the first few golden shafts of light broke the overnight darkness, announcing the coming dawn to the world. Kishan stood outside his tent, sipping on coffee, watching the sunrise. This was his favourite time of each day: the promise of a new beginning.

A small figure appeared over the crest of the hill, dressed in a bright, floral frock. Kishan smiled and put the coffee down. Little Shreya, all of ten years old, ran into his arms; he picked her aloft and spun her around before setting her down again.

"Thanks so much for inviting me!" Shreya cried, happily.

"What are friends for?" Kishan grinned.

He led her around the campsite to where the larger tents were situated, housing lions, elephants, and the more important performers of the show. "Have you ever seen a circus before?" Kishan asked, looking down kindly at her.

Shreya shook her head. "Ma can't afford it," she said, simply.

Kishan felt a twinge of pity. Though he had never been

particularly wealthy either, he was certainly better off than Shreya's family. Her father had died a month before she'd been born, and her mother had worked three jobs trying to support her all these years.

"Do you want some cotton candy?" he asked, hoping that buying her food would alleviate his guilt. She nodded excitedly, so he bought her two different colours. She ate the candy happily as he led her through the tents. Shreya was a very smart girl, and she had a penchant for adventure that Kishan had only ever known in himself. If she'd been older and closer to his age, he thought he would have liked to marry someone like her, someone who was smart, kind, gentle, and had an unquenchable thirst for experiencing life.

"If you could work in a circus, what job would you like?" he asked her.

She didn't answer at once, but chewed on the cotton candy while she pondered the question. "I would… like to do something exciting," she said, "Like walking on the rope that's really high-up, or else eat fire or dance with bears or something."

"Dance with bears? You'd need bigger shoes," he said, making her laugh.

"What work do *you* do?" she asked, eagerly.

"Oh I help out here and there, that's all," Kishan said, in a small voice. "I wish I had an exciting job but I don't. One day though, maybe my dream will come true."

"What's your dream?"

Kishan smiled. "I want to be a clown."

Shreya laughed. "Really? Why?"

"*Why?*" Kishan said, pretending to look scandalised, eliciting another laugh from Shreya. "Because clowns have a wonderful job, that's why. When you're a clown… you're someone *special*. You wear some make-up and a costume and you just disappear. You become someone else, someone who people like and laugh at. Imagine how much happiness you can bring to others when you're a clown… it's what I want to do."

"You *should* be a clown," Shreya said, thoughtfully. "I think you'd be good at making people laugh. I would pay to come see you."

"You would?" he laughed, picking her up again and spinning her in the air.

She squealed happily and then when he set her down, she reached into her little handbag. "That reminds me. I have to give you something."

"Oh? What's that?"

Shreya took two coins out of her purse and placed them in his hand.

Kishan looked down at the coins. "Fifty pence … What's this for?"

She shrugged. "It's a thank you for bringing me here."

He gave the coins back. "I *wanted* you here. You don't need to pay me."

"I know that but," she said, dropping the coins into his shirt pocket, "It's always polite to show gratitude for a nice gesture."

"But Shreya…" he began, but thought better of finishing the sentence. He wanted to tell her that he couldn't possibly accept that money, because she and her mother *needed* it. But how could he tell her that without hurting her feelings? Taking people around the circus was his privilege, something that he enjoyed doing, and he certainly didn't need monetary incentive for it; *especially* since Shreya meant the world to him. He tried to find the right words to say it.

"If you don't take it, I'll be very upset," Shreya said, putting on an adorable pout.

Kishan smiled at her. He pulled the coins out again and looked at them. "Where'd you get these?" he asked. "I've never seen 25p coins before."

"They're supposed to be comm… commem… commemor…"

"Commemorative," he helped her, and she looked thankful. "I

knew that, I'd just never seen one before. That makes these coins ever more special, Shreya, thank you."

She beamed at him. "Good. Now you can continue taking me around."

He smiled, took her hand, and led her through the circus.

❁ ❁

Kishan had been surprised when Shreya had agreed to have ice cream with him. He had never been to the ice cream shop before, but it was not the thought of ice cream that excited him, but the prospect of spending time with Shreya. He had spent a restless two days since asking her out, wondering how he could make the day perfect. He had clung to the fifty paise that Arun Nayar had paid him as though his life depended on the two coins.

On the morning of their date, Kishan decided to groom and dress himself impressively, a task that was perhaps easier in conception than in execution. He had just the one shirt and the one pair of old, patchy shorts, but he washed them both in the river that morning. He scrubbed the shorts with the little bar of soap his mother used for the dishes, but he scrubbed so hard that he made holes in the fabric. He took a bath right after, using the same dish soap, and then greased his hair back with some old stove oil. He had found a tattered old leather belt in the garbage pit two weeks ago, and it was his prized possession, so he now secured it around his waist—not atop the shorts though, but atop the *shirt* instead. He understandably attracted some amused looks as he left the slums and wandered into the posh side of town to meet Shreya.

He waited outside Shreya's school for her. She came out with a gaggle of girls around her, all of whom sniggered openly when they saw Kishan walk up to her side. Shreya glared at them, afraid they would hurt his feelings. Kishan however seemed oblivious to any of this and merely stood expectantly beside Shreya, grinning happily at her. Shreya and Kishan left the other girls and set off

19

into town. She didn't seem to have noticed any change in his appearance, or if she did, she didn't comment on it. They walked largely in silence, interspersed with Shreya telling him about her classes and about anything to do with school that Kishan wouldn't know.

Kishan had always been fascinated with her school, by the fact that all the children wore clean, crisp, matching uniforms, and read books that held many messages and meanings that he hadn't a hope of deciphering. He stared longingly at their colourful lunch boxes, and did his best to eavesdrop on the classes through the open window; but he was always chased away by the school watchman. Shreya was therefore Kishan's only eyes and ears into that school.

At the moment though, Kishan wasn't concerned with school. He was walking into an ice cream shop for the first time in his life, and more importantly, he was walking in with Shreya at his side. His eyes widened with unabashed delight when he saw the glass counter filled with several trays of various flavours of ice cream. He looked quite literally like a kid in a candy store, stunned into a trance by the abundance of colourful, delicious food.

With his attention fixated on the ice cream, Kishan didn't notice the amount of interest he and Shreya were garnering amongst the people around them. *Everyone* appeared to be watching them. Shreya noted the surprised faces, the visible nudges, the obtrusive stares and the irritating smirks. She felt herself turn red as they stood by the window, where passers-by now shot them piercing looks. Kishan had remained quite oblivious to all this attention, and had been acting rather like his pants were on fire, for he had bustled all around her, trying to ensure she was comfortable, and yet had never appeared to have moved an inch. He had kept by her side loyally, opening the door for her, forging a path through the crowd for her by nudging people out of the way; and now when they reached their table, he briskly pulled out a chair for her.

When she'd been seated and was comfortable, he prepared

to squat down on the floor right beneath her feet, but she caught him in time.

"Don't be so silly," she said, half amused, half embarrassed, and forced him to sit on a chair. "We're equals, Kishan. I don't like you sitting on the floor even when you visit me at home, but you certainly won't do that out in public. We are friends, you understand me? Friends are *always* equals, no matter what."

Kishan nodded and rather hesitantly sat on the chair. He smiled happily though, and then pushed the complimentary tray of biscuits towards her.

Shreya smiled back and shook her head. "No, thank you. They're stale."

Kishan's face fell dramatically as he withdrew his hand. He seemed to be conflicted about something and it took Shreya a moment to realise what the issue was. "*You* can still have some if you want," she said, hazarding a guess that he was hungry.

He grinned and began attacking the mouldy biscuits with both hands. The waiter that materialised at the table shortly after, cast Kishan a look of deep disgust, before turning a leering gaze upon Shreya. Because of her fair skin, and her "plump" appearance—plump only in comparison to the half-starved population that inhabited the town—Shreya was often ogled at by both men and women alike. To them she was something akin to a rare, exotic fruit, or to put an *even* finer point upon it, an exotic *flower*, grown unblemished amid a barren desert.

But despite how often she'd endured their curious, probing stares, Shreya still felt a chill whenever she noticed the greedy look in their eyes as they scrutinised her.

"Good evening, Miss," the waiter said to her. "You would like some soda?"

"Er… no, some ice cream I think." She looked across at Kishan, whose face remained expressionless. "What flavour would you like?" she asked him.

Kishan shrugged.

The waiter, Shreya noticed, did not even spare Kishan a glance.

He stared at her unwaveringly, his eyes threatening to pierce right through her clothing. She instinctively brought her arms in front of her chest, before ordering two vanilla ice creams. The waiter nodded with a kind of a bow, during which he glanced at her fair legs, before disappearing into the back.

"He gives me the creeps," Shreya told Kishan, shivering slightly.

Kishan nodded, his eyes widening with understanding.

"I hate such men," Shreya said. She then closed her eyes and took a deep breath. "But let's not let him ruin our afternoon. Tell me about *you*, Kishan. Have you read the books I gave you? I know they're difficult, but your reading is coming along so well."

Kishan had a guilty expression on his face as he squirmed uneasily in his seat.

"What's the matter?" Shreya asked.

Kishan half-shrugged and muttered something inaudible.

But Shreya seemed to have guessed what he was struggling to tell her. "Your father sold the books, didn't he?" she asked, shrewdly.

Kishan looked down at his hands.

"It's all right," she smiled kindly at him. "It's not your fault. I'll get you more books. Only, this time I'll keep them at my house so they'll be safe. You can come read them whenever you like. That way I'll be able to teach you in person."

Kishan seemed to brighten considerably at this suggestion.

There was a sudden intrusion at their table. Three boys, who had a moment ago been talking to the waiter while casting overt glances in Shreya's direction, now approached their table. Shreya thought they looked like ruffians, with their shabby hair, their intentionally dishevelled clothing, and the slow, taunting manner with which they moved. But more than their appearance, it was the perverted, almost sinister looks in their eyes that troubled her.

Two of the boys sat on either side of Shreya, pressing up

tightly against her. The third sat beside Kishan and put an arm around his shoulder. "Look at this, guys," the third boy said to the others. "The pretty Brahmin girl is having an ice cream with the slum rat."

The others laughed and Shreya glared at them.

"Sister, you can do better than this prick," said the boy to her right, as he ran a finger through her hair. She slapped his hand away, and the three boys started to laugh.

"He's just a *kid*," the one on her left said, as he dipped the little plastic spoon into her ice cream and raised a mouthful to her lips. Shreya slapped his hand away too, and the spoon fell on the counter, while the ice cream splattered on Kishan's hand. The boys laughed, and the one by Kishan's side lifted his arm up and said, "Good idea, make him white before you do him."

Shreya tried to get up but the boys beside her pushed her back down. "Where are you going, sweetheart?" the one on her right said, as he ran his hands over her blouse and slowly slipped them down to her skirt. Shreya struggled out of his grip, slapped him across the face, and then ran out of the store. No one sitting at the other tables reacted or even looked in her direction. Kishan got up and made to follow her, but one of the boys caught him by the shirt collar and yanked him back. "Oy hero, who's going to pay for this?" he asked.

Kishan fumbled in his pocket and pulled out the two coins Arun Nayar had given him. The boy looked at the money and laughed. "This won't even cover a spoonful," he said, shaking Kishan roughly. "It's two rupees *each*. Cough up the money."

Kishan shrugged, looking helpless and defeated.

"I don't think he's got any money," one of the boys said with mock sympathy. He then suddenly pulled Kishan's shorts down and slapped the ice cream against his crotch. Wincing with pain, Kishan hurried of the store, pulling his shorts up as he ran, while the laughter from inside the store echoed after him. The memory chased him the rest of his life.

⊠   ⊠

Kishan led Shreya towards the admission tent, where there were a lot of vendors selling plastic toys, jewellery, hula-hoops, animal figurines, and candles.

"Pick out anything you want," he said to her. "Anything at all and it's yours."

Shreya's eyes widened as she considered the abundance of treasures before her. The only toy she'd ever owned was a headless doll—it hadn't been headless when her mother had brought it home, but during that first night the doll had spent in their house, a rat had chewed off the head. Shreya had nevertheless played with the doll for months after, and still looked upon in with fondness as it sat idly in her room. To her it was an invaluable treasure, despite its deformities.

Kishan watched her run around the little stalls, examining the different items on sale. Shreya was very mature for her age, and he often felt like he was conversing with a young woman when he spoke to her, and not a ten-year old girl. But at rare times like this, Shreya showed the true innocence of her age, and it pleased him to learn that despite the harshness of her everyday reality, some of her naïve, endearing, child-like qualities still remained. Children *must* remain children after all, for as long as life will allow them.

Every time she found something of interest, Shreya ran to Kishan and led him by the hand to come look at it. He always agreed with her opinions, trying to match her interest and excitement, and when she proceeded to explain at length to him why she liked a certain item, he listened with rapt attention. There had been a time, quite long ago, when Kishan himself had been a child as impressionable and as easily pleased as Shreya; but the adults around him had slowly squashed the excitement out of him through their pragmatic, near-cynical approach to life. He saw in Shreya now the same naïve enthusiasm he himself had once been

full of, and he was determined to help her hold onto that youthful quality for as long as she could.

He insisted on buying her every item she showed him, but she politely refused each time, claiming not to have *really* liked it. It was a façade, he knew, but he hoped that when she came across something that really, overwhelming appealed to her, that he would be able to recognise it and buy it for her. This hope came true a mere moment later. He saw it in her body language first, for the bounce in her step vanished when she laid eyes upon it. Her body went limp and still, as she stared at it with open fascination.

It was a large cage, covered with an old, ragged sheet.

Kishan knelt beside her.

"What's inside?" she asked him.

He shook his head. "I don't know, sweetie."

He gestured to the man running the stall, which had a selection of odd antiques and artefacts, too plastic and ugly to be worth much of anything.

The man, an older, surly looking fellow, lumbered over to them with a frown that looked like it had been residing on his face almost as long as his eyes or his nose had.

"Morning, Manny," Kishan said, warmly.

Manny nodded curtly.

"What's in the cage?"

"Can't tell ya."

"Why not?"

"Haven't you seen the signs?" Manny said, gruffly. "It's 5p to look at it."

Kishan laughed. "You're kidding me!" He leaned in towards Manny and said in a low voice, "I know it's some kind of bird, Manny. So what's the mystery?"

"That's for *you* to find out, isn't it?" Manny replied, slyly. "5p."

Kishan looked at Shreya, who was staring at the cage quite earnestly. He had never seen such a solemn, intense expression on

her young face before. "You want to see what's under this sheet?" he asked her. She nodded without turning to him.

"Here," Kishan said, handing Manny a coin. "Now show us."

Manny pocketed the coin and then lazily pulled the sheet off the cage. Inside was a beautiful short-toed snake eagle. Kishan regarded it with modest interest, but Shreya stepped closer to the cage with utter fascination etched onto her features. The eagle's large eyes regarded her with equal curiosity, scrutinizing her every move as though she were a potential threat.

"She's beautiful," Shreya said, her voice echoing the awe displayed on her face.

"Yes, she is," Kishan agreed, studying Shreya with more interest than the eagle.

"She's unhappy, though," Shreya announced.

"Oh? Why do you say that?"

"You can see it in her eyes," she said, simply.

Manny grunted loudly and then muttered something that sounded like "… it *always* looks like that, it's a bloody eagle…"

Kishan knelt beside Shreya and put an arm around her. "Where do you see her sadness, Shreya?" he asked, curiously.

She simply nodded to the eagle, which now turned its piercing gaze onto Kishan. "Just *look* at her," Shreya said. "She wants to fly… to hunt, find her mate and have children."

"I think she just wants to be fed," Manny said, with a cackle.

"Manny, be quiet," Kishan said.

"Or maybe she just wants to be left alone so she can try and make me some money," Manny said, irritably. "If I don't put the sheet back on, no one's going to pay me to take a peek. So I think you two have had enough of a look—"

"Give us a moment," Kishan urged him, as Manny approached the cage.

Shreya seemed unaffected by all this, and merely stared at the eagle. She put her finger into the cage, and both Kishan and

26

Manny prepared to warn her, but the eagle had already ducked its head and nipped her finger affectionately. Shreya stroked its head and beak with her finger, talking in a soft, assuring voice to it the entire time. The eagle made a soft, whistling noise, which was musical and lovely to hear. Shreya laughed happily.

"I think she's the prettiest thing I've ever seen," she said. She turned to Kishan for the first time since they'd approached the cage. "I think we should set her free."

"You think wrong," Manny said at once, bringing the sheet out to cover the cage.

"Manny, hear her out," Kishan said.

"The bird's not going anywhere," Manny said, "Not till it makes me some money."

"When did you get it?" Kishan asked.

"Two towns ago," Manny replied. "Caught it when I was out fishing. They're pretty rare, you know. Never seen one in this country before. I was lucky to catch this one."

Shreya looked imploringly at Kishan. "Please... we *need* to set her free."

Kishan watched the eagle, as it brushed its head against Shreya's finger. Was it just the power of her suggestion or could he *actually* see sadness in its eyes? He imagined it soaring gracefully over mountains and valleys, scouring the earth for its natural enemy, the serpent. He could almost *see* it swooping down sharply, its talons deftly gripping the snake's body within its short toes, as it took flight again and climbed to a high vantage point where it could devour it. Such a beautiful, graceful creature... Shreya was right, Kishan thought... it deserved to be free.

🀄 🀄

Kishan and Shreya stood in a large meadow, filled with thousands—no, *millions* of yellow roses. It was a sea of yellow, rippling like currents in an ocean, as the wind gently swayed the

plants. Kishan held a flower in his hand and Shreya held one in hers.

Kishan plucked a petal and gave it to her.

Shreya plucked a petal and gave it to him.

They shared the flowers, giving each other a petal, one after the other.

When there were no more petals left, Kishan reached into his pocket and gave her a quarter. Shreya took the quarter in one hand, and pulled out another quarter from her purse with her other hand. She regarded the two coins with a hungry look in her eyes. Then she turned and ran away from him. Kishan stood alone, staring after her.

"Manny," Kishan said. "Name your price."

"Five pounds."

"That's absurd."

"That's my price."

Kishan looked helplessly at the eagle, which met his eyes and held his gaze, as though hoping to persuade him to pay the price. "I don't have five pounds—you know what I make working here. If I give you five pounds, I won't be able to eat for a month."

"Then the bird stays."

Kishan looked at Shreya's eager face. "You got the bird for free, Manny," he said, and then reached into his pocket to pull out a pound note and the fifty pence Shreya had given him. "Take this… it's all I got and it's the best I can do. Take it and set the bird free."

Manny looked down at the coins in disbelief. "But this won't even cover a feather," he said, outraged. "I don't care if the bird *was* free… *this* is insulting."

"They're commemorative," Shreya added, but Manny ignored her.

"Manny," Kishan reasoned. "Has the bird made you *any* money so far?"

Manny paused and then shook his head gruffly. "Only your 5p."

"So I'll bet he's costing you more than he's earned you, right?"

Manny nodded shortly.

"So what's the problem?" Kishan said. "Take the pound and the fifty pence cut your losses."

Manny grumbled something gruffly, but pocketed the coins all the same. "Fine! Well go ahead you rotten thieves, stealing money from an old man like me, and..." the rest of his mutterings drowned to gibberish as he walked away from them.

Kishan went up to the cage and unlatched the door; he swung it open and stepped back. The eagle seemed hesitant and unsure of what to do. Shreya put her entire hand into the cage and stroked its feathers. It nipped at her gently and then hopped onto the edge of the cage. Shreya kept petting it, hoping it would relax and follow her out of the cage.

A few moments later, the eagle launched off from the cage and soared into the skies. Shreya and Kishan watched it take flight eagerly. Many others around the circus watched it with fascination, and even Manny spared it a glance. It flew gracefully around them, whistling a lovely tune with what sounded to Kishan like gratitude, before it disappeared into the distance.

"Now *that*," Kishan said, putting an arm around Shreya, "Was worth 50 pence."

❈ ❈

There was an old, musty smell inside the shop. Kishan approached the clerk hesitantly. He tried not to look around at the odd cages stacked all around him on pedestals, shelves, cabinets, chests, or even just the floor. He cleared his throat softly.

The clerk looked up. "Yes?"

"Uh... I'm looking for something," Kishan said.

"And what is it that you're looking for?" the clerk asked, with a slight sneer.

"A best friend."

The clerk didn't appear at all surprised by Kishan's declaration. He merely nodded and came out from behind the counter to lead Kishan through the shop. Kishan allowed himself to look at the merchandise, at the people cooped up in the little cages, their expressions ranging anywhere from indifferent to hostile. He walked through them cautiously, determined to avoid their gazes for the most part, for he found it disturbing to glimpse their eyes.

"And what is the price range you're looking at?" the clerk asked.

Kishan reached into his pocket and extracted two coins. He looked shamefully up at the clerk, whose derisive grin only grew wider. "I have... fifty cents."

"A fortune, no doubt," the clerk said, harshly. "In that case, sir, I have only *one* item in this store that will suit your needs." He took Kishan to the far end of the shop, where on the lowest shelf of an old, dusty cabinet, there lay a rusty, brittle-looking cage. Within it sat a young girl, with pretty, delicate features, and large, expressive eyes. She regarded Kishan apprehensively, but with fascination.

He smiled kindly at her.

She did not smile back.

"Is she... nice?" Kishan asked, doubtfully.

"You get what you pay for," the clerk replied.

"What are her qualities?"

"That is for *you* to find out, sir."

Kishan knelt beside the cage and smiled at her again. This time, the girl within the cage managed a weak smile in reply. "What's her name?" Kishan asked the clerk.

"I don't know. I never asked."

"What's your name?" Kishan asked the girl.

She looked up at the clerk and then back at Kishan before answering. "Shreya."

Kishan nodded. "It's a very pretty name."

Silence fell, as they considered each other quietly. Then Kishan stood up and gave the two coins to the clerk. "I'll take her," he announced. "But please let her out of that cage at once. She's not an animal or some kind of criminal."

"Oh?" the clerk said mockingly, as he unlocked her cage. "Then what is she?"

Kishan helped Shreya out of the cage. He took her hand as she put weight on her feet gingerly, and supported her as she tried to walk. "She's my best friend."

※　※

Shreya hadn't been home in many years. She had left town when she was still a child, and time had made a mockery out of her plans to return here one day. But she'd finally made it back, and now she had a husband to share her memories and experiences with. They walked arm in arm through the streets that she no longer remembered vividly, yet hadn't forgotten entirely. Everything had changed so dramatically in the twenty years she'd been away; the buildings were new or just larger than she remembered; the streets were paved and equipped with crosswalks and lampposts; there were cars and bikes and buses thundering past them; the population had swollen by at least five hundred percent, and she didn't recognise *anyone* she came across. It was, she realised mournfully, as though she was in a different town.

As they turned into a narrow lane, Shreya's eyes fell upon a beggar on the side of the street. He lifted his head as they came near and stared overtly at her. She felt that she should turn away, but somehow found herself equally fascinated by him.

When they walked past him, he held up his bowl and shook it pleadingly.

"Do you have any money?" she asked her husband.

He made an impatient noise with his tongue as he dropped her hand and reached into his pocket to extract his wallet. Shreya stared at the beggar, who now avoided her gaze entirely and stared solemnly at the pavement. Her husband gave her a couple of coins, which Shreya then offered to the beggar. He did not meet her eyes. He bowed his head, in gratitude and in shame, and held his arms aloft, with the bowl between his hands—the two coins were dropped into it.

"Thank you, Miss," he said. "God bless you."

"And you," she replied.

The couple left him and walked a few paces, when Shreya stopped and considered the building they were walking past. Time had changed it. The structure was the same, but it had been improved dramatically, and outfitted with modern designs and facilities. It was no longer the same establishment either: it was now a stylish, high-priced restaurant.

"There used to be an ice cream parlour here," she said.

"Oh?" her husband said, feigning interest. He checked his watch when she wasn't paying attention. "Honey, it's late. We should be getting back."

"It must have been... almost thirty years since I was here," she said.

"Brings back memories?"

Shreya nodded. "Funny thing is... I didn't even eat any ice cream that day."

"What were you doing here then?"

She smiled, remembering. "I was meeting a friend."

She then took his hand and they walked away. As they turned the corner, she cast one last glance at the beggar; he was smiling.

They are on the shores of eternity, beside the immortal river.

Shreya is lying on the boat, her arms folded across her chest. Kishan stands on the shore, looking down upon her.

"For the boatman," he says, and puts two coins on her eyes.

He gives the boat a gentle nudge, and the current pulls it along. He watches the boat disappear into the distance. He hears footsteps behind him and notices Shreya standing there. He looks at her enquiringly, and she points to another boat bobbing along the edge of the river, right by his feet. He climbs in willingly and lies down.

"Close your eyes," she tells him.

He obliges.

"For the boatman," she says, placing two coins over his eyes.

A moment later the river pulls the boat away from the shore. He drifts downstream, leaving behind mortality, existence, friendship and division. He is glad the end is near. Too long have they both been alone, clinging to one another to find solace. But now, upon the immortal river, all would change. Somewhere along the way, the two boats and the two bodies within them would become one. Only the fifty cents would remain behind, as eternal payment.

# III

## At First Sight

Her name is Emma. I have no memory of her, of our past or our present relationship, and yet I am undeniably in love with her. I gaze at her with a sort of mad desperation, as though our fates are inextricably entwined: as if we are one soul, one entity, split into two people. She smiles at me, and I notice that her soft features are warm and pleasant. We are coasting down a busy city street at night, weaving through hundreds of dazzling lights, moving with unnatural speed and precision. I know I'm driving, and can feel my hands on the steering wheel, but I have no control of the car, and have no sense of where we're headed.

I turn back to her, and gaze into her beautiful, enchanting face.

"You seem distracted," she informs me, "Is something on your mind?"

I try to grip the steering wheel tighter and stare determinedly out the windshield again. "Not really," I tell her, with what I hope seems like a nonchalant shrug.

A silence falls, broken only by the soft pattering of rain, and

the squeaks of the wiper blades. I can see her turn to me from time to time, for I too am stealing glances at her, and yet our eyes never meet. Are we both pondering the same thing, I wonder?

"Storm's picking up," she says, peering out into the darkening skies.

As I look up, the sky erupts into strange convulsions—the black, smoky clouds start churning wildly at an inconceivable pace. It looks as if a celestial pipe is continually pumping fresh clouds into the skies, causing a turbulent, almost violent storm. It's mesmerising to behold, for coupled with the intermittent flashes of lightning, the storm creates an impressive, larger-than-life atmosphere. And in the distance, far beyond the roofs of the towering skyscrapers, I can see an enormous funnel cloud descend into the middle of the street.

"We'll have to leave this road," I say to her, the words coming out of my mouth without my mind having formed a decision to utter them.

"We have time," she replies, unfazed.

The street is suddenly deserted, and the funnel cloud is now almost upon us.

She reaches out for the steering wheel with her left hand, in a kind of sudden panic, and turns the car into a narrow gulley between two buildings. I can hear the wind howling wildly, and can feel the tornado sidling forward, approaching us.

We are somehow out of the car, standing against the wall of the building. She's bleeding from the leg, though I don't know how. I try to treat her. I feel panic, worry, and a sense of heaviness that has nothing to do with anxiety for her well-being, but apprehension for the words I'm about to share. I push her up against the wall and grip her shoulders. "You have to get out of here," I urge her. "You *have* to survive: you have a life to live. You have Raymond to live for."

Raymond? The name echoes into my mind from a past I cannot discern, and yet the name bears meaning, and stirs within me a deep sense of bitterness.

"If we go, we go together," she argues.

I press myself tightly against her, to keep out the wind and any debris that might come our way. She holds me close, not with desperation or urgency, but with fondness. We stand in close embrace, as the tornado whips past us. I don't hear the wind anymore, nor do I feel its powerful gusts. I only feel her touch, which is at once new and familiar.

"I fell in love with you," I whisper, and as she looks up I add, "At first sight."

The café was warm and cosy. It was snowing outside, and the windows were covered in frost. We were seated at the table closest to the hearth, and its healthy fire kept us comfortable. I was watching Emma greedily, appreciating her every feature.

"It was an uneventful sort of weekend," she said, taking a sip of the hot chocolate. "Except for this one fight Raymond and I had. We had the same argument we've had since we started dating, but this time I think things are going to turn out differently."

Inwardly, I reacted the same way I always did when I heard Raymond's name: by cringing and pretending he didn't exist. Outwardly, I feigned interest. "How's that?"

"Well," she said, a smile slowly forming on her beautiful lips. "I think he's starting to realise what I want out of the relationship: I think he's starting to listen to me."

I felt a deep sense of foreboding, and knew I wouldn't like what I was about to hear. "Well, that's good," I said, hoping the conversation would end there. But it didn't.

"I think," she said, excitement bubbling within her, "He's going to propose."

The café exploded around us: the roof was blown away, the tables, chairs, counters, and everything else rose in a cloud of smoke and dust, but somehow Emma and I sat at our table, sipping our drinks, unaffected. She leaned across the table, and

I found myself naively hoping she was going to say something intimate and affectionate, maybe even something revelatory like "But I don't love Raymond, I love *you*."

I leaned in too, blind hope building within me.

"I think," she said, a mischievous grin on her face, "We may just elope."

I sighed, in spite of myself, but fortunately managed to turn it into a kind of happy, breathy chuckle, so that she wouldn't get suspicious. The café was gone. We were simply hovering in space, sitting at a table, sipping our drinks.

And my heart had just been broken.

❋  ❋

The tornado is gone. We take a cab to the station. We step out and I turn to look inside the window to pay the driver, but he isn't there. The driver's side door is left open, and he is nowhere to be found. I look all around the busy parking lot, but I don't even remember what he looks like. I turn to Emma, but she is already walking into the station.

I follow her, but as I reach the front doors, a surly man shoves me back. He is the taxi driver. He accuses me of trying to cheat him out of payment.

"But you left," I insist, looking back at the empty cab. "You weren't in there."

"I went to the washroom. You should have waited," he argues.

People turn to us; Emma stands by the door, looking back with a mixture of pity and disapproval on her face. She's expecting me to stand up for myself, to prove that I'm the kind of man she can be with. The driver's rant echoes distantly in my ears as I turn away from Emma and face him. I yell—no, I *roar* at him. He steps back, surprised.

"It's not my fault you left the cab unattended," I growl. "It's not my fault you didn't even tell us where you were going. I was

ready to pay you—look, I even have the money in my hands. This is *your* fault and nobody else's. You're a coward and a cheat."

And then I strike him; the feel of fist against jaw is incredibly enthralling, as is the sight of him flying back twenty feet and crashing into the wall. The entire station erupts into delighted applause; people start cheering for me, whistling, and singing my praises. I turn expectantly to Emma; I find her standing by the door, her expression still disapproving. Shaking her head, she turns away and the door closes behind her.

I took our drinks from the bartender and made my way back to her. She was suddenly surrounded by a group of gossiping, giggly girls. These were the friends she'd spoken about all these years, and I recognised them without having ever met them before. I couldn't tell if they were pretty or not. In fact, I honestly didn't even notice. They resembled the type of young, adolescent girls that I personally came across too often: tittering, uncoordinated and shy, while still being loud and caustic. And it didn't seem like they had a collective I.Q that would reach double digits. But despite all of their shortcomings, I knew (without even looking at them) that I *needed* their approval and their validation, more than I needed anything else at that moment.

Emma pulled me close to her as she faced them and said, "This is my boyfriend. We have a kid together." She was smiling, and her hand reached for mine, as if she really were my girlfriend. I felt my insides doing cartwheels at her statement, but my mind argued that she already had a boyfriend, and reasoned that she was simply trying to make me feel good. Perhaps I should have played along, but bitterness found me.

"I'm not her boyfriend," I said, laughing politely—I hated myself for every single word that I uttered. "She's just kidding— she already has a boyfriend, and *they* don't have a kid yet. But

one day they will, because she loves him more than anything or anyone else."

Her friends broke into laughter and she joined in, as if they were all in on the joke.

"I'm not gay," I declared, as their giggles abated.

❈    ❈

"I want to know something," I tell her, as we make our way through the station. "Is there any *particular* reason you never found me attractive?"

She shrugs, determined not to meet my eyes. "Not really," she says, evasively. I know I am making her uncomfortable, but I don't care. "You're not my type."

"Neither is Raymond."

"No, but I love *him*."

I ignore the stab. "But you found him attractive before you loved him."

"Of course." The response is immediate, almost instinctive.

"What was it that you found attractive about him?" I probe further.

"I'm just… not attracted to *you*," she says, skirting the question. "And don't pretend that doesn't mean you're not attractive. You're just not right for me—you're too emotional and I'm not. You're just not someone I could be in a relationship with."

I consider her words and then laugh, like I have never laughed before. Her words ring through my head, reminding me of how repulsive I am: how utterly worthless and without merit. I don't blame her for rejecting me—I would have rejected myself, too.

"I think your best friend is really cute, though," she adds suddenly, and twists the knife she's stuck in my chest. "I think your dad is pretty hot, your brothers are gorgeous, so are your uncles, your cousins, your grandfathers, your great-grandfathers, your sons, your grandsons, your neighbours, your bosses, your subordinates, your councilmen, your attorneys, your accountants,

every man in your life, and every man in this world but you. They are *all* very, very attractive."

I keep laughing, even though the searing pain has paralysed my every thought and feeling. I continue laughing, until the laughs echo into the silence and turn into tears.

I suddenly remember the conversation we'd shared by the lake.

We were on the edge of a lake, throwing stones into the water. "There's something I need to tell you," I said, not turning to her, for I was nervous enough without having to look at her.

"Hmm?" she said, casually.

A duck swam leisurely before me, without a care in the world. How easy its life was, I thought: how utterly simple and without complication. What made its life simple? It needed the very same things I did to physically survive: food, water, and basic everyday health. It wanted a mate, as did I. But perhaps what separated us were our egos. He didn't know what he was; only what he *needed* in order to remain, to exist. I on the other hand knew myself, my surroundings, my world, my past, my world's past, and much more. I knew so much that I could even afford to imagine, and that imagination led me to think I was special; special *only* because I existed. But mere existence was not worthy of pride, or else this duck would be proud too. It was pride that made me fallible, that made my life complicated, and made that moment with Emma so tense.

"You're not saying anything," she observed.

I inhaled deeply. "I love you…" I said, and the words came out of me before I could stop them. "Emma," I added, just so she knew I wasn't talking to the duck.

There was a long silence. Or perhaps it wasn't that long at all, but felt long because I was left standing on the edge of a knife, wondering whether her reply would tip me over. In that moment, while I waited for her response, I felt like I was alone in the world,

naked, vulnerable, and mortal. My fate was in her hands, and that was a feeling I didn't particularly enjoy. I felt oddly embarrassed, as though I was placing too much value in a matter as trivial as love. There were more important things in life, surely. Yet I could think of nothing more significant at that moment. My ego had been risked, and her answer would determine the outcome.

"Oh…" she said, breaking the silence.

I turned to her. She was looking into the water, her expression a mixture of gratification and apprehension. For one fleeting instant, I thought the gratification was reflective of her similar feelings for me, until I noticed a frown appearing on her features, suggesting annoyance. I understood—she was happy that I loved her, because it gave her validation as a woman and a person. But it also annoyed her, because she didn't love me back.

We sat in silence, watching the duck swim around us.

We ride the escalator in silence. The pride I'd felt after emasculating the taxi driver had evaporated upon seeing the look of disapproval on Emma's face. I feel like myself again now: useless, worthless and insignificant. As we reach the ground floor, she instinctively reaches for my arm to steady her. I take her hand, but let it slip through my fingers. She trips at the edge of the last step and falls forward. I try to catch her but can't, and she falls to the ground.

"Emma, I'm so sorry," I mutter hastily, as I pick her up.

"No worries," she says, getting to her feet and examining her arm.

I notice a fresh, heart-shaped bruise on her forearm. "Cute, don't you think?" she grins, looking up at me. "When I was a kid, I had a bruise the shape of a bell."

"So did I!" I reply, with a laugh. "And that's not all; when I was younger I had some freckles on my arm that lined up like a question mark."

"Hey, I did too…" she says, amused and taken aback. "Are we just a couple of mutants then, with some kind of invisible, undetectable connection?"

"Perhaps," I smile. "But if that's the case, I'm not complaining."

"Oh? Why not?"

I kiss her hand. "I can't think of anyone better I'd like to have a connection with." I am then surprised (and offended) when she bursts out laughing.

"I'm sorry," she says, holding a hand up to her mouth to try and stop the giggles trying to burst through her. "It was just one of those moments, you know? It just got kind of corny there, like something out of a movie." She smiles. "I'm sorry."

She is so different from me that I wonder how we might have ever found common ground if she *had* loved me, which she however never did, does not, and never will.

⊠    ⊠

She'd wanted me at her wedding, so I attended. It was a beautiful ceremony. She looked stunning. I was glad she didn't elope, because she would have missed out on the happiest day of her life, and the worst of mine. At the reception, she came to find me.

"Mrs. Raymond Darren," I said, and the words nearly choked me, though I did manage a weak smile to mask the inner pain. "It's a pleasure to meet you, ma'am."

She smiled back, her face flushed with joy and excitement. "I can't believe I'm married! I was afraid this day would get screwed up, but it didn't. It was perfect."

"Perfect," I repeated, with the same smile, but a hollow voice.

She took my hand and squeezed it; she was happy I was here, and I thought this would be our moment, the moment when she would say how much it meant to have me here on this important day. I thought she would tell me that she loved me, and that she

always would, even though she was married to someone else. I wanted her to know I loved her too, more than she would ever realise. Tears streamed down her cheeks, and made her look (if possible) even more beautiful than she already did. She wiped the tears and looked up into my eyes. "I'm so grateful to God for bringing Raymond into my life."

I felt like a drain hole had been unplugged in my chest, and that everything of value within my heart was emptying rapidly, while I sat powerlessly, unable to stop it.

"So am I," I lied.

Overcome with emotion, she pulled me into a hug, and then disappeared into the crowd. I stood there alone, watching the woman I loved dance, laugh, cry, and celebrate her marriage to another man. I didn't think I had ever felt worse in my life.

It was then that I saw Raymond standing to the side of the dance floor, talking to his brother. I had never gotten along with him, and never understood what Emma saw in him. I wanted to believe that he was a decent man, and that he would *never*, not under *any* circumstance, take her for granted. I wanted to believe he loved her as much as I did, or even *more* than that. But above all, I wanted to believe that he would make her happy, in *every* sense of the word. For Emma, amazing as she was, deserved nothing less than utter, unequivocal bliss.

Raymond laughed at some joke his brother had made, and the expression lit his features flatteringly. There was innocence in his laughter, a sincerity that touched his eyes; it made him appear honest and straightforward. In that one short moment, I found myself relating to him, even (dare I admit it?) liking him. Because I realised he and I weren't that different. As people we were polar opposites—we were nothing alike, had nothing in common (except love for the same woman, and a mutual dislike for each other), and lived contrasting lives. But we could so easily have led each other's lives. I could have been born as him and he as me. It was chance, or God's sleight of hand that had placed us in our respective lives. And underneath all the circumstances that

separated us, we were basically the same person. The world was one single, living soul, and we were its broken fragments, scattered into fate and circumstance.

He scratched his forehead as I watched, and that pulled the unbuttoned cuffs on his shirt down the length of his arm, revealing a heart-shaped bruise on his forearm. I frowned, scrutinising it. It looked familiar. In fact I had seen a similar bruise elsewhere, on almost the same spot. I noticed that his brother, standing next to him, also had the *exact* same bruise on his arm. I moved through the crowd, studying everyone's arms. I grabbed people's arms randomly to check for tattoos; they regarded me nervously, as if I was crazy, but I didn't care. Every one of them had the *exact* same bruise, on the *exact* same spot. How could that be possible?

As I stood in the middle of the reception hall, my eyes met Emma's.

"I love you," she mouthed, and her eyes twinkled with desire.

I thought she was looking at me, but she wasn't. I turned around and found every man in the hall mouthing back to her, "I love you too."

We stand on the platform, waiting for the train that will part us forever. We take this moment to say our farewells, and to prepare us for a lifetime apart.

"Well, this is it," I say to her, my voice brittle with emotion. "Tell Raymond that he better take good care of you, all right? Because I'll be watching..."

She nods and smiles. "He's a good man, you know."

"I know."

"You two have that in common."

I laugh mirthlessly. I look at her longingly, the woman of my dreams, the girl that stole my heart and refused to give me hers. I realise that I still love her, as much as I ever did, and I know

this love will never diminish. "You *deserve* happiness," I tell her, sincerely.

She seems to recognise the earnestness, for her answering smile is warm and appreciative. "We *both* do," she replies. "Why not attempt to find mutual bliss?"

I raise my eyebrows in surprise. "You mean together?"

She nods and flashes me another irresistible smile. "We can pretend, can't we? Just for today, just for now..." she says, and takes my hand in hers. "Tell me, my dear, did you fall in love with me as soon as we met?" she asks.

I smile and gaze down to notice a heart-shaped bruise on my right arm. I had seen it before, this *exact* same bruise, only it had been on a different arm. No, I realise, with an inward smile, actually it had been the same arm. I had thought it was different, but I'd been proven wrong now. It is this same arm that balances the entire world on its hand.

"Did you hear me?" she asks, and I lift my gaze to meet hers. "I asked if you fell in love with me the moment we met," she repeats the words, sounding a little worried now.

An old memory, one of my earliest, surfaces:

*Parted from an all-forgiving womb, I rested in a crib, my new home, and examined my new limbs. It was a fat, shiny arm with a pudgy hand, little chubby fingers, and a curious birthmark: a heart-shaped mark on the forearm, a kind of bruise. I examined the arm at length, turning it around for my eyes to scan it, while I giggled in amusement. And then, as if to test my level of control over it, I moved it into my mouth. I giggled again, but happily this time, for I knew this hand was mine, and would remain mine, no matter how many years passed, and no matter how many avatars it took. For me, there was only one arm, and it was mine.*

*I was in love...*

I smile at her. "Yes, of course," I answer. "At first sight."

# IV

## *Reality's Dream*

It's daytime… Or is it simply night, lit up by a passing swarm or fireflies? I must be going crazy, for I can't see the sun anywhere. I can't really pivot my head either, so I can't check to see if it's merely hiding somewhere behind me. Oh well, I'll figure it out sooner or later. Night or day, this is a beautiful setting. Clear blue skies, and an even clearer, bluer sea.

The urge to sneeze rushes onto me suddenly and I indulge it without much thought. The sneeze erupts into a snowstorm, and the golden beach around me turns white with snow. Then I inhale, and all the snow evaporates into my nostrils. The world returns to its former setting.

There is a madness that befalls dreamers, an all-consuming dearth of reason and relevance that consumes the dreamer in its convoluted reality. Gazing out into this apocalyptic sea, a helpless invalid, I cannot help but wonder if the madness has found me.

A farmer strolls by, leading a cow behind him.

"A drink, please?" I ask of him.

"It is not my decision," he informs me. "Ask the cow."

The cow's large, beautiful eyes pivot to find mine, and her expression is enquiring.

She takes pity on my predicament and offers me the only aid she can. The taste of fresh milk from a cow is delicious. But this milk tastes even sweeter, because the cow has parted with it willingly. Her milk lends me the strength and the clarity of thought I have been lacking.

As the farmer and the cow, two anomalies in this bizarre landscape, disappear into the distance, I am allowed an opportunity to reflect upon my condition. I attempt to realise my situation, and recognise any possible solutions. But there are no solutions. That fact becomes obvious after just a moment's contemplation. I am in the middle of a large, bizarre dream.

The effects of the milk are short-lived. A fog settles over my thoughts as I watch the hypnotic movement of the tide. I feel confused, dispirited, and helpless.

She is a young girl, no more than four years of age. Chasing a butterfly, she stumbles upon me quite by accident. "Are you playing a game?" she asks.

For a moment, I wonder if I actually *am* in the middle of some kind of a game. But somehow, through the fog, I find a clear answer. "No, this isn't a game."

"Are you hungry?" she reaches into the pockets of her skirt and extracts a piece of chocolate. "Open wide," she says, and I willingly oblige. The chocolate has much the same effect as the milk, and once again, I am allowed a moment of lucidity.

There is a pattern to be discerned amid this chaotic existence: a rhythm to the sea, a symmetry to the landscape, and a purpose to this eccentricity. *I* am the solution.

The dream, if it *was* a dream, vanishes as seamlessly as it appeared.

There is no chocolate in my mouth, and there was no girl.

The reason collapses, and the world reverts to chaos.

One fact that has survived this world, despite the absence of logic, is the truth that dreams are hopelessly fickle. Like a

butterfly that flutters teasingly outside the arc of a lepidopterist's net, dreams ever dwell on the edge of reason, just beyond the dreamer's understanding. They exist in the dreamer's sensory field, and yet, since they hover beyond the scope of logic, they do not exist—or rather, they *could* not exist. The dreamer is therefore left questioning existence itself, dismantling its very structure in an effort to unearth an answer.

My current existence is worth dismantling, for it is at much real as it is devoid of logic. I stand buried under a tree, with only my head above the surface, while the sea eats away at the world around me. I try to remember when the earth imprisoned me here. It must have happened recently, for I still bear memories of walking, of running wildly, climbing trees, swimming through streams, and soaring off high cliffs. I had been alive, my limbs roaring with youthful vigour and reckless passion. The world had been my playground— there had been no fences anywhere, no rules, and no boundaries. And then suddenly I'd fallen... or had the earth risen? Either way, I'd crashed into a reality so harsh and so true that it stripped me of hope. For how could hope survive where dreams couldn't? How could one paint a rainbow, when no colours remained? I became a caged bird, imprisoned in a dreamless world.

Yet now I sit in the middle of a bizarre dream.

My nose itches.

Do I still have arms and legs beneath the earth? My mind calls out to my limbs, asking them to answer if they're still there. I have been here so long that I cannot remember if I had been buried or if I had been decapitated and my head left here. Instinctively, I believe my hand can break through the soil and alleviate this itch—I even *expect* it to happen. But the earth remains unbroken, and the itch only grows stronger.

Many horrendous tragedies befell the millions that came before me in this world, and I give due respect to their suffering. But the frustration of being buried neck-deep with an itchy nose is unlike any other. It is a fate that would likely drive even the

sanest to madness. More than the unpleasant sensation, it is the simplicity of the condition that I find frustrating. It would take but a moment to scratch my nose, and yet I am unable to do so.

I pause to consider the value of friendship. In the past, when I've been helpless and vulnerable, I've usually had a friend nearby to rely on. But now I'm not only incapacitated, but I'm also apparently alone in this terrifyingly small world, devoid of companionship.

"Help me!" I cry out into the sheer silence.

A squirrel appears by my side, his own nose twitching as he hugs the earth, searching for food. He stands before me, oddly entranced. My head must seem to him like a giant nut. He comes closer to investigate. I can imagine him pulling out a measuring tape to check whether my head would fit in the trunk of his car. Or he might have been wondering whether his wife would approve of such an extravagant purchase. Humourless as my predicament is, I cannot help but smile at the idea of this squirrel possessing such human characteristics. His nose twitches again as he contemplates me further. He *does* appear human... perhaps even more than I do.

I feel an odd sense of kinship towards this creature. I remember having driven down a dark street one night, when a squirrel appeared suddenly before my car. I had swerved desperately to miss him and had crashed into a parked car as a result. My mercy had cost me a fortune in insurance. Perhaps this squirrel is here now to repay that act of mercy. It might not have been the same squirrel, but perhaps it came here on behalf of its kind.

My hope turns to impatience though, when the little critter merely stands still. "Do something," I demand. The itch is becoming unbearable, and I begin yelling curses and profanities at the creature, threatening its life and the lives of all squirrels everywhere if it does not come to my aid soon. But despite all my abuses, it remains unmoved. I begin to wonder if it is here simply to mock me. Days fade to night, and nights drift into days...

The squirrel hasn't left my side—in fact, he's hardly stirred.

There was a time when I had caught butterflies with my fingers, a time when I had chased birds away with a wave of my hand, and frightened squirrels just by walking towards them. Is that why I have captured this squirrel's interest? Perhaps I had chased it away once, back when I'd been a large, looming monster, fearsome and capable. And so he beholds me in disbelief now, wondering how I became this pathetic, helpless object, unworthy of awe or fear. He obviously doesn't fear me, for he knows that with my circumstances being what they are, I don't pose any sort of a threat to him or any other living creature. I can yell and threaten him till I lose my voice—he won't budge, because he knows I can't follow through on my threats.

*Helplessness.*

To a living creature, there is no word more frightening than helplessness. I say so with confidence, because I myself am helpless now. Whether I live or die depends on sheer chance. I am utterly reliant on the hands of fate, as it shoots darts into the board of my life. I start to wonder if I had ever possessed any control over my fate, even back when I'd been a fully functional, mobile being. Or had the reality I had taken for granted been the most consuming dream of all?

Am I dreaming *now*, or is this real? Am I real, or is this a dream?

I consider how similar those questions seem, and yet how different they actually are. In one question I am the dreamer; in the other, I myself am the dream. It had taken me a lifetime to recognise that distinction, and even longer to understand it. But understanding the difference now hasn't helped me decipher an answer. What I find frustrating is not the absence of answers, but the sheer abundance of them. They're everywhere, and yet, like fruits that dangle teasingly from atop a towering tree, they are beyond my reach.

The itch is still there. Its persistence has been met by my defiance, and the two are locked in a battle for supremacy. However I have a more pressing concern: boredom. I am bored and have

50

grown weary of this tedium. I crave some colour, something eventful—*anything*, really.

As if in answer to my wishes, a lone traveller passes by. He carries nothing on him, and is dressed in a black suit, with a tall top hat. He bows to me, quite ceremoniously, and I indulge in a chuckle as I imagine myself trying to bow back. Thankfully, my behaviour doesn't offend him.

"Who are you?" I ask.

"A performer," he declares, with another bow.

He juggles artfully, emulating the skill and prowess that I myself had once boasted. His timing is impeccable, his routine ambitious, and his execution flawless. At the end of the first act, he bows again, but with pride this time, and a sense of accomplishment. When he tips his hat to acknowledge my cheers, a squirrel jumps out of it. Boldly, it scurries up to the other squirrel already staring at me, and the two sit together, still as stone. The magician (much to my annoyance) doesn't appear to have noticed either of them, and continues with his act.

He rubs his hands together, while smiling knowingly at me. Flakes of lovely, white snow fall from his palms. The world around us turns dark, and the noise of his low whistle drifts eerily through the silence. His eyes never leave mine, and they shine with the brilliance of the silver white rain. His whistles echo loudly until the wind answers them with long, mournful howls. With the wind comes more snow, falling directly from the sky itself and not just his hands. He spreads his arms and gazes at the Heavens, as if claiming the skies as part of his act. I recognise the smile on his face, for I myself have often worn it. At once proud and reckless, it reveals a man who is smart, wise, and yet undeniably naïve. I find him so familiar that I wonder if he and I are the same person, trapped within a common world. Or rather, is the world trapped within us?

His body suddenly explodes and turns into ten more squirrels. They leap over and around each other, before assuming positions adjacent to the two already present. A dozen of the little critters

now sit before me, with rapt attention and unwavering curiosity. Are they real or am I imagining them? The first one appeared when I wished for relief from my itchy nose, and yet it didn't help me. Why? I had expected it to help; I had *wanted* it to help. I *still* want it to help—

The first squirrel hops out of line and approaches me. Paw outstretched, it reaches for my nose and somehow scratches the exact spot where the itch troubles me. The touch of the squirrel lifts the fog over my thoughts. I feel my consciousness growing. My awareness drifts beyond just my mind, further and further still. It reaches the first squirrel, then the others, the trees, the sand, the sea, and the skies; it spreads far and wide through this world until it encompasses this *entire* existence. I feel as if as if I am one with this reality.

We are *one*.

I think of the cow, the farmer, the butterfly, the girl, the squirrels, and the magician. I think of this earth, of this sky and even that marauding sea. We are all one and the same. Our consciousness is shared, and our existence entwined. This then is the ultimate answer: the Universe is *one* person, one mind, and I am merely a part of the consciousness. But one question remains unanswered: is all this a dream or is it real?

I awake with a start.

Sunlight floods in through the tiny gap between the drapes. What time is it, I wonder? The nurse must have forgotten about me, because I've been left here by the window all night. My eyes pan down mournfully to the rest of my body, sitting lifelessly in this old wheelchair. Fragments of the dream echo within my mind... I remember the helplessness of being buried, unable to move my hands or my legs. The vulnerability I'd felt then was no different to what I feel now, to what I feel every day in this life.

I hear a muffled crash from somewhere behind me, and my mind orders my neck to pivot so that it can determine the source of the noise. But my mind and my body don't communicate

anymore. They haven't communicated in many years, I would assume.

My nose itches.

I grit my teeth and hope that someone checks on me soon. My hands lie folded under this blanket, unresponsively. I frown at them, concentrating hard in the hope that I might beat my condition, produce a miracle, and regain the use of my limbs. But, like the thousands of other times I've tried this, nothing happens.

I think back to the dream... it had been haunting because it had seemed so real. It wasn't very different from my current reality. In fact, in an odd sense, I might have preferred that existence to this. To sit in a wheelchair and watch my life wither away is torture. But to be buried from the neck below, and left in the middle of an apocalyptic world... in a strange sense, it gave me more control, because the world was within my mind, and I alone controlled it.

I hear a little girl laughing.

The noise startles me. It had come from outside the window, just beyond these concealing drapes. I close my eyes and listen carefully:

I hear the gentle voice of a cow; the rhythmic pattering of a magician juggling; the chatter of many squirrels, and I even hear the low rumble of a hungry sea.

The nurse walks in just then, talking animatedly as she tidies up the room. Normally, I would have treasured this opportunity for conversation, but now my thoughts lie in disarray. I review my past as far as I can remember. What had happened the previous night? What had come before the dream? The questions circle my head uselessly, but I find no answer. I know that the answer lurks beyond these drapes. I could discover whether I am caught in a labyrinth of dreams, or merely paranoid, pushed to the point of imagining sounds that aren't there.

"Anything I can get for you before I bring in your breakfast?"

the nurse asks, at the end of a long speech that I have carelessly missed.

"Yes," I reply, my voice trembling. "Could you open the drapes?"

The drapes fly open in one crisp, fluid motion.

I gaze into my reality.

# V

## *Reflection*

I was told that these stairs would take me home.

"But I live far, far away," I had protested, gesturing to the distance, beyond the oceans where memories swim, and the mountains where children grow, and even past the sunrise, where dreams begin. "How can these stairs lead to my home? There are so few of them."

I was wrong. The stairs rose into the persistent fog, and they climbed steadily, while the hours passed reluctantly. I could see nothing through the mist but half a dozen stairs at a stretch: three beneath me, and three above me. The rest of the way was hidden.

I had expected exhaustion to set in, but there was still ample strength in my legs, and enough vigour in my heart. The choice of giving up and climbing back down was always available; but my curiosity had been aroused. I had to know where these stairs led.

In the chilly silence, I heard voices within my own mind. My mother told me that I was inconsiderate, "You should have told us

you would be off climbing stairs, so we wouldn't have worried."
As her voice faded into the echoes, my father reminded me that I
was a failure, "You could never climb *all* those stairs. You know
our neighbour's son? The doctor? Well he could have climbed
those steps *three* at a time. In fact, I bet he'd have already reached
the top."

Their voices renewed my will and I picked up my pace, daring
to even sprint a few lengths. Suddenly the stairs ended, and I
came upon a dark room. The moment I entered it, a bright screen
appeared on the far wall. It was some sort of a theatre, and a movie
was about to start. I marched down the aisle and sat at the front.
I picked up a tub of popcorn.

A couple appeared on screen, cradling an infant in their arms.
They were my parents, only younger than I'd ever seen them.
They were smiling at the camera and showing off their new born
child. I was a beautiful baby. I watched my younger self on film
greedily, a luxury I'd never indulged in before. It was odd to see
myself that way, to have no clear memory of those times, of that
day or even that one single moment. I kept putting my hand in
my mouth, as my large eyes darted this way and that, curious
yet confused by the voices of the adults, who kept asking me to
look at the camera. I smiled at my younger self and gazed into
my own eyes, brimming with more innocence and hope than I'd
ever had since. I was filled with a sense of... disgust... *disgust?* Yes,
disgust. I was disgusted. I wanted that child to die in its parents'
arms. I hated it, despised its glaring weaknesses, its fragility and
its obvious vulnerability.

"Destroy it!" I cried at the couple on screen. "Drown it! Bury
it! Kill it!" I threw popcorn at the screen, broke off the armrests
on the chairs and hurled them too. I tore the chairs themselves in
anger, wept in frustration, and screamed in agony. I wanted that
child to die!

The screen faded to black, and the room went quite dark.

I sat down, breathing heavily. The silence and the darkness
were both comforting. I was confused and embarrassed, but

mostly I was disappointed. I had expected these stairs to take me home. However, I had merely been returned to my past, and exposed to feelings that I neither understood nor recognised. I felt cheated. These stairs had promised much and delivered little.

I paused long enough to compose myself, and then returned to the stairs, prepared to climb back down. But as I left the room, I realised the stairs hadn't ended yet—they climbed higher still, beyond this theatre. Where did they lead to, I wondered?

I set off climbing again. Clouds swirled around me. It rained for a while, and I shivered in the cold. It was uncomfortable, but I couldn't abandon the quest and walk back down, so I continued. Thankfully, the sun soon shone again, bright and clear. I was very high up, and looking down I could see a vast, beautiful world. It looked oddly small from up here, and seemed somehow insignificant. I couldn't help but feel that these stairs were more important, and that my quest to reach home was more relevant than anything else on earth. Perhaps that was just my ego stretching its muscles, but I felt distinctly detached from the rest of existence. I was alone, and I recognised that this journey was one of personal significance.

An hour later I came upon a circular platform, which looked like a kind of observation deck. I approached the railing at the end of the deck and gazed out into a vast, open field. An enormous army stood beneath, poised ready for a long march.

"There you are, sire!" a man called from behind me.

A General approached me, donned in military gear, and decorated with many medals and ribbons. He looked relieved to see me. "The men were growing restless waiting for you."

"Waiting? For what?" I asked, startled.

"For you to lead them, my Lord," he answered, equally surprised by my answer.

"Lead them?" I gazed down at the army. "I cannot lead them…" I murmured, my voice trembling even as I considered it. "I am no soldier."

He wasn't listening. He opened a closet in the corner of the

room and rummaged through it. "Your armour, my Lord," he said, when he returned.

In his hands lay censorship, honesty, conformism, and prejudice.

"I cannot wear these," I declared at once.

"But these are our weapons, sire," he said, regarding me as if I had lost my mind. "What else can you carry out into battle but the army's standard issue weaponry?"

"If I am to fight, I will carry my own weapons," I insisted. I showed him individuality, tolerance, imagination, and fearless rebellion.

"This is madness," he cried, all trace of respect lost from his manner. "If you insist on carrying *those* in battle," he said, eyeing my weapons with disgust, "Then you will march alone, and *without* our protection." Saying, he left the room in a cloud of disgust.

I went back to the railing and gazed down at the army. I saw the General ride out on his horse. He was soon at the head of the ranks, issuing orders to them. Then slowly the entire army marched forward. Their pace was remarkably sluggish; at this rate they would never reach far. Had I an opportunity, I would have preferred to ride alone, to ride fast and without restriction, even if I would have been left vulnerable in their absence. I would have been unprotected riding alone, and would perhaps have suffered harm or eventual death, but I would have seen much more of the world before my death than they. It would have been the price to pay for freedom.

But my purpose was not to fight battles or lead marches.

I returned to the stairs and resumed climbing.

The next door I came upon led into a circus. I had never glimpsed an arena so large, or an audience so boisterous. The stadium seemed to stretch for miles, and each seat was filled with an eager, vociferous spectator. In the middle of the stadium was a large, circular stage, and on it were the performers. They were many, and varied in talent, skill and persona. The audience

cheered loyally, laughing at the jokes, marvelling at the feats, and celebrating the triumphs. Personally, I was more interested in the audience than the performers, and studied their reactions intently. Their praise was genuine, motivated by sincere appreciation for the performer, rather than a mere obligation to respond. They seemed to share in the performer's success, as though they themselves had been part of the act. And I realised it was because they *were* a part of the act, a most integral part at that, for they acted as a kind of stimulus and motivated the performers to do better. The more I watched them, the more compelled I felt to earn some of their praise and appreciation. Shamelessly, in an effort to share in the performers' accolades, I too chased the limelight. I leapt upon the stage and performed for the audience.

First I juggled, and did so skilfully. My dance routines were complicated but artfully executed. The animals responded to my commands loyally, never once failing to obey. I swallowed swords, breathed fire, stood on nails, walked high wires, climbed burning ropes, and even leapt from a ninety-foot platform into a tiny barrel of water. And yet, when at the end of my performance I took an expectant bow, there was no applause.

The spectators sat silently, their expressions ranging from bored to indifferent. The other performers waited beside the stage, their arms crossed, tapping the floor impatiently with their feet. Had I not amused *any* of them? Had I not entertained? Flawlessly I had performed, borrowing only the best routines and the most daring acts. And yet I had failed to draw even a single cheer. I turned back to the audience to demand an explanation, only to find the stands suddenly empty. How could this be? They had been filled with thousands not a moment ago.

I gazed out into the empty stadium, devoid of even a single living being, and I felt alone.

Unsatisfied, I trudged off in disappointment.

When I resumed climbing the stairs, my mood was sour. So far these stairs hadn't led anywhere useful. They had teased and taunted, promising much but delivering little. I was beginning

to feel very sceptical about the promise that they would lead me home.

The next room seemed quite promising. As soon as I entered it, I recognised the wallpaper pattern, the poor but cosy furnishings, and the all too familiar layout. I was home. The stairs had indeed led me where they had promised. Eager to know what I would find here, I walked through the foyer into the main hall. The place was crowded, filled to capacity with people that I knew and loved. Tears streamed down my cheeks as I gazed into faces I hadn't seen in ages. I went up to each of them and opened my arms in greeting, but they did not respond. They spoke amongst themselves, laughed, danced, cried and celebrated each other's presence, but they did not notice me. Was I invisible? Indeed not, for they could see me. They frowned when I interrupted them, recoiled when I touched them, and turned away if I addressed them. It was as if I was a stranger, or worse still, an enemy. Yet in reality I was neither. I was their friend, someone they loved, and someone whose company they had once cherished.

I had never known such sadness before. To be around my loved ones and not be able to share in their love was a fate beyond mere cruelty. It resurfaced insecurities I had long kept supressed within myself, and these renewed fears now began to weaken me; they fed on my positivity, and thereby strengthened every negative thought I had ever possessed.

I couldn't bear to be in this room any longer. I returned hastily to the staircase. I didn't know if this was the home I had been promised, but I wanted to believe that there was something better awaiting me, something more redeeming. So I decided to climb further, to try and reach a warmer place, a sort of salvation even. I wept uncontrollably though as I resumed climbing, for I felt as if I had reached the lowest depths of misery. Since first entering this stairway, I had failed to conquer weakness; then I had failed to lead; I had failed to win attention, and now I had failed to earn the affections of those I loved. What other misfortunes would these stairs bring?

The stairs climbed higher and higher still.

At one point I was certain I was being chased. Though the tenacious fog that hovered over the staircase concealed most of my sight but for half a dozen stairs, I was certain I had glimpsed something behind me, something sinister. At first I only heard its footsteps, echoing faintly but not distantly. But then its shadow fell over mine, and I turned to see its ghastly silhouette through the mist. I ran up the stairs in panic, and its footsteps followed, its own pace quickening. My lungs burned with effort, and my limbs ached for rest. And yet my fear was so great that I knew I couldn't pause. It wasn't long before my body collapsed, refusing to move another inch. I fell on the stairs and turned in anticipation of the attack.

The creature's shadow loomed over me, but it did not come near. Its hesitation took me by surprise. I waited long enough for my legs to recover, and then I resumed climbing. I didn't push myself as hard this time, and was content to merely keep a brisk pace. Again the creature followed, matching my now more conservative speed. But it still didn't attack. What was it, I wondered? It persevered relentlessly, almost loyally, yet never revealed itself. Over time I grew accustomed to its presence, and learned to disregard it, as I would my shadow.

The next room I stumbled into was some kind of a control centre. There were all sorts of machinery and computers inside, with control panels, large screens, keypads, gauges, meters, and other equipment that I didn't recognise. The most distinctive feature of this room wasn't the machinery however, but the personnel. Dozens of gnomes were scattered in every station, busily taking readings, filing reports, and issuing orders. They ignored my presence and kept at their work. I ambled around the room, peering over their tiny shoulders to see what they were doing.

In some of the screens I saw my family and friends. In others I saw people from my past, acquaintances, co-workers, and even enemies. Some screens showed movies I had seen; books I had read;

articles I had glanced at; pictures I had viewed; conversations I had participated in or else had been privy to; music I had heard; ideas I had developed; emotions I had experienced or else had invoked; thoughts I'd had, ranging from sinister to inspiring; dreams I'd had; fantasies and wishes I had indulged in; the knowledge and the skills I had gathered in my lifetime. Some of this information appeared in printouts, which the gnomes filed in cabinets.

The cabinets, I discovered, were actually enormous vaults with drawers. I opened a few of these drawers and perused the files within. I came across information from my own past, things I myself had forgotten. I came across *every* conversation I had ever had with every person I had ever met. I found files detailing my prejudices, my dislikes, my weaknesses and errors. I came across an alarmingly large file that listed all the lies I had ever told. Another file listed my regrets and grievances. Others still detailed my accomplishments and my happiest memories. The files were endless, as were the cabinets. How did the gnomes keep track of all this, I wondered? More importantly though, how had they come by this information? Was their sole purpose to spy on me, and record every detail of my life, no matter how trivial?

A dial on one of the stations showed a word that described my current mood: confusion. The other titles on the dial ranged from ecstasy, joy, wonder, pride, satisfaction, idle contentment, idle jealousy, doubt, anxiety, anger, sorrow, to devastation. Confusion sat in the dead centre of the dial, between idle contentment and idle jealousy.

I moved forward to get a better look at the dial.

Deciding to venture a guess, I tried to recall a joke from my past. I soon remembered one that I'd heard at a friend's wedding and retold it within my head; the dial shook slightly, and then veered ever so slightly from "confusion" to about halfway towards "idle contentment." I tried to stimulate a stronger reaction. I thought about the love of my life, a woman who had failed to reciprocate my feelings for her, and had instead announced her love for my brother. The dial swung sharply towards "idle jealousy,"

and then oscillated between "doubt" and "anger" before settling finally on a mark halfway between idle jealousy and doubt.

I was fascinated by this machine. How could it gauge my mood so accurately?

Perhaps as fascinating was a screen adjacent to this machine, which depicted a picture of that very screen at this very station, in the middle of this *very* room, as seen through *my* eyes. I pivoted my head slightly, and the image on the screen moved accordingly to capture what my eyes were viewing. Remarkable! I was being spied upon from within. Though disconcerting, it was a realisation that posed more questions than concerns within my head. The gnome at this station, unperturbed to my presence like the others, wrote down details of anything and everything I perceived, including the resulting opinions, concerns and questions. It was odd being documented like that, to have my every thought and feeling witnessed, measured and then recorded for an unknown purpose. I tapped the gnome on the shoulder to question him, but he waved me away irritably, without even turning around. I found it funny in a sense that he was too busy recording my life to spare me a moment's consideration. It was like working for an employer and failing to acknowledge him when he came around for an inspection.

I left the room and tried to return to the staircase, but it had disappeared! In its stead I found a corridor. It was narrow and dimly lit. Many doorways stood on either wall, with closed doors. I opened the first door: it led into a staircase that spiralled downwards. Was this the highest point on the stairway then? Perhaps this doorway would lead me back down. I went to the adjacent door and opened it. Inside was another staircase, only these climbed *upwards*. I opened yet another door and found yet another staircase, though this one climbed in both directions. Each door led out onto a stairway. Where did each stairway lead, and how many such stairways did *they* each lead to? How many stairways, how many doors, how many rooms and how many memories would I have to endure before I reached my promised

home? And was there indeed a home for me to reach, or had that promise been a blatant lie?

As I stood in that corridor, a door opened to my right and I saw myself come out of it. I gazed at him, my reflection, and he gazed back. We stood in silence for a moment, regarding each other as though we were strangers. And then he opened another door at random and disappeared through it. I stared after him, dumbstruck by what I had just seen…

I thought back over everything I had seen since I'd climbed that first stair. Everything I had come across within this labyrinth had been familiar and relevant. I wondered if the stairway had been built around my life. Or rather, had the stairway been built *into* my life?

No, I decided; the stairway had been built within my *mind*. All these stairways and all these doors… they were within my consciousness. I was lost within the labyrinths of my own mind. It explained why I had been promised that these stairs would take me home. These stairs *were* my home. I had explored my desires, my memories, my doubts, my insecurities and every other aspect of myself. I had been chased by my own fears, and confronted by my own demons.

I stood poised in front of a random doorway, leading into a random stairway. My reflection was out there somewhere, wandering this labyrinth as I was. If I entered this doorway, I might be lost forever. But then, I realised I had always been lost.

Knowing where I was had never meant I'd found my way. No, life (not unlike my mind) was a labyrinth of questions and answers. My purpose had never been to find my way through it, but to simply make the journey. I would have to walk as far as my time allowed, see as much as was there to see, and understand whatever I could. My existence *was* my purpose.

I entered the stairway, without expecting it to lead me anywhere. In fact, I had no expectations. This puzzle was larger than me. These doors travelled further than just my mind. They extended beyond the mortal reaches of the world, past the obscure

borders of the Universe, into the realms of existence itself. For the Universe is not altogether different from the mind. Shrouded in mystery, they are both comprised of infinite labyrinths, and though a traveller might roam them eternally, he will never succeed in opening every door, or learning every secret. But he won't be alone; he will always be pursued by his eternally loyal shadow—*reflection.*

# VI

## *An Apple Branch*

Max and Macs were born on the same apple tree. Their nests were built on different branches, and their families lived in symbiotic harmony for years. But then came a famine and a flood, and all the other members of their families slowly died out. Correspondingly, the apple tree bloomed less and less with every passing season, until all the apples it bore grew on just one branch. Max and Macs, both desperate and hungry, migrated to this branch at the same time.

Though not strangers, Max and Macs had never really been acquainted in all the time they had lived in this tree. Faced now with a territorial dispute, they regarded one another with a sense of apprehension, unsure of how the other would act under these circumstances.

Max spoke first. "Pardon me, but this is my branch."

Macs was quick to respond. "Indeed? Where is your nest?"

"Up there," Max replied unabashedly, gesturing to a branch several feet higher.

"Then how can you claim ownership of *this* branch?"

"I arrived here first, therefore it's mine."

"On the contrary, I landed here the same time as you did."

Max hesitated, for he had no suitable rebuttal. They were both aware that since they had arrived on this branch at the same time, it would be difficult to decide who had the right to stay.

"When did you first settle down on this tree?" Macs demanded.

Max pondered the question. "When did *you* settle down on this tree?" he asked.

Macs was too smart for that. "Long before you."

Max turned to a different strategy. "My great, great grandfather carried the seed of this apple tree and planted it here, so this tree should really belong to me."

"Well, it was *my* great, great grandfather who showed your great, great grandfather *where* to plant this tree, so really the tree belongs to me."

Max glared at his counterpart, but then decided to adopt a subtler approach. "Why don't I draw a line in the middle of the branch? Then we can divide it into two halves. My half will be from the line to the tip of the branch. Yours will be from the line to the armpit of the tree. Neither one of us must then cross over to the other's side. Agreed?"

"But your half would contain all the apples on the branch," Macs argued.

"That is the tree's choice; I am but the innocent benefactor."

"In that case, I would argue that by extension, along with *my* half of the branch, the rest of the tree also belongs to me," declared Macs.

"How do you figure that?" Max asked, outraged.

"If everything on *that* side of the line is yours, then everything on *this* side of the line is mine. Therefore the rest of the tree, along with any and all apples that may grow upon it in the future belongs to me. Agreed?"

"Certainly not."

"Then I am afraid the issue is still far from settled."

They sat in silence for a while, each lost in his own contemplation. The branch remained unclaimed, and the apples aged slowly, wondering if they would ever be eaten.

"Can you fly?" Max asked, eventually.

"Most certainly, I fly like a bird."

"Good one."

"It was there for the taking."

"I haven't flown in years."

"How come?"

"My wings were injured in an accident. I have lived on this tree for so long now that it is my entire world; I know nothing of, nor *care* for anything beyond its branches."

"Do you know that I am blind?" Macs said.

"No! But then how do you fly and move about?"

"Instinct. Wisdom. Imagination."

"You imagine the world you fly into?"

"Quite literally."

"Well, isn't that dangerous?"

"No more than flying with full vision. The world is full of predators, and having sight will only enable me to suffer through an additional sensation of death. But by flying blind, I imagine a world devoid of danger, disease and death. In my world, there is no suffering."

"What happens if you fly into something and hurt yourself?"

"Oh I don't fly at all."

"You don't? But you just said you fly with imagination."

"By never leaving this tree. Blind as I am, I sit in my nest and imagine the sensation of soaring through the clouds, gazing over a world that is lush green, with streaks of blue, ridges of golden brown, and deep pools of mesmerizing turquoise."

"Then both our fates are similar," Max concluded.

"Do you dream of flying, also?"

"No, I prefer to walk with my eyes open. I have scoured every

inch of this tree on foot, and learnt that to know this tree is to know this world. I do not need to fly."

"Perhaps, but we are both in need of this tree, and in particular of this one branch."

"It would seem so."

They fell silent.

"Do you know there was once a farmer who tried to cut this tree down?"

"Indeed! How was he stopped?"

"The axe wouldn't go through the trunk. Try as he did hew after hew, there was not even a scratch upon the tree. The axe eventually split into two, so he gave up and went home."

"Isn't that remarkable! I guess the tree has predators, too."

"Certainly. I used to think the world was the largest predator in existence, but I was wrong. There are larger ones—the Universe, for instance. Even beyond that, existence. And there might be one larger still, though that is too large for me to know about."

"Existence is a predator?"

"It feeds on itself. It devours all that exists, whether it be living things, mountains, lakes, seas, or memories and time. Everything gets ingested and eventually regurgitated into life."

"Rebirth?"

"Something like that."

"But how do you know of this? You said you've never left this tree!"

"Indeed I haven't. But this tree is larger than this world, and it holds as many riddles as the entire Universe does. It is this tree that taught me all I know today."

"It seems silly suddenly to realise we were fighting over a mere branch."

"Do not call it a 'mere' branch, for nothing is mere and insignificant. Just as this tree is larger than this world, this branch is larger than the tree. The apples it holds might be portals into another existence. You and I might each be larger than an entire Universe!"

"But I feel so small and insignificant."

"So? The Universe itself is tiny. My sneeze might blow it away."

"Stop, you're being facetious."

"What if you and I are the creators of all existence?"

"Now you're being blasphemous."

"I think I lost my wings for a reason. The world shrunk while my wisdom grew, until this tree and everything within it became larger than life. What need do I have then for flight? If I could fly, then I would delude myself by roaming uselessly around a barren, listless existence. But now I see existence for what it is: it is alone, tiny, and rather insignificant. Much as we are."

"You're speaking in riddles."

Max hopped over to one of the apples and began pecking at it.

Macs called out to stop him, "Beware! That apple might be poisonous!"

"How do you figure that?"

"Every one of my family members died after they ate an apple."

"As did mine," said Max, remembering.

"So the apples must be poisonous."

"Perhaps it is *we* who are poisonous. We poisoned the apples."

"But the apples poisoned our families."

"*After* they poisoned the apples."

"Then we too are poisonous. We too are apples."

"Don't be daft. I am a bird."

"I am an apple."

"Then I am poisonous to you."

"And you to me."

They shared a laugh over the matter. The laughter soothed their abrasive natures as each then conceded to the other. "Perhaps *you* should take this branch."

"I do not think I could, after all that has happened. You take it."

"And suffer the guilt of knowing I left you bereft of a home?"

"There are plenty of branches on this tree—I will find myself another home."

"I think I would miss you if you were not near."

"I would certainly miss you. Perhaps you should stay near."

Their attention was stolen by rising smoke. One saw it, while the other sensed it. The tree was on fire. Max and Macs weighed their options and found them to be limited.

"The tree will not survive. We cannot linger here."

"It is too late! Save yourself, fly away."

"How? Blind as I am, if I leave this tree I may never find another home."

"But if you stay here, you will surely burn and die."

"Then that is my fate. Could you not hop away?"

"The flames are too vast. Wherever I hide on this tree, I will be found. It is over."

"Then I am glad for your company."

"As I am for yours."

"Tell me what you see."

"A flood approaches. It has vanquished everything, from the mighty mountains to the vast forests, and has levelled the earth entirely. There is nothing left but water."

"And this tree."

"And this tree."

"Now tell me what *you* see."

"I am blind."

"But not dreamless. Tell me what visions your mind has conjured for you."

"I am soaring over a vast, beautiful land. There is colour and laughter everywhere, acres and acres of it. There are millions of trees just like this, filled with fruit. Birds roam everywhere. I am above this world, flying proudly, freely. I feel fortunate."

"You *are* fortunate."

"How do you figure?"

"You are blind to reality, but your mind is awake to fantasy."

"Yours isn't?"

"Not anymore. I have seen too much to dream. It is the curse of vision."

"If only I could live in my dreams."

"If only I could dream."

"I will share my dreams with you."

"Then I will share my sight with you."

There was a pause, as they regarded each other with compassion. The flames rose steadily; most of the tree was now on fire, but for this branch and everything above it.

"In this end, are we so different?"

"How do you mean?"

"We fought for the rights to this branch, as though our lives were independent of each other. But alas our fates are entwined, more so perhaps than any two living beings."

"More than a pair of close friends, or siblings?"

"More than a mother and child."

"More than a husband and wife?"

"More so even than God and His creatures."

"Then should we not be one?"

"Perhaps we *are* one."

The flames rose to the level of the branch. Searing pain and suffocating smoke surrounded Macs and Max as they stood in a tight embrace, awaiting death.

They conversed till the very end.

"Is this tree not a living being also?"

"Indeed it is."

"Then is it not also a part of us?"

"Of course. That's why we are all dying together."

"Then the tree *is* one with us. We are all *one*."

"Take me into your dream."

"Which one?"

"Your choice. Just take us all away from this fire."

"I am dreaming of a world that is neither fair nor pure. There is abundant darkness, and yet there are golden hearts everywhere, scattered like gems over a field of dirt. It is a world different to ours: there are trees, there are apples, there is an apple tree, and there is you and there is me; but in this world that I dream, we do not know that we are all one."

"An all-consuming dream."

"Indeed."

The branch was on fire. Max and Macs were surrounded by the flames.

"Take us into the dream. I will follow."

"But in the dream we will be ignorant, much as we were before we spoke. We will not remember. Would you rather not die here, pure and enlightened?"

"To live is to think, to dream and to hope. That is what I wish for."

"Then let us be rid of this world, and reside instead in a dream."

"Farewell! We shall meet elsewhere."

"Inside a dream, within a dreamless existence."

The fire consumed the tree, the branch, the apples and both Macs and Max. Yet their spirits were not conquered. In another world, within another existence, immersed in a different dream, Macs and Max were reborn. They were not birds in their new lives, but they were neighbors. And in between their houses stood a tall, proud apple tree. Macs and Max, like all living creatures, were children of circumstance. They were now within a different reality, and yet a new dream had begun. The apple tree, however, was still the same.

# VII

## *Touch of Reality*

Most good stories involve conflict, engaging plots, vivid characters, and romantic settings. They are not mere tales, but fragments of a reality blended so artfully with colour and imagination, that even the most skilled reader cannot discern fact from fiction. Yet in my experience, I have found that the most interesting stories are ones that bear none of the traits required of a "good story." There are mere glimpses of conflicts or none at all; the plots, which are hardly engaging, threaten to collapse before the reader even gets through the first page; the characters are dull, while the settings are about as romantic as bus depots. But what makes them good stories is the ambiguous, almost malleable nature that they each possess. Every reader has the opportunity to absorb an entirely unique translation, individual to that reader alone.

I have one such story, built more out of fact than fiction, which bears close, personal significance to my life. If it is a good story, perhaps it will transcend the limitations imposed by the

empty words that define it, and translate importance to each of its readers.

My memories of that delightful night are hazy, but not because the occasion wasn't significant enough to remember—on the contrary, its sheer worth as a memorable event exceeded the grasp of my mind, and most of the details were dropped by the clumsy fingers of my feeble memory. But though the facts are somewhat fuzzy, the emotional impressions left upon me are strong and clear, and I daresay they will remain with me for a long time to come.

It began, somewhat ironically, with disappointment.

I was in the lobby of a grand, luxurious reception hall, with thousands of people flocking around me, speaking to ushers, to security, and other theatre personnel. A few grim ticket collectors were checking the receipts of the crowds before allowing them access into the stadium, and I was harshly aware that I myself was ticketless. I saw V.I.P ticket holders bypass the rest of the crowd, receive special treatment and considerations, as they filed into the theatre and took their seats amid celebrities and fellow V.I.Ps. I watched them with envy.

I was continually jostled by the crowds, who were in a mad rush to enter the stadium before the show started. I eventually left the reception hall and made my way to the elevators. I stepped inside one and as the doors were about to close, I heard a sweet, sultry voice ask me to hold the door, so I promptly obliged. A tall woman with a delightful coffee-complexion, large brown eyes, lustrous black hair, and long, slender legs, entered the elevator and left me breathless. It was not her beauty alone that floored me, but the fact that she was someone I knew and recognised better than my own reflection, for I was her greatest, most loyal fan.

"It's you..." I said in something of a steady exhale, as the doors closed.

"It *is* me," she laughed, and I practically shivered in delight. "Hello," she then added, politely. She chose the fourth floor and looked at me enquiringly. "What number?"

"The same," I said, breathlessly. I was dimly aware that I was gaping at her, my expression no doubt suspended somewhere between a state of awe and having been clubbed on the head. She looked across at me and smiled again, though nervously this time.

"I… I can't… I can't believe it's *you*," I said, grinning so widely that my face ran out of room to accommodate the gesture. "You're the reason I came here tonight. I wanted to see your performance. Actually, I wanted to see *you* up close, if possible. I mean… when I say 'up close' I mean I thought I would get to see you like across the lobby, separated by like over a thousand people, or else in the stadium, separated by fifty rows… *if* I was lucky. But I certainly didn't expect to see you standing next to me on an elevator… Oh my God, you're standing next to me on an elevator. I'm *talking* to you… I can't believe I'm talking to you…"

She laughed warmly, but said nothing in reply to that nervous rant.

"I can't believe I'm standing next to you," I said again, with an excited chuckle. "I've been a huge fan of yours for ages and ages! You look even more beautiful up close, if that's even possible. I mean, forgive me for saying so. I don't know if that's rude or not, but it's the truth."

She smiled shyly, looking flattered but modest.

"I'm sorry, I must sound like an idiot," I said, embarrassment finding me at last.

"No, of course not," she said quickly. "I think you're very sweet."

It was only then that we noticed the elevator had zoomed past floor number four without stopping. She frowned. "We missed our floor…" We watched as the elevator display climbed steadily, past 10, 20, 30, 50, 80 and eventually rested at 84, the top floor.

"Odd," she said, and selected 4 on the console once more. The elevator dropped back down again. She looked nervously up at the roof of the elevator, and then rocked on her heels uncomfortably;

it took me several seconds to realise it was because I was still staring at her.

"So..." I said, still not bothering to look away.

She turned to me.

"You're performing tonight," I said, rather ineffectively.

She nodded. "And I'm running late. I should have been here an hour ago."

40, 38, 36, 34... the counter display kept dropping.

I had a rapid and violent struggle within my mind, as I searched despairingly for something to say, something clever yet relevant and pleasing, something that would interest her, amuse her, and perhaps tempt her to remain in my company for just a little while longer.

18, 17, 16, 15...

I wanted to show her that I was intelligent, and that I could hold a conversation on any topic of her choice. But I also wanted to demonstrate my sensitivity and my emotional prowess. Yet perhaps the most attractive initial gesture would be to display my sense of humour. I needed a joke... but I couldn't just turn to her and say "Knock knock..." No, I would need to set it up...

8, 7, 6, 5...

It was too late... In a moment she would step out of the elevator and I'd never see her again. My *one* chance to impress the most beautiful woman in the world, and I'd missed it.

4...

I closed my eyes and sighed...

...but the elevator didn't stop.

3, 2, M.

"Again?" she exclaimed, hitting the panel with frustration as the elevator opened on the ground floor. "What's wrong with this stupid thing?" she said, annoyed. "Why won't it stop at number four? Do you think it's broken?"

"We could try it again?" I suggested.

She shrugged and hit floor number four again. The doors closed.

I realised as she stood there in frustration that I had been given a second chance to impress her. A good joke would now break the ice perfectly.

"Your fly's open," she said, turning to me.

I looked down at my trousers, at the shirt flap sticking out through my zipper and hastily readjusted myself as the lift shot upwards again.

2, 3...

I'd lost yet another chance.

4.

...5, 6

"Damn it!" she said, and chose floor ten, but the elevator kept rising. She chose 15, 28, 32, 49, but it didn't make a difference, the elevator refused to stop until it hit the top floor again.

"Now what?" she said, turning to me as the doors opened on the 84th floor.

I was flattered and excited that she was asking for my opinion. I was also painfully aware that I didn't really have a suitable answer ready for her. As the doors closed, inspiration struck.

"We could... take the stairs?" I suggested. "We'll try number four on the way down again, and if it doesn't work again, we'll just take the stairs from the ground floor."

She paused and then smiled. "Now why didn't I think of that?" she said, as she hit the ground floor button. "I wish I'd taken the stairs to begin with."

I privately disagreed, because if she *had* taken the stairs, I never would have had these few minutes alone with her. As the elevator dropped back down yet again (I was starting to feel a little sick, but there was no way I would admit that to her), she looked at me with unexpected gratitude. "I'm glad I'm not going through this alone," she confessed. "I'd have lost my head if I was by myself. I think having someone around who was calm and relaxed made a difference."

I smiled in what I hoped was a suave, nonchalant manner. I

wanted to say something cool and smart, but my tongue seemed to be glued to the roof of my mouth.

The elevator, almost predictably, didn't stop at number 4 again, and the doors opened instead on the ground floor. We stepped out into the chaotic scene of mad crowds thronging into the stadium, and she seemed at once to regret her decision. She looked around and hesitated, clearly unsure of where to find the stairs in the midst of this madness. I pounced on the opportunity by offering to lead her. "I can show you where the stairs are," I said, politely.

"You will?" She sounded surprised and suspicious.

"Of course."

"I can't be seen," she said, slipping on her sunglasses and covering her face with her right hand—ironically, though I didn't say so, this only made her more conspicuous.

"I'll hide you," I said, walking closely by her side. She looked at me with sudden gratitude and then ducked her head in my chest as we walked, so she wouldn't be seen.

"So where are the stairs?" she said, in something of a whisper now, because people were bustling around us, and I gathered she was afraid her voice would be recognised.

I felt embarrassed, for I'd passed the stairs on my way to the elevators and yet was unable to locate them now. I was worried that she would think I'd lied to her just to be in her company a little longer. I looked around the large, posh lobby, which now looked more like a massive shopping mall than anything else. "There was a sign... I saw it when I came in here," I told her. "It was of black stairs against a yellow background. It shouldn't be hard to find, should it?"

"Let's hope so," she said, taking charge of the hunt. She now led me through the crowd, and I kept pace with her as though my life depended on it. Blind to everything else, I searched desperately for the sign I was sure I had seen earlier.

"Maybe there aren't stairs in this place," she finally said, sighing in frustration.

But I had just spotted what we were looking for. "This way," I said, and weaving through the bustling masses, I led her to a doorway right below the symbol of the stairs. The stairway was deserted, and she briskly ran up the first flight. As I prepared to follow, I noticed something strange: this stairwell didn't have an echo. Almost all stairwells have echoes, probably because of the abundant spaces, but this stairway sounded like a tiny closet. Yet it was 84 floors high.

It is when this realisation dawned upon me that the details of my memory began to warp and erode. Quite suddenly, the stairwell disappeared, and we found ourselves in a hallway. Though I was aware of the abrupt change in location, I neither commented nor paused to reflect upon it, for I was made aware of a new task: she and I were both looking for a place where she could take a bath. I don't know what happened to our trek through the stairway, or why she wasn't in her make-up room, re-united with her assistants, managers and hairdressers. All I knew was that we were wandering down this hallway now, looking for a washroom.

This wasn't real... it couldn't be... logical questions began to encircle my head at this point: why would anyone want to take a bath in a washroom, where there was neither a bathtub nor any other facilities conducive to bathing? If she was late for her performance, how could she afford to wander through hallways with a stranger looking for a washroom to bathe in? Where were her assistants and managers? Why was she alone in a stairwell with a stranger, looking for a washroom? The entire situation was ridiculous, yet my consciousness seemed oddly immune to this absurdity, and was instead keen on winning her approval. I was clear about the task at hand: to find a washroom and fulfill her request, thereby earning her trust and gratitude.

Once again we made our way through thronging crowds and eventually found a washroom in a narrow corridor. "Here you go," I said, panting slightly as we reached the doors.

"Thank you," she said, smiling gratefully at me as she disappeared into the room.

I waited outside. Instead of pondering the bizarre circumstances that had led me to this hallway, I took the time to reflect upon how much she meant to me already, even though we'd only known each other for a few minutes. In fact, I already found myself missing her terribly. Barely had this thought registered though that the door opened and she walked out.

Her expression was a mixture of amusement and embarrassment, and she seemed to be fighting back a smirk when she said, "How am I supposed to take a bath in a washroom?"

As I frowned to consider the validity of her question, she burst out laughing.

I watched her laugh greedily, studying the pleasing effect it had on her already beautiful features. It was the sincerity of the emotion, I realised, which made her laugh so attractive. People laugh for a variety of reasons, all of which are driven by an effort to communicate. For instance, when told a joke, people laugh to communicate the fact that they enjoyed the joke, and not always because they *truly* found it funny. People laugh to break tension, to relax, to pose like they're having a good time, and for a host of other similarly vain reasons. But few laugh in spite of themselves, in spite of any conscious, planned thought. Her laugh lingered strongest in her eyes, and radiated to her other features, enhancing her entire appearance.

"Now what?" she asked, shrugging and looking defeated.

I knew that this was my opportunity to come to her rescue and make sure she remembered me for a long time to come. "I have an idea," I told her confidently, and led her down the hall. But here my memory turns patchy once more.

For as far as I can remember, we next found ourselves in a hotel room that had been stripped of almost all furniture and decorations—it looked like it was being renovated. But in the bathroom was a large tub, and we both stared at it. "There's no water though," she said.

"Don't you worry about that," I assured her.

I was soon shuttling kettlefuls of steaming hot water back and forth from a stove in the kitchen to the tub, as she undressed in an adjacent room and came out wearing a robe. The tub was soon full of hot water, and she looked at me with clear gratitude. "I don't know how to thank you," she told me. "I don't think anyone's ever done something so sweet for me."

I mumbled something incomprehensible, too shy to meet her eyes, for she was standing excitingly close to me, wearing nothing but the robe. I left her to enjoy the bath and offered to wait in the next room. I heard the robe drop softly to the floor—I would have gladly signed away all the treasures in the world to be a fly on that wall. I heard her climb into the tub and gently splash about within it. She called out to me suddenly, asking if I could hear her.

"Loud and clear," I told her, from the other room.

"Then talk to me," she said, with a small laugh. "I'll get bored sitting idly in this tub."

And so we talked, as though we were two friends reunited after years apart. We didn't bother getting to know each other— we already seemed to know everything of importance. Instead we told jokes, swapped memories and anecdotes, and laughed merrily as if time were a patient spectator, content not to budge until our conversation was complete.

Perhaps it was because I was in the other room and unable to see her, but I no longer regarded her as a world-famous actress and performer. Her celebrity status seemed irrelevant as we bonded, for beneath all the glamour that surrounded her existence, she was still a human being, and (I sensed) in need of a friend, just as I was. I had the impression that we talked for hours, yet I remember mere seconds of it, and logically, considering that she had a show to perform within minutes, we could *only* have conversed for seconds. But how could someone take a bath and make a friend in mere seconds? It was as if we were in some kind of a time warp.

Looking back, I don't remember a single detail of the conversation we shared, but I do remember how much joy I

derived from it. Regardless of the impracticality of it, and of the inexplicable timeline, I knew I would cherish the sentiment for years to come.

"I have a problem," she called from the next room.

"What is it?" I asked, getting to my feet.

"Come in here."

I entered the room, which was bathed in steam. She stood by the tub, wearing her robe, looking resplendent but anxious. "What is it?" I asked her again, concerned.

"I don't have slippers," she told me. "How can I make it upstairs with bare feet?"

I looked at the floor, and found that it was layered not with carpet, but with rows of inch-long nails. How had I not noticed this before? "Well, don't worry," I assured her.

I was soon carting her through a labyrinth of hallways on a wheelbarrow, as she giggled with amusement whenever I took a sharp turn, or else sprinted a short distance just to please her.

In a pragmatic corner of my mind, I wondered where the wheelbarrow had come from. Perhaps more importantly, I wondered why I hadn't merely carried her. If I admired her, liked her, maybe even *loved* her, wouldn't carrying her have been a more intimate and romantic gesture? Wouldn't it have been an ideal opportunity to get closer (quite literally) to her?

In answer to these questions, my consciousness claimed that the only thing that mattered was her happiness and contentment. It lauded me for having managed (through inexplicable and bizarre circumstances) to yet again come to her rescue.

We entered the make-up room. A gaggle of girls emerged from the corners of the room, speaking incomprehensibly over each other, fawning at her, questioning her disappearance and thanking the heavens for her return. She was plucked out of the wheelbarrow and taken into an adjacent room. As they carried her through the doorway, she looked back at me briefly: our eyes met like two lovers sneaking glances in the middle of a crowded room.

I stood awkwardly in the doorway, unsure of what to do.

There was a mirror in the corner of the room. I hurried towards it, deciding to take the opportunity to fix my appearance and make myself look like someone she might be interested in. I stood before the large, cheval mirror and gazed at my reflection: only, it wasn't a person.

There was a pond in the midst of a little wood. Tall, elegant trees bordered the little pool, casting the water in a serene, emerald shadow. A small, cherubic-faced boy sat on the edge of the pond, with a silver ball in his hands. He spoke to it fondly, though it didn't answer him. He cared for it, bathed it in the water, nurtured it, loved and cherished it, yet it sat unmoved like stone. When he was finished caring for it, he saw his reflection within it. He spoke to the reflection and it spoke back. He seemed happy and content. They smiled at each other.

"How do I look?" came her sweet voice, from somewhere behind me.

I turned away from the mirror to face her.

Dressed in a gleaming, pearl-white saree, atop a stylish, velvety blue blouse, she practically sparkled in the dull lighting. The saree, draped over her right shoulder, circled back around her to eventually rest stylishly over her left arm—not many women would have looked as sophisticated and as effortlessly beautiful as she did in an outfit that was the perfect blend of a traditional design reworked with modern flair. Her dress aside, the rest of her appearance was equally flawless: her long, black hair fell in elegant, wavy curls just below her shoulders. Her make-up, if there was indeed any upon her, was barely discernible, and served only to accentuate her already beautiful features. She wore simple jewellery in the form of silver earrings, which matched the colour of her saree, and a matching bracelet upon her exposed left wrist. Her look in its entirety was unassuming yet mesmerizing, for it allowed her natural splendour to shine through. Her radiant smile flashed brighter than the cameras that would click furiously tonight, in a futile attempt to capture the full effect of her limitless

beauty. Her eyes, large and reflective, studied me eagerly, with unrestrained anticipation. She was waiting for my response.

Only, I was unable to find the words at once.

"You look stunning," I eventually told her, breathlessly.

"Thank you," she said, softly.

We stood in silence, our behaviour awkward and hesitant. I wanted to say something sweet and thoughtful; I wanted to take her in my arms and kiss her. But before I could do either, one of her assistants emerged from the other room to inform her that she was due on stage.

Almost suddenly we were backstage, and a large red curtain towered over our heads. Assistants, spot-boys, technicians, and other theatre personnel scrambled here and there, barking orders and replies at each other. I felt rather out of place, and conspicuously in the way.

"You should take your seat before the show starts," she told me, urgently.

I hesitated. "I… I don't have a ticket," I confessed.

She seemed confused. "But didn't you come here tonight to see the show? You told me in the elevator that you were here to see me, and—"

"*See* you, yes," I said, "But I meant somewhere in the lobby, surrounded by a hundred bodyguards, or else as you stepped out of your limousine. I didn't come here tonight for the show—I… I couldn't afford a ticket. I was just hoping to catch a glimpse of you… I never dreamt that I would spend all this time with you."

She looked at me with a mixture of pity and gratitude, but didn't say anything.

"Your show's starting," I told her, in an effort to break the silence.

She nodded and slowly walked away. I felt my heart shrivel with pain and disappointment. She was drifting out of my life. But just then she paused and turned back: an invisible hand clutched my heart tightly, delaying its demise.

She came forward, tilting her head and frowning. "I want

to see you again, though," she said, and it sounded like she was having an internal debate about the matter.

"So do I."

She danced forward and beamed at me. "Then come with me," she said, her eyes twinkling. "We can perform together. That way I won't risk losing you."

Perhaps I should have paused here yet again to wonder why she didn't just bother to get me a ticket... it was *her* concert, after all, and it would have made more sense than inviting me on stage. But again, none of these logical inconsistencies seemed to matter to me at that point.

"But I don't know *how* to perform..." I told her.

"I'll show you," she smiled. She went to a cabinet and opened it; hundreds of large, beach-ball sized tennis balls fell out, and she picked one up and tossed it to me. The background dancers and other performers materialised out of nowhere and each grabbed a ball, too.

This seemed rather strange... where had the life-sized tennis balls come from? This almost definitely felt like a dream now. A dream... Something clicked within my mind. I reflected over every moment she and I had shared since our meeting, and realised that most of it had been strange and nonsensical, almost dream-like. My recollection of our time together already felt disjointed, as though the significant moments had been meshed together without any logical, linear chronology. I thought back to before tonight, to before I had met her... I had almost no memory of my past life, up until the moment in the elevator. I realised I didn't know where I was, or how I'd gotten here. Had I driven? Taken a cab? Could I have afforded a cab? Did I have a job? And for that matter, a larger question surfaced: who was I?

If this was a dream, then it would follow that *she* wasn't real. Or was she? I remembered her, remembered my feelings for her, and knew her as a person to be real. But was she actually, *physically* here with me? Or was she part of the dream? Considering how famous she was, how exclusive and utterly inaccessible to a

common person she would be, how had I managed to meet her unprotected on an elevator and spend an entire, bizarre evening with her? Was our friendship truly plausible? Or was this all just one large, indulgent dream?

It was then that something happened to shatter the illusion, yet strengthen the importance of the moment. She glided forward and took my hand. The moment I felt her touch, I knew this was definitely a dream, for her hand lacked the warmth and texture of a human being. And yet, her touch possessed the overwhelming thrill of a fantasy turning real. The mere sentiment of holding hands with a celebrity that I had admired from afar was so overpowering that I surrendered myself to the deception. I had found a friend, a *real* friend, and our friendship (though strange and even somewhat absurd) seemed likely to last through eternity. I was in love, and perhaps more importantly, I sensed I would *be* loved.

"Are you coming?" she asked, looking at me expectantly. She was still holding my hand intimately, as though we'd known each other for years.

She was me. If this was a dream, then she was quite simply just a projection of my own imagination. But so what? She would never fall in love with me in real life; but here, within the confines of my subconscious, we would make a perfect couple. Did it even matter whether I was dreaming? The touch of her hand was exciting, and the promise of a life together was intoxicating. If anything, the knowledge that this was all a dream had somehow sweetened the experience. Reality is incomplete, for it is governed by a rigid, predictable set of rules that paints a colourless existence. But dreams are effervescent, structured in such a manner that the dreamer can extract as much colour from each moment as possible. I could never have had such a night with her in reality, not even if we actually *were* close friends. But there is something magical about the absurdity of dreams, which presents the dreamer with a sentiment, without all the unnecessary residues of plausibility and rationale.

I was glad that this was a dream. The only thing was... I didn't want it to end.

"Hey..." she said, her eyes stealing my thoughts. "Coming?"

"Right behind you," I told her.

She took both my hands in hers, and facing me, led us towards the curtain. I was anxious, apprehensive, even afraid, but her eyes stayed with mine, assuring me silently that everything would be fine. She was so beautiful... Smiling, she led me through the curtain. I didn't know what I would find behind it, but as I relished the touch of her hands within mine, I realised I didn't care. Whether I found an audience, or else woke up alone inside a cold, grey reality, it wouldn't matter. Dream or not, I knew I would never forget her touch. It was the touch of reality.

# VIII

## Soul Mate

I am happy—no, *more* than happy… I am content. I approach each day with a sense of clarity that was once beyond even my mere reckoning, let alone my reach. I see the world for what it is, yet the darkness and the shadows that my eyes discern are promptly colored with laughter, joy and fantasy. Like a powerful wizard painting a better world through a masterful wand, I augment everything negative that I come upon, until it too radiates with the kind of positive energy that now bubbles within me. I feel immortal, indestructible, almost god-like, and I owe this enviable prowess to an incident that occurred a few years ago.

I was in the middle of some kind of a market, surrounded by hundreds of bustling people. I refer to it as a market, but whether it *actually* was one, I have never found out. For though it looked, sounded and smelt like a market place, it also possessed some considerable abnormalities: for one, the people didn't seem to be bustling about calmly shopping for the best prices, but rather appeared tense and frenzied, as though their lives were at stake. Their behavior and the looks in their eyes reminded me not so

much of Sunday shoppers at a bazaar, but desperate sinners lying prostrate outside the doors of a temple. The market itself was quite unlike a "typical" market: there were neither dozens of shops scattered about, nor a host of cunning vendors running them, but only *one* store and one very large queue that led into it.

I found myself standing in the middle of the queue. There were all kinds of people assembled around me, of all ages, genders and ethnicities. It made it difficult to guess what city I was in; the overall surroundings suggested this was a small, somewhat impoverished town. The buildings looked archaic and in ruins, yet I was unable to guess the time period based on their designs. The street was dusty and unpaved; the sky was dark and overcast; there were no mountains or defining land features, and I saw no tree or any other form of vegetation that might hint at the identity of this location. There weren't any cars or other automobiles to be found; the people were dressed in distinct and varied attire, ranging anywhere from suits and robes for men to dresses and sarees for the women. I felt as if I was in a town not of this earth.

I turned to the man standing behind me, who was wearing a bulky overcoat and a fur-lined hat. He appeared to be Russian, though he had darker skin and heavier features. His accent however was undetectable, and felt out of place in relation to the rest of his appearance.

"What is this place?" I asked him, hoping language wouldn't prove to be a barrier.

"Dis a soul market," he replied at once, much to my relief.

"Seoul?" I said, surprised. "Are we in Korea?"

The man looked at me like I was a rabid dog. "Soul market, like *soul*, huh?" he said, tapping his chest with his finger, hoping I would follow him. "Dis ain't Korea, man."

"Soul market," I repeated, frowning. "What do you buy here?"

"Ha, you buy nothin' man," he said, cackling suddenly. "You go' nothin' to buy but everythin' to be bought, huh? Des people

dey won't think twice of selling you if dey got to. You *leesen* to me, huh? Take what dey gives you and don't ask for no more."

"Yes, but *what* do they give me?" I asked, somewhat impatiently.

He tilted his head and grinned at me. "Man, dey gives you a *soul*," he said, bunching his fingers together and kissing the tips. "Dey gives you de soul you meant to be with, huh?"

"You mean I don't have a soul right now?" I asked.

He looked animatedly annoyed. "No man, no," he said, waving his hands as though he was trying to land a jet. "You have soul *now*—but is alone. Dey gives your soul a friend."

I frowned at him. "Like a soul mate?"

He looked relieved and slapped me on the back happily. "Dats it man, dats it," he said, laughing. "Soul mate; you go in der man and dey gives you a soul mate, huh?"

Soul mate… I didn't know what to make of that revelation. A myriad of logical questions assembled before my mind, demanding equally logical answers: how could a soul-mate be bought or even sold for that matter? How would this place be able to provide people with soul mates? How would they even *recognize* a person's soul mate? Why were all these people so desperate to find their soul mates? How had I wound up here, standing in line like the rest of them? There were so many questions and yet no conceivable way of having them answered.

Equipped with a few theories, I looked around the market place again, but with a different perspective. A lot of what had confused me before, now seemed to make sense. The market as a whole resembled a small town in Africa that I had a vague, detached memory of having once visited. In that town, aid workers had set up a small camp to give out rations to the public. The people I had noticed standing in line then had been half-starved, malnourished and in a state of desperation that not many outside of a third-world country could have imagined. The people standing in this queue around me weren't half-starved or malnourished in that same sense, but they looked intensely depressed, lonely, and

seemed deprived of emotion. The desperation within their eyes wasn't different from what I had seen amongst the starving public in Africa, except that while the latter had suffered physically, the suffering of *these* people appeared to be largely emotional, if not even spiritual.

I remember having decided upon that trip to Africa that human suffering was not a curse or a bane of existence, but rather a trivial, inconsequential passage of life—inconsequential only when considering the larger scheme of things, for suffering can actually be enlightening. Echoing the old cliché of suffering being good for the soul, there is a lot of insight one can derive from enduring pain at the rawest, most basic human level. For suffering provides clarity of thought. Joy and contentment can disillusion even the most accomplished seer into abandoning the tools of introspection, for happiness tempts an individual to remain within a reality that has been kind. But suffering forces an individual to look beyond the present, beyond the good, the real, the factual, and to delve instead into fantasy: a realm where through the aid of imagination, suffering can be dismantled, disabled, and eventually discarded.

However, to evade reality altogether is difficult, if not impossible. For those of us unable to immerse ourselves wholly into fantasy, we require the aid of something more tangible than dreams, something equally intoxicating, but more adept at surviving reality.

Love is one such aid.

Even in the midst of that tense, cheerless market, I could remember the heady, overwhelming joy of being in love, and more importantly, of *being* loved. It was strange, I thought, that while I seemed unable to recall my own name, my past, my whereabouts or anything even remotely tangible about myself, that I should nevertheless be able to remember with clear precision the potency of love. The mere memory of it brought a smile to my face.

"You look happy," said a voice nearby, pulling me out of my reverie.

I turned and found a young woman looking up at me curiously. She was sitting on the ground, apparently too exhausted to wait on her feet any longer.

"I'm talking to *you*," she said, when I didn't answer. "Why do you look so happy?"

"I don't... I'm not..." I muttered, suddenly flustered.

"It's all right," she said, comfortingly. "I'm just curious. I haven't seen someone looking happy in a very long time. You must be new around here."

"I think so... but... I don't remember. Where are we?"

She grinned: it was a hollow, lifeless expression. "Somewhere between heaven and hell I figure; though personally, I think it's closer to hell."

I frowned. "This isn't earth?"

"Earth?" she frowned back. "You really are new around here. Earth doesn't matter here anymore than a car or a job or even your name. Nothing matters here but your *soul*." She didn't say the word with reverence or any kind of significance, but rather with a skeptical, somewhat disdainful undertone. "Till you find what you're looking for, nothing else matters."

"And we're looking for a soul mate?"

"That's what they tell me," she replied, rolling her eyes.

"You don't seem convinced," I noted.

"Of what? Their fairy tale about how a soul mate can change my life?" she replied, scornfully. "They have no idea who I am, how I think, how I feel, or what I've been through. But somehow they're convinced they can pair my soul off with a perfect match? How do they even *know* I have a soul? I haven't seen it. I don't feel it. So I don't believe it."

"Then why are you here?"

"Where else can I be?" she said at once. "You think I caught a bus and came here? That I bought a ticket to stand in this line? How did *you* end up here?"

"I... I don't know," I admitted.

"Exactly," she said, meaningfully.

She reached into her pocket and pulled out a little box of small, square tablets.

"What are those?" I asked at once.

"Love pills," she said, as she took a handful to her mouth and swallowed gingerly.

I fought back a sudden, childish giggle. "What are love pills?"

"They suppress your emotional appetite," she informed me, oblivious to my amusement. "If I don't take them regularly, the pain becomes unbearable." She gazed into the distance, as though trying to recall a long-forgotten, distant memory. "It was different once," she said, in vague, almost dreamy tone. "I didn't need these pills and I never felt any pain. I believed in love. It was everywhere. I bathed in its calming, healing waters daily, and I was happy."

"What happened to change all that?"

She shrugged. "I came out of the forest. I found light, and it showed me the world for what it was. In the forest everything had seemed larger than life; but out in the light, I realized the word was tiny—smaller even than I was. How could I lose myself into something *that* small and insignificant? So I grew sad and sadder still, until the pain nearly swallowed me whole."

"I don't understand," I told her. "What's this forest you were in?"

"*The* forest," she said, as if I ought to know. "We all begin there."

"Me too?"

"I should think so, yes," she said, after a moment. "The forest is more than—" she began, but was interrupted by a sudden uproar amongst those gathered in the queue, a kind of mad panic that infectiously captured every innocent bystander in its terrifying embrace.

"The Narcissans!" cried several voices, with terror and awe.

I followed the direction of their alarmed gazes and found a group of the most beautiful creatures I had ever beheld. They

appeared human, yet unlike any human I had ever laid eyes upon. They were each so tall that our heads reached below their waists, yet they did not lumber along like lethargic giants, but rather moved with the quick, graceful gaits of antelopes. Their skin, bathed in a striking golden hue, sparkled with an ethereal, flattering glow that lit their proud, strong features with enviable clarity. Their eyes were the most gorgeous shade of violet imaginable, and complimented the deep maroon of their lush, curly hair. Their strong, nimble bodies rushed past the crowd majestically, and as they passed us, they extended their arms as if asking for friendship. Many in the crowds reciprocated the gesture, and the moment a Narcissan touched someone, that person transformed into a similarly beautiful, god-like creature. This tempted many at the back of the crowd to abandon the queue and offer themselves for conversion. In this manner dozens were taken away, as the Narcissans deftly picked up armfuls of people and kept running, until like a passing storm, they drifted out of sight.

It took a while for the dust to settle and calm to be restored. There was a great deal of excited chatter and murmuring amidst the leftover crowd, and I confess that I felt a surge of bitterness at the fact that I hadn't acted quickly enough to be picked up by the passing herd. I turned back to the young woman I had been in conversation with, and found her curled up in a tight ball on the ground, her head shielded within her arms. I knelt beside her.

"Are you okay?" I asked.

"Have they gone?" she asked, cautiously.

"Yes, of course," I replied. "Do you fear them?"

"More than anything else," she said, slowly lifting her head up to look at me. I noticed that terror still lingered in her eyes, as she scanned her surroundings cautiously to confirm that the Narcissans had indeed left. "They are demons, darker even than the nameless heralds of death that roam these lands, for to die is not to suffer. But the Narcissans do not kill... they *destroy*. They lure you into an existence devoid of humanity. It is a fate worse than death."

"But they were beautiful," I argued, as if that was a valid point to consider.

"More beautiful than anything you or I would have ever seen," she agreed. "And they share that beauty with those they capture. But it is a fickle quality, their beauty, and it does not allow hope, faith, reason or enlightenment to seep through its stubborn hide. No, I would rather remain as I am now, even if I am ugly, for at least I have a measure of myself."

I considered her words as my eyes wandered to a father and child, standing a little way before us. The father was carrying his daughter, who looked to be no more than three or four years old, and he was speaking reassuringly to her about what was to come.

"The storekeeper won't hurt you," he was saying, in a soothing voice. "He'll just ask you to look around and choose what looks best to you. That's all, sweetie."

"What am I supposed to choose?" his daughter asked, anxiously.

"I honestly don't know, sweetheart," the father admitted. "That's something you have to find out by yourself. But it's nothing to be afraid of... you'll see. It'll be all right."

It only then occurred to me that I ought to have felt some kind of apprehension about what was to come. It had sounded simple enough when I'd been told that I was standing in line to find my soul mate... but what did that *mean*, exactly? What did this line lead *to*? Who was this storekeeper that the little girl feared? I looked around at some of the others standing around me, and noticed that most of them looked similarly concerned.

"What if I don't find the right one?" a woman asked a man standing beside her.

The man grinned somewhat arrogantly. "I know a lot of people who've been to this store. Some of them tried other places first, but they never succeeded. Then they came here. So far, no one who's come here has returned empty handed. Trust me, you'll find the right one."

The woman sighed. "Promise?"

"I'm not selling insurance here," the man laughed. "But sure, I promise."

He sounded so confident that I found myself believing him, too.

I wondered if my soul mate would look like a Narcissan: tall, grand and beautiful beyond description. Or would I not be that lucky? Perhaps my soul mate would be an animal, a donkey or a meerkat or something... or maybe the shopkeeper wouldn't be able to find me a soul mate. Perhaps he would inform me that he was out of soul mates, and that I was therefore destined to spend the rest of my existence alone. Would that be so terrible, I wondered? Solitude was not something I was unfamiliar with. But it would have been nice to share life with another... four eyes instead of two, to witness the world's beauty; two hearts instead of one, to match life's steady pulse; and two pairs of feet instead of one, to tread that winding path to salvation.

"Careful," the woman beside me suddenly said, holding out her hand to prevent me straying to the side. I stepped back and then looked down. There was a low, rumbling noise as the ground seemed to part into a large hole, just beside my feet.

Within this newly formed crevice, I glimpsed a splendid sight: mounds and mounds of shiny gold, amassed along with gems, diamonds, and other treasures, far beyond even the most ambitious pirate's dreams. I gasped out loud, greed building within me.

"Mammon!" cried several voices around me, and then suddenly some people started hurling themselves headlong into the hole. Their actions stole my attention long enough to notice that most of the people in the queue had turned away, as though in fear. I sensed that I ought to do the same, for this treasure pit might have just been another hurdle in my path to finding a soul mate, and if so, then I would have to muster enough will-power to resist temptation. Chaos ensued for several minutes more, as people kept throwing themselves into the pit, while others screamed in terror and panic, until eventually I heard a low rumbling noise

again. When the rumbling subsided, the screams died down, and a sense of calm ensued.

I deemed it safe now to turn to the woman who had so far enlightened me about much of this reality, and ask her what that hole in the earth had been. But when I turned around, I found her missing. She was nowhere to be seen. I could only assume that she had succumbed to the temptation of treasure. If so, then she was lost in the depths of the earth…

I wondered what that hole in the ground had been. Was it merely a temptation thrown in our path to see which of us had the resilience to withstand it? Or did it serve some larger purpose? What would have happened to those that had fallen in? I had many answers, but none that bore any real validity. I wouldn't discover the real answers until I too met my end. For death was the ultimate answer: it was the lifting of the proverbial blindfold, the revelation at the end of a riddle, the climax at the conclusion of a convoluted story—death was salvation.

Yet life had taught me so much, so much more than I could hope from death. What would my soul mate teach me? Would I be taught the value of love? But I already knew it…

I had a sudden vision of being a child, and running into my mother's arms.

She set me on her knee and rocked me gently as she held me in her tight embrace. The moment her arms wrapped around me, I forgot all my concerns and relished her warmth, the warmth that only a mother could provide a child.

"Would you love me this much if I wasn't your son?" I asked.

She stopped rocking me. "What do you mean?" she asked.

I looked up to meet her eyes and challenge her. "If I wasn't your son, we would have never met. How could you have loved me then, if I was a stranger?"

She opened her mouth to speak, but seemed unable to find her voice. Her mouth opened and closed like a fish, but she remained silent. Nevertheless, I got my answer.

There is no selfless love. Through our actions and words, we don't so much express what we feel, but more what we desire. She did not love me as a person, but only as *her* child. I was a part of her, forever. It is how I would have loved my child, too. We love selfishly, only that which is ours, or that which is near to us. I can love the apple tree in my yard, for it feeds me apples. But will I love the apple tree in my neighbor's yard? It does not feed me anything.

I was so engrossed in my thoughts that I was startled to find myself being pushed into the store. I wasn't sure how I had reached the front of the line so quickly, but nevertheless here I was, inside the store. The door swung shut behind me.

The sudden silence was deafening, especially after having spent so long waiting amidst the agitated thousands outside. I could still sense their restlessness, even through these closed doors—they wanted me to hurry. But now that I was inside, time felt irrelevant. I didn't care if it took me an hour or all of eternity. I wouldn't leave this store until I found my soul mate.

There was the storekeeper, standing behind the counter. He was old, with a few wisps of silver hair atop a large egg-like head. He had long, thin limbs that made him look rather like an insect, or a really tall bird. He stooped considerably, even when standing upright, much like a vulture. He had a large, curved nose, which only accentuated his bird-like appearance.

"Welcome," he said.

No more was said, and there didn't appear to be any need for more words. It was apparent why I was here. Somewhere within this store was my soul mate. I would have to find it.

The storekeeper watched me intently, with genuine interest. He did not comment as I walked through the shop, studying the thousands upon thousands of random, diverse, seemingly worthless objects. He shadowed me loyally, his hands held behind his back in a casual yet respectful gesture. I grew weary of his presence, and of the profound silence, so I spoke.

"I see no people here," I said.

"No? That's strange," he said, in a crisp, clear voice. "What do you see?"

I turned to him in surprise. "What do you mean? Are you blind?"

"Not literally, no," he answered, indifferent to my insensitive question. "But for me, this store is empty but for *one*, single object, which you have not come across yet. Everything else in here is for my customers' eyes only, for them to see, judge, and decide upon."

"But you're the storekeeper. How can you not know what items you carry?"

He smiled. "You seem to take analogies literally," he said. "I am neither a storekeeper nor a store. My duty is to lead those who come before me to their eternal partners, to their *soul mates*, and in doing so I hope to impart upon them wisdom and salvation. When you find what you're looking for, I will be able to recognize it and guide you accordingly. But until then I am virtually blind. The choice and the accompanying responsibility are both upon you."

"This isn't an analogy though," I argued. "This is real life."

"If you say so."

I eyed him curiously and then turned back to the many objects littering his shelves. "Isn't a soul mate supposed to be a *person*?" I said. "I don't see anything here but objects."

"I'm afraid that's beyond my comprehension."

"You're supposed to help me though, aren't you? Help me."

"This is *your* store now. Everything you see is yours. How can *I* help?"

I was annoyed, but what could I say or do? I kept walking through the store, examining the objects and simultaneously considering his words. So if this store was empty to him but for *one*, single object, then shouldn't the same have been true for me? Why was all this junk thrown in my path? There was a basketball, a lampshade, a fishing rod, several clothes, a cricket bat, a bicycle pump, a flashlight, a stapler, several flasks and thermoses, folding

chairs, umbrellas, a globe, a variety of bookends, a witch's hat, many books without covers, empty jars and bottles, picture frames, and hundreds of similarly useless, trivial, everyday objects.

I was about to turn around and demand that he give me some answers, when I caught sight of it from across the store, past dozens of objects, some of which were perhaps more appealing and eye-catching. Yet I knew what I was destined for.

"I see it," I cried, pointing to the distance.

The shopkeeper came up to me and looked where I pointed. "I see it, too," he said, with a satisfied smile, "Which means that your choice is right and true."

He took a ladder to the far shelf and climbed it all the way to the top to reach the cage. He brought it down gingerly, for it was fragile and worth far beyond mere reckoning. "I see you are blessed," he said, as he handed the cage to me. "Not many before you have had the foresight to choose the right one as you have. Many choose from their hearts, but *you* chose from the mind, and thus your choice is true. The heart chooses for the body, but the mind chooses for the soul."

I wondered if perhaps he had gotten those words mixed up, for I would have thought the heart chose for the soul, while the mind chose for the body... but what did that matter? I had my soul mate in my hands, so nothing else mattered anymore.

"Your soul has now found its partner,' he told me. 'I congratulate you."

I gazed at it through the bars of the cage, feeling fortunate and grateful. I was still overflowing with questions, was still frustrated, confused, helpless, and anxious about the future. But I knew that my soul mate would lend me the insight I required to find those answers.

Inside the cage was a large, shiny object within a sturdy oval frame: a mirror.

# IX

## Hangman

I was in a dimly lit room, washed in a disturbing shade of red. The room had only two walls, one in front and the other behind me. On either side of the two walls, the room opened out onto empty spaces, cloaked in impenetrable darkness, such that I couldn't tell if the space was only about a foot wide, or was larger than the entire Universe. The walls and the floor were a striking hue of red and contributed more to the atmosphere of the room than any other feature. There was no ceiling, only an empty space again, covered in solid blackness. In the middle of the room was a round wooden table with two chairs. On one of the tables sat Death.

He was not at all like I expected, for I had always imagined Death to be a short, goblin-like figure that skulked into houses in the middle of the night and stole souls from sleeping bodies. He was tall, practically gigantic, with an enormous frame beneath a heavy, red cloak. His long, skeletal limbs protruded from within the cloak, whose hood concealed his face in shadows. He had enormous hands, each larger than my head, with long, spindly fingers.

I was seized with the urge to flee, but found myself rooted helplessly to where I stood.

"Come, come," he said, in a surprisingly cordial manner. "Have a seat."

I did not dare disobey. I took a seat at the table, feeling dwarfed by his colossal, menacing figure. I still could not see his face; there seemed to be nothing but darkness underneath the hood he wore, and yet he spoke as though he had a mouth within.

"Do you know where you are?"

I did not look at him. "In hell?"

To my surprise he suddenly laughed, loudly and with considerable relish, though the gesture lacked any warmth or *actual* mirth. "Yes, I can see what led you to that assumption," he said, in his deep, powerful voice. "You are somewhere in the nebulous realm between life and death. But your fate lies in your own hands. If you so wish, you may return to life."

"So I'm not dead?"

"Not entirely, no."

I frowned. "So what happened? How did I end up here?"

He shrugged. "You were killed."

"But I'm not dead?"

"No, not yet." He said the words plainly, without menace, and yet the threat loomed clearly behind the remark. "Whether you live or die is your choice."

"I want to live."

"I thought you would say that," he said, with something of a sneer. He turned his head to the side, ever so slightly, and I too looked in that direction. From within the darkness, a tall T-shaped pedestal appeared, with a noose tied to one end of the bar running across the top.

"But I said I wanted to *live*," I said hastily, though with enough fear and respect in my voice, so as not to offend him.

"I *heard* you."

A piece of paper appeared on the table between us, and

on it ten dashes were drawn. My stomach tightened slightly as comprehension dawned upon me.

"Let's play hangman," he said, smoothly.

"Hangman?" I said, shakily.

"I *know* you've played this game before," he said, in what I imagined was as cheery a tone as his voice could reach. "Indulge me. Play a game of hangman."

"Are we just playing for… fun? Or is there a purpose to this?"

He chuckled. "There is *always* a purpose."

"So if I lose…" I said, hesitantly. "Then I die?"

His answer was immediate. "Very good! You're sharper than I expected."

I stared at the word, at the ten spaces I would have to correctly fill out in order to survive. The long, skeletal fingers of his hands met atop the table in a contemplative gesture. But I found the sight of his hands rather intimidating.

"Do I get a clue?" I asked, tentatively.

"Oh, silly me," he said, slowly. "But of course—the word is the answer to life."

"The answer to life," I repeated, nervously.

"The rules are quite obvious," he said. "You will guess *one* letter at a time. If your guess is correct, the letter will appear in the corresponding space. However, if your guess is wrong, then a part of you will be strung onto that noose. If you accumulate enough wrong guesses, then *all* of you will be dangling from that noose, and you will most certainly die."

I felt my palms sweat with the tension.

"Come, come," he sneered, with mock sympathy. "You have led an interesting life. Surely you cannot tell me that it will be a tragedy if you do not get to return."

Truth be told—and I suspected that he already knew it—I didn't remember anything of my past life. I had appeared here suddenly, without any prior memory or instance to look back upon. I didn't have an identity, a purpose, a past, or a clear future.

All I knew was that my survival depended on my success in this game of deduction and chance.

"You may begin," he said—it was an order and not a request.

"Um… okay, uh… 'A'," I said, deciding to start with the popular vowels first.

"Good choice," he said with a hint of disappointment, as the letter "A" appeared on the ninth space on the word. "Tell me, why do you want to live so badly?"

I was nervous enough about the prospect of guessing correctly to save my life that I didn't particularly feel like answering his questions. However, to not answer would have probably been foolish and near-suicidal. "I… uh… it just seems like the right choice," I said.

"Does it?" he said, and I sensed that he found my answer humorous.

I stared at the empty word on the paper:

_ _ _ _ _ _ _ _ A _

"Um… my next guess is 'O'," I said.

"People do labour under many misconceptions, don't they?" he sneered, as the letter "O" was etched onto the paper, not in one of the spaces, but *above* the word. Once written, a line was drawn across it. Almost at once, I felt a sharp, searing pain along my shoulders—my arms were being pulled by some invisible force. I tried to resist, but how could I? With a resounding tear that induced a piercing scream from me, my arms were wrenched free from my body. They now hovered beneath the noose, as if attached to an invisible body. I had never known such pain before, and I didn't think I would survive. I screamed at the top of my voice, and the noise echoed around the room until he very calmly but authoritatively said, "Enough."

I stifled my screams at once, for I didn't dare disobey. Hot tears streamed down my cheeks as I writhed in pain and misery, but he didn't even flinch.

"I'm afraid 'O' was not a correct guess," he said, with

considerable delight in his voice. "Tell me," he carried on conversationally, as if my arms hadn't just been torn off my body. "What do you think death is? What does death mean to you?"

Breathing hard with panic and agony, I did not answer him at once. I contemplated his words through a fog of pain, before answering, "It means… release."

"Do explain."

"Death… is an escape," I panted. "Life is predictable, even at its most turbulent and unexpected moments. But death? Death is an escape from everyday reality."

"What sort of a release do you think death brings?"

Though I was answering him, my mind was busy contemplating my future. What if I guessed the word correctly and my life was subsequently spared? Would my arms be returned to my body and this agonizing pain erased from my memory?

"I suppose… it must be something like salvation," I said.

"So it's a spiritual release?" he said, derisively. "So that's what you expect will happen to you in death. You expect God will ride down on a golden chariot and rescue you?"

I nodded, not daring to look at him. I stared at the blank spaces in silence before deciding to risk another letter. In an ever so small voice, I said, "E."

Though his face was hidden beneath the hood, I could sense his ugly features twisting into an evil grin. "Tsk, tsk, tsk," he said, with mock sympathy. "Wrong again."

I had never known that the human body could withstand so much pain and yet survive, for my legs were then similarly twisted, stretched and ripped from my torso. I *had* to be dead, for no living being could sustain so much torture. But if I was dead, then why was I still feeling pain? Wasn't death a physical end? Shouldn't my body have been dead by now?

All that was left of me now was my torso—with the head attached—hovering loosely above my chair, while my arms and my legs dangled in mid-air beneath the noose. On the paper,

next to the "O" the letter "E" had been added with a similar line struck through it.

"How... how much more?" I asked, through gritted teeth.

"Keep guessing," he said, simply.

I closed my eyes and tried desperately to think of something that would mask the anguish, but nothing worked. I felt as if my body had been set on fire, and I could already feel the effects of phantom pains, for it felt like my limbs were searing with latent wounds.

"Keep guessing," he repeated, in a brusque tone.

I hastily thought of what my next guess would be. I had two more vowels to consider, so I decided I might as well try them. Surely a word of ten letters would have more than just the *one* vowel in it. So I chose "I" next. At first I sensed more twisted pleasure emanating from within him, but that soon shifted to outrage as he hissed loudly at me. The letter "I" appeared in three spaces: the first, the fourth, and finally the sixth. Relief washed over my beaten body.

"Well done," he muttered. "But you still have *six* spaces to guess before you live again, while just *two* more errors will condemn you to my dungeons for eternity." Then he laughed, and what a chilling, cruel laugh it was! My very bones seemed to shiver at the sound of it.

I _ _ I _ I _ _ A _

I stared at the word with the four spaces filled, and wondered if I ought to risk guessing "U." In hindsight perhaps I should have, but I wasn't thinking clearly with the effects of the pain. So I pondered many letters at length before choosing my first consonant. "T," I said.

I knew at once that I had guessed wrong.

This time my torso was torn free of my neck. I could never accurately describe the tearing, twisting, excruciating pain of having one's neck separated from the torso, but I was sure I had endured what no other living being had endured before; for decapitation would normally *certainly* kill, and yet I was still very

much alive now. The body dangling below the noose was nearly complete, but for my head and neck, which now hovered above the table, facing Death.

"One last chance remains," he told me.

"What will happen if I guess wrong and die?" I asked.

There was a long silence before he answered. "I do not know," he said at last, with a hint of bitterness, as if he lamented the fact that he didn't know the answer.

"Will I go to Heaven?"

"I do not know."

I sighed. The word was right in front of me, and yet I couldn't figure it out. I thought of consonants that would probably most likely be in a word: I thought of N, M, D, S…

"D."

I could feel him seething with rage as two 'D's appeared on the third and the seventh space of the word. It now spelt: I _ D I _ I D _ A _

I stared at the word for a long time, hoping some form of inspiration would strike, but it didn't. I couldn't endure this torture anymore, so I guessed blindly. "S?" I said, in a small voice.

It was over.

The moment I said it, I sensed the sheer delight radiating from within him. He stood to his feet as my head was torn from reality, from the living, and reunited with the rest of my body. The noose was tightened around my neck and I dangled lifelessly before him.

"The answer, for I know you are *dying* to know, is 'Individual,'" he said, and laughed coldly. "For it is the *individual* that is at the heart of all existence. We define our lives by that notion, by putting the individual before the collective, and yet we fail to realise that the collective *is* the individual. It would perhaps interest you to know that the God you worship is within you, just as he is within me. We are all *one* individual." Saying he removed the hood that covered his head, and I stared into a face that I realised was my very own.

# X

## Immortal in Death

I clutched the knife in desperation, but it was too late. I felt hot blood gush onto my hands as I fell to the floor, crippled with the fatal wound in my chest. My eyes spun around the room one last time before they closed forever. The animals looked down upon me, their expressions cold and hostile—it was fitting perhaps that I should die where I had restored them.

Death isn't instantaneous. A soul that has suffered through a mortal existence, encased within a living body, does not part with its circumstance willingly. When a body dies—or to put it more aptly, when a body *ceases* to function, the soul trickles out slowly and reluctantly. Unsheltered and vulnerable, it floats unheeded in a metaphysical ocean. Space doesn't embrace the freshly liberated soul with warm hospitality, for it is still a foreign matter, best left encased within another body. Thus it is bullied, or quite simply *coerced* into the nearest available body. But until such time as a suitable accommodation can be found, the consciousness drifts in a sort of celestial limbo, not unlike a patient in the waiting room of a clinic.

My eyes closed within the shop, but awoke in a forest. I was walking beside an adult zebra. We were already deep in conversation, and I seemed to be full of many questions.

"And in the summer," he was telling me, in a casual, charming voice, "When the herds migrate east towards the river, I commence my personal quest for meditative salvation."

"Oh? And how do you do that?" I enquired.

"Through observation," he informed me. He had a pleasant manner about him, yet I sensed a great deal of arrogance within, a trait best reflected in his voice. "I walk, I think, and at times I merely exist, allowing the Universe to educate me with its endless wisdom."

I nodded. We were surrounded by gigantic trees, and seemed to be in a very dense part of the forest. The air was cool and humid, yet I neither shivered nor perspired. I tried to look down to see what I was wearing, but my gaze wouldn't shift. I seemed incapable of controlling where my eyes could focus, and it felt much like I was watching the world through a television screen, which pivoted and moved by its own will rather than mine.

"You seem distracted," he noted.

"Do I have a body?" I asked.

He did not turn to me—maybe he couldn't control his vision either. "Oh yes," he answered at once. "But it's still new, so you must give it time to accommodate you."

"It's new?" I said, surprised. "So who… or *what* am I?"

"You are who or what you were before."

I tried to remember who I'd been before, but for the life of me (no pun intended) I just couldn't recall my past. I remembered having suddenly awakened here in this forest, walking next to this talking zebra, but I couldn't remember anything prior to that.

"Let us not speak of the past for the moment," he said, gently.

"Are we dead?"

"*You* most certainly are."

"What are *you*?" I asked, annoyed. "Suspended?"

To my surprise he laughed. "Yes, and rather permanently," he said. "Ah… look."

He stopped in his stride, as the trees suddenly thinned around us, and we looked upon an enormous valley, populated by thousands—no, *millions* of weasels. They sat idly, climbed about, danced around, or merely hung upside down from trees. I didn't know weasels liked to hang upside down from trees, or even that they were biologically adept at doing so, but nevertheless there were hundreds of them hanging from the branches of the few trees scattered within the valley. But the most distinctive about the entire population was that every single weasel was juggling ceramic pots, even the ones hanging upside down from the trees (with understandably poor results). The air was filled with the noise of ceramic pots crashing and breaking every second, and in large, echoing numbers. The weasels though never seemed to notice anything, and merely went about juggling the pots, while carrying on ever so casually with their normal activities. I studied a few particular weasels, and noticed that every time one broke a ceramic pot, another one appeared readily in its hands, out of thin air. They juggled continually—each weasel broke about a dozen pots a minute! I watched them with fascination.

"Ah yes," the zebra said, smiling (do not ask me what a smiling zebra looks like, I beg you, for it is a gesture more difficult to describe than a disapproving frown on a giraffe). "The valley of weasels—do you know what's going on down there?"

I listened to the steady sounds of ceramic pots crashing and laughed. "Mayhem, by the sounds of it," I said, as one weasel threw three pots into the air and then simply walked off.

"This valley bears close, personal significance to your life on earth."

I scoffed almost immediately. "You're kidding me, how?"

"Every time a ceramic pot breaks, an accident occurs in the real world."

I tried to let his words sink in fully, so I could better understand

them—an accident occurred every time a ceramic pot crashed? "What kind of accident are we talking about?"

"Dropping a plate, stubbing your toe, spilling your drink, slipping on a banana peel—you name it, these weasels cause it." He then lowered his voice and tilted his head towards me. "Between you and me, they seem to derive a great deal of amusement from the process."

"Well, of *course* they do," I cried. "They're weasels, and you've given them responsibility to such an important matter! Do you know how much trouble they've caused?"

I listened to the pots crashing in the valley with a renewed perspective. I had a sudden flood of visions within my consciousness: someone's birthday cake fell onto a tiled floor; a car backed into a mailbox; a cellphone was dropped in the toilet; a jar of pasta sauce shattered on a white Berber carpet; someone slipped on a patch of ice and broke a wrist; a cricket ball was hit into a window… I still had no solid, tangible memories of my former life, yet all these accidents reattached themselves to my memory, like disjointed fragments of an incomprehensible picture. And despite the fact that I neither remembered the significance of these accidents nor the consequences that arose out of them, I still felt remorse at the fact that they'd occurred.

And to think that these weasels had been the ones to cause them all! I tried to glare at them, but since I didn't know if I had eyes let alone eyebrows to accentuate the glare with, I doubt the gesture had the desired effect. I did however wince every time a pot broke.

"They don't have opposable thumbs," I said, sadly.

"Indeed they don't."

"So *why* are they trying to juggle pots?" I said.

"They're weasels. They're not particularly smart."

"So why don't you stop them? Do you know how many accidents they cause? In my life alone, they've caused hundreds and hundreds of stupid, needless—"

"I thought you said you couldn't remember your former life?"

I tried to turn to him, but my vision stayed rooted on the annoying weasels. "I can't, but I somehow *remember* a lot of accidents. I can't explain it, but I *know* it happened."

"Well, the weasels have a purpose and that purpose is being met," the zebra said, simply. "Accidents are a necessary part of existence, so does it really matter what causes them? Would you feel better if an accident occurred every time a hyena laughed?"

I watched a weasel try to catch a pot when it already had a pot in its hand, causing both pots to break upon impact. "It couldn't occur more frequently than this," I said. "That's what makes this so unbearable, is that it's *so* needless! So many accidents could be avoided."

"Oh believe me, the frequency of the pot-breaking is pre-decided," the zebra said, with a chuckle. "If an accident were to occur every time a hyena laughed, then all the hyenas in this existence would suffer endless tickling. That is to say, they would each still laugh as often as one of these weasels break a pot. That's how fate works."

"Well, then why *do* accidents happen? Who decides the frequency of them?"

"I don't know."

We watched the weasels attempt to juggle in silence.

When we moved on from the valley, I began questioning him on anything he might know about life, death and existence. I asked him if life was indeed a circle.

"I've always thought it was a straight line," he said. "But then my imagination is rather limited. For me, life is linear: there is birth, followed by existence, leading to an eventual death."

"Yes, but isn't there reincarnation?"

"Most definitely."

"Then wouldn't the line begin all over again? Leading to a circle?"

"Ah, I see your misapprehension," he said, with a small laugh.

"You asked me if life was a circle, but not if *your* life, or *my* life, or the life of a *single* person was a circle. Our existences are too irrelevant to be signified by either circles or lines. Our births and deaths and rebirths are inconsequential in the linear progression of Life. Life in its *entirety* is a line."

"How do we factor within it?"

"When you were alive, your body lost cells daily, but did it affect you?" he asked. "Death that occurs at such a level is inconsequential to your existence. Following that analogy, when diseases spread through life's body in the forms of war, genocide, natural disasters, and other such large-scale catastrophes, larger clumps of cells and even organs die. Is life affected? Yes. Is it impaired to the point of death? Not always. The death of life can occur at any time, due to any given cause. But we each alone are not significant enough to either cause or prevent that death. We are the tiny cells that occupy life's vast expanse for a brief period."

I thought about his words as we came into a tiny clearing in the woods, where there were hundreds of monkeys scattered about. They were everywhere: on the trees, on the ground, on boulders, within bushes, or even on the pieces of wood floating in a little brook between the trees. Chattering busily, they were all methodically picking lice off each other. It was a comical sight to behold; for though they were vocally animated, their antics were limited to the apparently scintillating task of grooming each other. I laughed aloud at them.

"I've never seen monkeys so excited but so calm at the same time," I said.

"Oh yes, they're very calm," he said, plainly. "They're working, after all."

"More like playing."

"It's not mere play, I assure you," he said. "Every time a louse is picked off a monkey, a death occurs within your world."

I gaped at him. "That's preposterous!" I cried, shocked by his declaration.

"It's the truth. Why does this disturb you?"

I watched the monkeys as their fingers searched the fur on each other's bodies and triumphantly brought out one of the little bothersome critters hiding within—I didn't laugh, because it wasn't funny anymore. To think that every time they picked a louse off, someone died on earth. Mothers, fathers, children, spouses, partners, siblings, friends, mentors, neighbours, colleagues, or mere strangers... so many deaths, affecting millions daily! And to think that *all* of those tragedies were caused right here, right before me.

"It was different with the weasels," I told him. "That was just—accidents are annoying, but death is... it's tragic and...this is *ridiculous*. Why would it be this way?"

"You would have been happier perhaps to learn that the Grim Reaper causes every individual death, when He roams invisibly through the earth searching for souls to feed upon?"

"No," I admitted, after a pause. "I just... I never realised death was so random."

"Who says it is?" he said. "Death follows a pattern, a precise, cosmic plan that you and I are ignorant to. But just as we play a role by living and dying, these monkeys play a role by picking lice off one another and inadvertently affecting lives on earth. They are not God, nor are they heralds of death. They are but links in a chain, much as you and I are."

I smiled wryly. "How much more are you planning to show me? Because I don't think I can take much more of this."

He smiled back. "You'll see." He showed me many animals, each of which had a purpose as strange as the weasels and the monkeys, if not stranger. He told me that every time a lion roared, a storm erupted; that when an elephant trumpeted, a fight or some form of conflict occurred; when an owl hooted, people woke up inexplicably; when a cheetah captured its prey, someone got caught either morally, legally or physically. Some of the correlations he told me about were just plain silly—for instance, he showed me hippopotamuses wallowing lazily in a stream, and told me that

every time a hippopotamus sneezed, two people fell in love on earth.

"Do hippos even sneeze?" I asked, after we spent what felt like hours watching hippopotamuses, waiting for one to sneeze.

He shrugged, but I saw a knowing smirk crack at the corner of his mouth.

"There is so much I don't understand," I told him, as we took a path through the jungle again. It was growing dark—the forest felt dangerous and foreboding all of a sudden.

"There is only a little you need to know," he told me. "But I will tell you a little more—death is the switch that flips reality to fantasy; birth is the switch that flips fantasy to reality. In other words, mortality is the bridge that connects the realms of fantasy and reality, much as sleep does. So as long as you dream in both worlds, you'll be fine."

"I still don't understand," I told him.

"You're not supposed to."

As we walked deeper into the woods, under the twilit skies, I wondered why he was my designated guide through the afterlife and not an animal that bore a more pronounced association with human beings, like a monkey or a lion or even an elephant. But then I realised that the answer could be found in the distinctive nature of a zebra's appearance, which is exotic, while still being somewhat domestic. For a zebra in essence is just a striped horse. The very black and white stripes that lend distinction to its appearance, symbolises the fusion of two contrasting halves: the plain and the striking. Through some imaginative license, it can even be argued that a zebra blends fantasy with reality, for horses are far more abundant and accessible than zebras, and are therefore a more concrete part of reality than their exclusive, striped cousins. So a zebra was in many ways the most suitable candidate to lead me, a lost soul, through the labyrinths of the afterlife, a realm that hovers somewhere in the ambiguous territory between the tangible, mortal world, and the near-whimsical paradise that was heaven.

"You will find colour in this world, wherever you search for it," he told me, rather abruptly, "But take care that you do not project this colour where there is none."

He suddenly stopped in his stride. I wished he wouldn't linger here—it was practically night now and the jungle was dark, eerily bathed in indiscernible but frightening shadows. I felt vulnerable and helpless, like a wounded antelope in the middle of the savannah.

"Death is nothing to fear," he told me, in a strange voice. "Death is like falling asleep, but it is also like waking up. It is a dream and it is real. It is a lie but is undeniably true."

I stared at him from a great distance, even though I was merely two feet away.

"You did not ask for a guide," he told me. "You were *sent* to me, and I was *told* to guide you. There is an animal you did not see today, with a higher purpose than the rest. Take comfort in the knowledge that you are being guided through life by something more capable than an ornery old zebra," he said, and his eyes twinkled. He then looked thoughtful again. "You asked me before if life was a circle. I dismissed the idea, but perhaps in *your* case, it is more circular than I expected." He leaned into me. "Remember this last truth: you are not real—you are one."

I heard his words, but they didn't mean anything to me just then. I sensed it would happen a moment before it did—I heard a thunderous roar from somewhere behind me, and before I could turn, was thrown to the ground. A great weight fell upon me—an inhuman weight, which crushed me as I fell. I felt searing pain spread through whatever body I possessed. I knew I was dying. I caught sight of the zebra's face before my world turned to darkness.

A bell tinkled as I stepped into the store. A large, tawny owl, magnificent and regal, peered down at me with lamp-like eyes; his gaze seemed at once inquisitive and accusatory. I fumbled through my mind for an explanation, for an answer that would appease his curiosity, before I noticed he was perched atop a wooden coat

rack. He wasn't real. From a distant corner of my mind, a corner where a few, frail remnants of a fading past lurked, I vaguely remembered having been told that I myself might not have been real. The circle continued.

# Epilogue:
# Absolution

## One

It is time.

Is it? I check the skies… but there is no giant digital watch floating in the skies. Have the arrows of pragmatism shot down every last feature of fantasy, I wonder? For though it is a cloudless sky that I gaze into, there is no alarm clock suspended in mid-air; there is no hovering time turtle; there isn't even a dancing sundial. Imagination itself has been shot down by reality.

The Banyan leaf and I are alone in this world. This sea is my home. But how long will I endure this existence, I wonder? How long will it be before the sea is drained? If these are my last few moments of life, then I must chronicle my every thought and preserve it.

I have no paper.

## Two

He dreams of a notebook and an ink pen; instead he is given a notepad and a pencil—his powers are weakening. Realising that the end is nearer than he feared, he prepares to hastily scribble down his every thought, even as it occurs to him. But as though shy of being captured onto paper, his thoughts refuse to fall into formation. He tries to coax them out by allowing his mind to ponder over this endless sea, the unblemished sky, and this plain Banyan leaf. But there is nothing here to stimulate thought. So he closes his eyes and meditates upon himself, upon his past and his present.

The sea watches patiently.

## Three

The world had once been teeming with people, scattered like ants

over a picnic lunch, and left to tussle with one another in their quest for food and survival. It took a lifetime for us to realise that we were all just one ant, and that the picnic lunch contained no food.

There are two versions to every tale, two tales in every truth, and two truths within every lie. Yet all we see is the lie, hollow and fickle, an unworthy residue of imagination. We discard it like we would the shell of a pistachio, and instead eat the nut. But the lie *is* the nut. Truth is the shell that guards the nut, and it acts like a noble camouflage, preserving the treasure within. The camouflage is clever enough to deceive most of us, for how many ever look past the truth? We seek it like we would air in a suffocating world. But air is a temporary solution to the curse of breathing. Lies on the other hand enlighten us to the possibility that there is no air, and certainly no need for it.

I haven't drawn breath in years.

*No wonder you're in the middle of a large, indulgent dream then...* says the small, pragmatic voice in the back of my head. *Your brain is starved of oxygen—you're hallucinating.*

So what if I am? Perhaps I am actually lying on a hospital bed, strapped to all kinds of machinery, while a group of medical experts hover over me like botanists over a rare, exotic specimen. But like the botanists, all the medical experts can do is *observe* me. They can manipulate my body however they wish, rescue or murder me per their whims, but they cannot enter this realm that I currently inhabit. Within this world, dream or not, I am a master of my own fate.

*Well,* the voice of reason with me says, *then why can't you dream anymore?*

# Four

Thoughts flood his consciousness and he releases them onto paper through the pencil. When he finishes his first thought, he takes the paper and tries to imagine a vessel into which he can

store it. A bottle appears readily by his side, but he ignores it. A message in a bottle is hardly an original idea. He strains his mind for an alternative, for something (for anything) that would be a distinctive, inventive substitute. But he finds nothing. The sea is draining, and the world is fast turning real.

So he puts the message into a bottle and casts it into the sea.

Over time he writes hundreds of messages and casts hundreds of bottles into the sea, such that he feels like a large wheel, endlessly conceiving new ideas, transferring them onto paper, and then releasing them into a world that is now deprived of colour and perspective.

He wonders if there is anyone left in this existence to find the bottles…

## Five

Sensitivity is a sieve into which we add our thoughts, our sensations and our experiences. The thick sludge of life that is poured into the sieve is then drained and purified into a crystalline potion of spiritual and emotion relevance. It is this potion that lends us clarity amidst a haze of delusion and distraction. The world that is painted in black and white is cold, harsh and angular. Sensitivity is the colour that softens the edges of this world, while adding warmth and character to its features. It is sensitivity that breeds the imagination, which ignites creation and gives rise to art.

Of course, not all of us are sensitive. There are those that thrive upon leading organized, pragmatic and ordinary lives. They do not dawdle away time by investigating the seemingly fruitless avenues of fantasy; they are content instead to serve humanity in another manner. It is due to the efforts of these realists in the everyday, practical fields of life that artists find the technological and economic support required to grow and develop their creations. Together, through the many diverse roles and duties that we each intentionally or inadvertently perform, we

construct the fabric of our society. All of our lives, whether we be artists, engineers, dreamers or realists, are connected.

So many thoughts... all these ideas and notions and theories that I have tortured myself with, what do I have to show for them except frustration? As a society, we tend to believe that knowledge increases understanding, but what if knowledge actually impedes understanding? What if it inhibits our ability to accept? Why else does life grow increasingly difficult as we grow older? As children we're ignorant, and that ignorance allows us to absorb answers and to understand them. But knowledge eventually corrupts that understanding, and dilutes it. Knowledge dispels all illusions, all fiction and all imagination. It leaves us intolerably vulnerable to that cruel nemesis: reality. And so, whenever we stumble upon an answer, we dust it off, measure it, and then finally hold it up to reality's expected standards. But more often than not, the answers fall short; so we discard them and move on. Until eventually, there are no more answers left.

I write all this down on another piece of paper, and drop the bottle into the sea.

Perhaps that *is* the answer then: stop searching for answers, stop looking for meaning, knowledge and understanding. Choose instead to live, dream and hope; for there is as much truth in fiction as there is in fact; as much truth to fantasy, as there is to reality.

And yet, dreams are infinitely better than reality.

So perhaps *imagination* is the real answer?

Illusions, dreams, fantasies, chimeras...

The sea swallows yet another bottle, but still appears hungry.

## Six

He notices the irony of the situation. Lamenting the drastic transformation of life from fantasy to reality, he transfers all the artistic ideas within his mind into sensible, logical messages. For

he figures that in a world slowly becoming devoid of imagination, it would serve him better to translate art into fact, so that the ideas may wander time without need for artistic interpretation. For fact is the *one* version of the truth that does not require sensitivity in order to be understood. So he jots down theories, draws diagrams, explains his ideas, and translates all the artistic concepts and creations that had once flooded his mind, into a plain, common form of language.

On the very last piece of paper, he composes not a work of art, but a summary of existence.

## Seven

The Summary:
**I**
I is the roman numeral One: the highest number, rank and position.
I is why insult translates as offence, and betrayal leads to revenge.
I is why a mother risks her own life to save that of her child's.
I is why a lover hesitates, fears, but still loves.
I is the cause, the motive and the purpose.
I is the unwanted residue of intelligence.
I is the intelligence *and* the imagination.
I is the answer to life and to existence.
I is the first letter of my name.
I is the individual.
I is Ishvar.

I stand alone under the Banyan tree.

Above the tree lies the vast expanse of cloudless, starless, formless sky. It is untainted by even a faint streak or blemish. The sea too is unmarked, and is swelling in the distance.

I watch with apprehension.

This tree is my last refuge, and my last friend; but how long can a tree stand in the face of an apocalyptic flood? I gaze up at the gnarled branches, knotted in and around one another like a

wooden cobweb. It bears no fruit or leaf, and yet it is maternal, for it houses me.

I watch the tide rise in the distance, swallowing another lap of land. It won't be long now before it consumes the entire world. Standing beneath the tree without shadow, I wonder how this came to be? Where did all this begin?

I was born, I lived, and therefore am special. In fact, I would like to believe that I *alone* am special. But I do not exist alone. I could not have survived without them, without the Banyan tree, the Banyan leaf, the sea and the sky. I am a part of them, just as they are a part of me. We are all one and the same. You, me and them. I is immaterial.

I, an individual, should not matter.

I, Ishvar, should not matter.

Ishvar is insignificant.

I is insignificant.

**God**

# Eight

I see a tree.

But there is no land beneath. The tree grows out of the water. It is a Banyan tree, much like the one from which the leaf I now occupy came from. I paddle towards the tree. When I reach it, I leave behind the leaf and climb the tree. On one of its branches, I find a small boy.

He is beautiful. His skin is dark, so dark that he looks blue. Or it is fair, so fair that he looks blue. He has wide, expressive eyes, and delicate, red lips. His thick mane of curly hair is adorned with three peacock feathers, and he wears golden anklets and bracelets. He smiles at me.

I stare at him, lost for words. And then he inhales. I am swept into his lungs along with the sea, the leaf, the tree and the skies.

Within his stomach, I find another Universe, another ocean, another leaf, another tree and myself perched on it, staring at this beautiful boy. But there are more Universes, millions upon millions of them. He has swallowed them *all*. I find myself sitting before him again, gazing into his resplendent face, etched with an ethereal, translucent beauty. I say translucent, for though he sits before me in a solid presence and I can see his features, his hair and his body, I also see everything *within* him, as though he is transparent.

I ask him to show me *Maya*, a kind of cosmic illusion.

So he opens his mouth in response, and I am once again inhaled into his stomach.

I awake in a meditative pose, alone upon a beach, beneath a Banyan tree. The sea sits idly before me, like a mere spectator to this grand show. I turn to examine the tree—it is the same tree as it has always been, except there is no boy perched upon it this time. I wish he would return...

I sit back down on the beach and meditate over this world...

The sea is rising. The skies are clear. I am Me.